THE ELK HEAD CREEK SAGA

McCannon's Country

McCannon's Country

JANICE MILLER

MOODY PRESS

CHICAGO

ISBN: 0-8024-7922-7

1 3 5 7 9 10 8 6 4 2

Printed in the United States of America

NOTE TO READER

Fort Davy Crockett existed in the early-to-mid 1800s at Brown's Hole (now known as Brown's Park) in northwestern Colorado. There is scant information about this region during the years recounted in this novel, and what exists seldom matches up. Therefore almost anything I write with regard to dates will offend one historian or another. Since I can't please all the people all the time, I have selected those dates that best fit my story, but in the interest of historical accuracy I offer the following facts.

The sparse historical data on Fort Davy Crockett indicates that the buildings were finished by 1837 but may have been built at any time between 1822 and 1837. I am assuming the fort was built gradually rather than all at once. At any rate, it seems to have been short-lived. Apparently it was gone by 1842.

The information about who Brown's Hole was named for is equally suspect. Therefore I have ignored the subject altogether with the exception of one short and speculative conversation.

With regard to the number of inhabitants and users of the area where the fort was built—both white folks and Indians—the historical numbers range from a handful of trappers to thousands of pre-fort Indians, so again I have used literary license as I try to bring the fort to life.

Other than these small issues, I have tried to be historically accurate with regard to dates and to characters who lived at that time. Nevertheless this book is intended to be brisk entertainment, a work of fiction with truth stitched between the lines. May you enjoy it as such.

Three people merit special mention for their contributions to my research: first my father, Irby Miller, who allowed me to use his account of his own arrival in northwestern Colorado in this book; thanks also to Dan Davidson, curator of the Museum of Northwestern Colorado in Craig, for his generosity in sharing his research; and thanks to Jerre L. Gamble, of the U.S. Fish and Wildlife Service, keepers of Brown's Park National Wildlife Refuge, for sharing the archaeological site surveys for what is almost certainly Fort Davy Crockett, as well as other valuable information.

And thanks as well to the trappers and fur traders, the Indians, and others whose bones are now dust but whose names live on in lakes, streams, "holes," mountain passes, and valleys throughout the West. I have come to know them in a haunting way; their ghosts rest in the streams of history. Looking into their lives, I have come to understand my own life and time and place much better.

I pray that you might do the same.

1

I couldn't have stayed in St. Louis. Not after the foofaraw I created during my eighteenth year. A young lady of my age and station had never been known to cause such a ruckus. One way or another, I'd have been tongue-lashed right out of town if I hadn't decided to leave on my own.

I didn't cause the scandal on purpose. No matter what they say, I wasn't pampered or spoiled—at least, not so you'd notice. To be sure, my parents were high-mucketymucks in the St. Louis fur trade. Some even called them highfalutin rich folk. But they were also good Christian people who raised me a whole sight better than that.

Truth is, I was headstrong.

The whole thing started one early spring day in 1822, when the robins were singing and the snow was barely off the ground—not that the Mississippi's big muddy banks often felt the taste of snow. St. Louis was noted for its mild winters.

I was on my way to Mrs. Effie Keeling's Haberdashery near the waterfront, an innocent act if ever there was one. All I planned to do was order a brand-new go-to-meeting hat to match the green mutton-sleeve frock I'd just received on the riverboat from Baltimore.

I was walking along, minding my own business, looking at the slapdash storefronts, and admiring my reflection in one of the occasional windows that showed goods and such. I was wearing my brown cotton cape with the mauve silk lining. Fawn, high-button shoes showed smartly beneath my hemline when I stepped high. I was carrying a beige French umbrella and wore kidskin gloves. Mother had done up my chestnut locks in a fashionable "giraffe," with all the sausage curls and ringlets pinned high at the back of my head, and my brown, mauve-trimmed bonnet was tilted to show off the style. The color set off the flash in my dark green eyes; my cheeks were rosy as new apples.

I was just passing by a liquor emporium, craning my neck to peer over the half-door for a look at the Wretched Lost inside, when who should appear but Mrs. Evelyn Farnsworth, the Reverend Farnsworth's wife.

She was a thin-faced, reedlike, carrot-topped specter clad in black homespun from the bonnet on her head to the sturdy shoes on her feet. At that moment she was also in high dudgeon, striding straight for me as she lifted her skirts to step over a mud puddle—the streets themselves were a scandal in those days.

"Emily Davidson," she said upon reaching me. "What a nice surprise to find you out and about. And such a lovely day."

I nodded politely and said nothing. Truth to tell, there was still a March chill in the air, and it looked as if it was about to rain. And I knew that Mrs. Farnsworth wanted more than a polite greeting from me or she'd have nodded and rushed on past.

"You are just the person I wanted to see," she said, confirming my worst suspicions. "I wonder if I might have a moment of your time?"

"Of course." I suppressed a sigh and walked with her past the haberdashery to the tea shop, where we sat down on high-backed chairs at a little round table and ordered a cup apiece.

She was of a mind to help some folks who'd been down on their luck for a long spell. That would be the Bridger family, who lived on a hardscrabble farm up near Six-Mile-Prairie. The mother and father had suddenly fallen ill and died some four years past, leaving young Jim and his sister to fend for themselves. Their aunt had come to take care of them, but she was a maiden woman with no resources of her own. So young Jim was forced into a man's responsibilities, and according to Mrs. Farnsworth it was high time for us womenfolk to lend the younger sister a hand.

"You have such beautiful frocks," Mrs. Farnsworth said. "I'm sure you have just dozens of trunks and such filled with perfectly good garments that you've totally outgrown."

Which was saying a good deal, since I'd reached four feet eleven inches in my sixteenth year and stayed there ever since.

But she was right. I did have more dresses than I'd ever use again, and the same with my younger sister, Sally, who had outgrown me by five inches when we were barely in our teens. In fact, I was the one who occasionally wore hand-me-downs. A fine pickle if ever there was one.

"It seems the young Miss Bridger has shot up like a cornstalk these past few months," Mrs. Farnsworth said. "She's turning into a regular young lady."

"Is she that thin, little tow-haired girl who comes to church now and again?"

"The same—though she's not quite so thin as the last time you saw her."

"Her brother is the apprentice at Phil Creamer's blacksmith shop?"

"Works himself to the bone, and he's bearing a heap of responsibility for a boy his age." She eyed me speculatively, then added, "I reckon he's about your age now, coming on to eighteen. Just imagine, Emily, if you had to support a family."

"I could do it if I was a man," I said.

She said, "Pshaw. Just imagine. They say young Jim is a fine hunter and keeps food on the table. But now that the girl is growing up, she's sprouted plumb out of her clothes, and I understand it's all the boy can do to keep her in shoes."

"That's a pity," I said kindly, for it truly was.

"The family hasn't been in church for a spell . . ."

"I don't believe I ever saw Jim there."

9

"The aunt says he works nigh unto all the time. But she and the girl attended regularly, if you'll remember, till a few months ago."

"What happened?"

Mrs. Farnsworth tilted back her head and looked down her long nose at me as if I'd caused the whole problem. "I can only imagine. The last time I saw the poor girl she was virtually wearing rags—and outgrowing those."

"I see," I said. And I did. "I do have some extra shoes she might have, if they fit her."

The Reverend's wife nodded, tight-lipped. "That's mighty kind of you, Emily."

"I'm happy to help."

"Yes, indeed," she went on. "It is hard sometimes to understand why the good Lord blesses some with such bounty, while others go wanting."

"And I have some dresses and such," I added, feeling just as guilty as she wanted me to, though I saw right through her wily ways. "If you would like to come by the house this evening, Mother and I would be happy to sort them out and donate them."

"Why, thank you, Emily. What a nice surprise. I shall arrive at seven P.M., the Reverend and I both. It's long past time that we called on your parents, and I do thank you for your kindness."

With that she braced herself as if sailing into a strong wind, then strode off.

I didn't mind a bit helping out the little Bridger girl. I was glad to sort those clothes and see what would fit and what wouldn't. But I did mind that the Reverend's wife felt she had to manipulate me into it when she could have just come right out and asked. All the same, I understood that most folks weren't so able to give as we were, and Mrs. Evelyn Farnsworth had her hands full trying to encourage her neighbors to love one another in this rough-and-tumble frontier city, where a person was as likely to take a bullet as a boot. And so I put my resentment aside and did my duty and felt the better for it.

At ten o'clock the next morning, Mrs. Farnsworth, Mother, and I took off to deliver a fine parcel of very nice garments, shoes, and unmentionables to the Bridger farm. The Farnsworths' buggy was sturdy and pulled by a brace of fine prancing roans. It was my first drive north to Six-Mile-Prairie. The ride up the river road from St. Louis took only an hour.

The Bridger home was a two-room, chinked wood cabin with a shabby outhouse, but there were wild flowers everywhere, and the dwelling was set in a fine woods. The harried-looking aunt opened the plank door and greeted us. She had a blunt face and gray hair done up in a bun. She was stooped and old before her time, like a well-weathered tree stump.

She thanked us and offered us bark tea. We were more than happy to accept her hospitality, and the little Bridger girl was overcome by the beautiful things we gave her. As she held up silk shirtwaists and homespun skirts, a light wool coatdress, a fine blue cape, and other garments, she looked as if she'd cry for joy. I could see the clothes would fit just fine. It made me proud to help.

We stayed only a short spell—the Reverend's wife had many another catfish to fry that day.

As we were leaving, Jim Bridger rode in on his bay mare with a brace of squirrels slung across the saddle horn, his rifle hanging in a buckskin sheath. He slid off and said a shy howdy. We nodded politely, and he went into the house. But by the time we'd turned the rig around and headed for the main road, he caught up with us and insisted that we take two of those dressed-out squirrels—one for us, one for the Reverend's family—in return for our neighborliness toward his sister.

We accepted, acting as if squirrel was the only thing we'd had on our minds for a week.

Young Jim was not at all ready to take any handouts. He was a lean, tanned, dark-haired lad with a broad nose and square jaw, and a rigid pride showed in the cut of his face and the set of his shoulders. He gave me a long, curious look as we drove away.

As it turned out, helping the Bridger family and meeting young Jim started the chain of events that set about changing my life. Still, the Lord has His own designs on our lives, and it's hard to tell where the fly will land, once you put out the ointment.

That Sunday the Bridger family attended church— all three of them, though young Jim looked about as comfortable as a cat without claws in a dog pen. He wore a starched homespun shirt, and wool pants held up by a strand of braided rawhide. He nodded politely to me as he left the service. The Bridger girl looked spruced up, and I have to admit that my pale yellow dress and beehive bonnet had never looked better, not even on me. The girl was indeed reaching the flush of young womanhood and turning right pretty. Even the aunt had found a plain, navy blue garment and matching cape of my sister's that fit.

But not all this story is quite so pretty as giving out charity and reaping smiles of thanks. After the scandal was set in motion, most folks forgot the goodness of my heart. Some wasp-tongued gossips even went so far as to call me unfit for decent male companionship—meaning their sons of marriageable age, of course, since I'd already written most of them off as dull and impossible long before I caused the uproar, and I'd certainly ruffled some feathers in the process.

Take Mrs. Dora McKenzie. The day the Bridgers came back to church she all but forced her poor son Barnabus to cross in front of the whole congregation and sit beside me, shame-faced and embarrassed, not daring to so much as look my direction. (She'd nudged and prodded him disgracefully until he finally had no choice.) His mother was always putting him up to such things. He had no more interest in me than a bird has in a broom.

But parents had more of a tendency to set their caps for me than some of their sons did. I was known as a good catch. There was no brother to inherit my father's prosperous fur business. I was the eldest daughter, and any son-in-law could rest on a soft feather. Or so some folks thought.

And wouldn't you just know, after the trouble Mrs. Dora McKenzie was the worst gossip of the lot. She said I'd had a knack for meanness and chicanery for a long spell, and she'd warned Barnabus to stay away from me just in time.

And Mrs. James Lee Bradley, mother of that no-good, rowdy Jed? She started the rumor that I might just be a little teched in the head, for what other excuse could there be for a young lady to behave so outrageously?

I certainly didn't do it on purpose. And most of it wasn't my fault. Some folks say that St. Louis itself wasn't a proper influence on a young lady back then. I suppose the time and the place played a part in my downfall as much as anything. You can't pry a person apart from the time she's born into.

Missouri had just come into statehood in August of the previous year, amid much confusion and anger. The federal government wanted Missouri in as a free state, but what with one politician and another we'd ended up entering the Confederacy in an act known as the Missouri Compromise. The compromise part was that they took in Maine as well as Missouri, to keep the balance of votes in the Senate equal among slave and free states—a fact that seemed to make nigh unto everybody mad, and most of all the mule-stubborn Missourians.

Slavery was an uncivilized state of affairs at best. But in those days it seemed to be the natural order of things, and I was hard put to figure out why folks were making such a fuss—so long as the slaves were treated decently, of course.

If a person beat or misused his slaves, why, that would be another matter. I heard folks I admired and respected condone it, and I couldn't see past the nose on my face.

Even at that, I knew that the small city of St. Louis was a long way from civilized, slave state or not. It was the principal market and outfitting point for the fur trade, which made it a boom town. Most anything a man or woman could put a wicked hand to took place right before our very eyes. In spite of my father's lofty position, there was no way *not* to see all the goings-on, and I got an eyeful.

St. Louis had its good points, though. I loved the big, flat, muddy river. I loved the carryings-on. We had a fine little steepled church, and Reverend Farnsworth was a decent pastor who preached the gospel right there on Church Street, where you could look out past the stained glass windows to see the new-fangled, fancy white steamboats tied up at the levee like floating palaces. Some had started bringing passengers and cargo all the way from New York back in 1819, what with navigable rivers connecting us with that august city. Who would have ever dreamed of such a thing?

We Davidsons also had a very fine house: two stories with white pillars and a wide lawn with groves of oak and cypress, just south of *La Rue Principale.* We could see the old stone towers that had been built, then abandoned, during the French-Spanish conflict almost half a century before. Tall oaks, dogwoods, and magnolias sloped off down to the river, and there we had a white-painted boathouse for the rowboats and a gazebo for picnicking. Father built the house so he could bring me, my year-younger sister, and Mother from North Carolina, where we'd stayed while he got his fur business settled. Mother would never have come with him if she hadn't had a fine house.

Mother was persnickety like the other North Carolina ladies of her social class, though I loved her dearly all the same. She was one of the Jacksons. She came from a sprawling plantation near Charlotte, not far from where Grandfather William Lee Davidson was killed while battling

General Cornwallis's troops at Cowan's Ford. But all of that had happened some twenty years before I was born, so I never knew Grandfather William at all, though his presence still loomed large and his stern-faced portrait hung in our St. Louis parlor.

I said to Father once, "Why are we highfalutin just because one of our ancestors got killed in a battle and some-one named him a hero?"

Father was wearing an especially fine, black brocade frock coat that day, with a plum silk vest and a diamond stickpin. He was a fine dresser even when he was just going to his office. He had it in his mind to keep up with that skin-flint John Jacob Astor, the high-muckety-muck in the fur trade.

Astor had ruled the business for nearly twenty years. He kept his main offices in New York City but had been doing business far and wide. He'd just opened up the first St. Louis branch of his American Fur Company, and that was a fine howdy-do. He had every fur trader within two thousand miles up in arms. Too many people moving into the local trade, folks were saying. A few people were bound to go broke sooner if not later. Not enough beaver pelts coming down the river to keep us all fed, Father said. Others were saying a heap more. It looked to me like trouble had moved in right on American Fur's tail.

But that was neither here nor there to me. I was intent upon finding out why I always had to toe the line. And when I suggested to Father that Grandfather William might have gone fishing or planted corn rather than die and be famous, he looked at me out of his black, measuring eyes and said, "What brings this on?"

"I don't want to go to the town social this afternoon. I'd rather pick berries."

"You have to go. It's expected of you."

"But why?"

"Because you're a Davidson, and you have to be there. You need to thank the good Lord for your blessings,

15

Emily, and mind your social obligations. Without your grandfather's sacrifices, we might well be paupers."

"Would a pauper have to spend an afternoon with all those preening peacocks?"

"She wouldn't have the chance. And mind your tongue, young lady."

"I'd far rather be a pauper," I said and flounced off to get ready for the social. But I didn't have an inkling of what I was saying. It was going to take some hard lessons for me to find out what being a pauper was all about. And it would take some even stronger lessons before I would learn how to hold my tongue.

2

Father had been wealthy all his life, and I thought that was the natural order of things. He was a baby at the time of Grandfather William Lee Davidson's death. By the time he grew up, his older brothers had already settled into running the family holdings, which were considerable by then.

After a while the four brothers started squabbling, and Father decided to make a fresh and independent start. He took a portion of his inheritance and came to invest in the newly booming fur trade. His brothers were glad to be rid of his never-ending complaining.

I could understand that. Though I loved him, Father was a hardheaded Scotsman who insisted upon constant perfection. I reckon I was just fed up with his trying to control my every move and thought. He and Mother were telling me all the time that I had to uphold a certain standard as their daughter, they being one of the first families in town. I expect that's why, when push came to shove, I did exactly as I pleased with no serious thought of the consequences.

By 1822, some four thousand folks called St. Louis their home—though to save my soul I never could see how anybody made the federal census count, considering that folks were always coming and going, blustering and blowing and floating through.

Most decent folks had built small stone houses beside the broad, churning river. Plenty of ungainly varmints boarded in the wooden lean-tos along the waterfront. The copper-faced Indians and independent traders and trappers set up camp just outside the city during the busy spring and summer seasons, laying out buffalo robes and bearhides, buckskins, even barrels of homemade whiskey.

It was no trouble at all for Sally and me to wander down to the waterfront to watch those stone-faced Indians as well as the boisterous French Creoles and rowdy keelboatmen, the sad-faced black slaves, the steamboaters, the Canadian indentured servants, the wealthy merchants in their tall beaver hats and ruffled shirts, the gnarly trappers and wilderness traders, and even a few fancy, painted women up from New Orleans, all of whom drew their luck from the river at one place or the other and from various depths.

And now we come to the real source of the trouble: That bothersome St. Louis waterfront.

That's where I first laid eyes on the broad shoulders and the strong, handsome features of Corrin Brevard McCannon, which means that's where I lost my heart.

The minute I saw Corrin, his warm hazel eyes caught mine, and I felt a little spark shoot between us, as if someone had ground two flints together and almost set a fire.

I'd like to blame Mr. McCannon for what befell me, though I might just as well go ahead and take all of the blame myself if I'm going to be honest about it. It was certainly my action that precipitated the trouble. Poor Mr. McCannon seemed to just get caught up in the flood tide, like a log spun downstream by a Mississippi waterspout.

When I first saw him, I had gone back to Effie Keeling's Haberdashery to pick up the hat I'd ordered the week before. He was arguing with a well-turned-out, gray-haired gentleman in a purple frock coat, a red polka-dot vest, and a gray beaverskin stovepipe hat. They were alongside the brand-new brick offices of John Jacob Astor's American Fur Company.

Both men's faces were agitated, hands motioning like hens in a pecking contest. The older man wore doeskin gloves, which I thought a bit pretentious, since most men were content with plain leather. I determined that the gray-haired dandy was fresh from back East and important as all get out, at least to himself. Perhaps he was even one of the partners who had bought in with John Jacob Astor.

It didn't surprise me to see two men in such a tizzy. I had learned at the dinner table the night before that a goodly batch of senators was fixing to throw out the law that allowed the federal government to compete in the fur trade. That meant a windfall, and any number of government traders were going to be looking for new markets. All the bigwigs from back East who owned the major companies were showing up regularly to make sure they landed on their feet when the beaver pelts started to fly.

Yet in spite of the human turmoil of the boiling waterfront, and in spite of all the arguing he was engaged in, Mr. McCannon caught my eye and held it.

He was a square-jawed, straight-backed, rust-haired young gentleman of some twenty-five years, who had come West several years back to try his hand at making a fortune in furs—or so he said when, to my surprise, Father brought him home for dinner four days later.

That's when I met him and learned his name. Father said he was a man of good family, a Scot—like himself. My family had known his folks back in the Carolinas.

Mother always set a fine table—with the help of the house servants, of course. That night we dined on venison steaks and beaten biscuits, bacon and collard greens and orange pudding.

Mr. McCannon's handsome eyes held an ornery sparkle as he explained what he was doing in St. Louis, as if it were all some big game he was bound to win. While he ate, he looked down at his plate as if he were shy.

He stayed a half hour after dinner and politely listened to Sally play "Hail, Columbia" on the pianoforte. Then he claimed that he had a prior business appointment and rushed out. As he left, he darted a bashful, sideways look at me, and I felt that little spark shoot between us again, as if someone had ground two flints together and almost set a fire.

After Mr. McCannon left our premises, Father made a point of sitting down beside where I was doing my needlework. I was by the fireplace, working on a quilt that featured cats, some fluffy and white, some calico, some gingerbread colored.

At forty-two, Father was straight as a board and strong as a tree. A solid, no-nonsense, dark-haired, determined Scotsman who seldom stopped to visit with anyone, much less the womenfolk in his family. Now, he complimented my work, then said, "That young Corrin McCannon cuts quite a figure, wouldn't you say?"

"He's handsome and well-mannered. He'd be just right for Sally."

Father laughed. "And he's not a bit interesting to you, I'd venture."

"I am not husband hunting, Father. I'm thinking of going back to Charlotte to get a degree in teaching. I can stay with Uncle John. Then perhaps I'll go on farther west. They say new towns are beginning to mushroom up all over the place out there, due to the fur trade."

"That may be a bit of an exaggeration. There are a few very small towns a bit to the west—but as you get farther away, it's only forts dotted here and there, and they're plenty rough. No womenfolk but Indians."

"Forts or towns, they'll be needing someone to teach their children. I believe it might be a good life for me."

Father laughed again. He never took me seriously. He said, "Mr. McCannon has been out West. He spent a couple of years trapping at some forlorn place on a river called the Sheets-Kadee. Fortunately he had the good sense to return to civilization to build a decent life brokering furs. You should ask him about it some time."

"I'm sure that's all good and well for Mr. McCannon." I was getting uncomfortable.

20

"Well," he said, sitting back and lighting his foul-smelling pipe. Mother would be in any minute to make him put it out. He said, "That young man certainly took a shine to you. In fact, I believe I'd invite him to your eighteenth-birthday party."

"I'm sure that would be kind, since you knew his family back East. But if you don't mind, I'll let you extend the invitation."

Father laughed again, and I blushed. It was as if he'd seen my heart flutter at the thought of seeing Mr. McCannon again.

I went to bed humming a little song I'd heard some folks singing in a saloon down on the waterfront as I'd walked quickly by.

"For the Love of Barbara Allen" was the song. It was an old Scottish ballad, and for some reason the words got me moonstruck that night. I got to wondering at the power a woman could have over a young man's heart.

It made me wonder if a prince would ever come along to carry me away, perhaps to the seashore or the mountains or the vast, wild western forests, where we would live in love and splendor in a snow-white palace amid a vast, adventurous, savage land. I wasn't ready to settle for any other sort of man than the prince of my dreams.

But then I thought about my friends who were married and having babies, sewing and mending and cooking and cleaning, growing old already and never having a free moment to themselves anymore. Anyway, I'd reached the age when I wondered if God would ever send the right young man to me, prince or no.

Sometime before I fell asleep, I thought about it some more, then sent up a small but sincere prayer asking God to leave well enough alone. There was too much to do and see in this world, without being burdened by a husband and family.

At my eighteenth-birthday party the following week, Corrin Brevard McCannon took an open shine to me. My folks sat back smiling, and I could see that they'd definitely set their cap for him as a son-in-law.

By early evening it was apparent even to me that Mr. McCannon was seriously courting me. He asked me to dance over and over, me in my pale pink, gossamer-satin gown. Fifty whole dollars Father had paid for it—he'd had it made special and sent up from New Orleans, though it had to be fitted locally.

Some folks were kind enough to say I was a miniature beauty in the rough, needful of some polishing, but I always wanted to be tall and willowy like Sally and Mother. For a long time I'd hoped I'd grow some more, but the past few years had quenched my hopes. Yet, even though my nose came only to the top button on Mr. McCannon's gray silk frock coat, I felt as though I'd been spit-shined and polished and grown full-size that night. I was also wearing brand-new white kidskin shoes, high-buttoned, and that added an inch or so.

I knew I cut quite a figure. My long chestnut locks were pinned high atop my head and held there with pink velvet tea roses; my mother's rose-colored pearls were around my throat and on my ears. Mother kept pulling me aside and pinching my cheeks to put color to them, and each time Corrin put his arm around me and led me to the center of the room to dance, I felt my heart sing.

Before we'd finished out the evening, Corrin and I managed to evade all the chaperons and were sitting alone in the parlor. The lantern wick was trimmed low. The big window showed a low, golden moon riding behind the trees and glinting off the broad, tar-black river. The scene was perfectly framed by Mother's plum velvet drapes with gold fringe.

"Look," I said. "Isn't it beautiful?"

"Yes. But there are far more beautiful places. Maybe someday I'll take you to see McCannon's Country."

"Where might that be?"

"The Far West. The far side of the Rocky Mountains." A faraway look indeed came into his eyes and a longing for something in the distance.

That's when I asked him about the Far West, just as Father had suggested. And that played a part in the coming scandal too, the things he told me. So I reckon that some of the fault for the trouble was Father's after all, him and his interfering ways.

Mr. McCannon painted me a picture, all right. A beguiling, mesmerizing picture of the far-off Rocky Mountains: tangled, remote, and wild. He sketched it out with his warm, deep voice, his glorious hazel eyes, and his charming crooked grin. He filled it in with colorful words and feelings I couldn't comprehend, and then he brushed his hand shyly across his crop of rust-red hair, smiled, and reached out and held my hand to draw me right into the picture.

The Rockies. Fur trapping. The freedom of a new land where there were no rules and no limits—"a place where you could grow to be full-sized" was the way he put it—and no other person around for a thousand miles, if you so wished.

Once I heard Corrin McCannon's version of the West and its challenges, I was hooked like a gar on a gig. I was going to go, one way or another. It was just a matter of how and when.

"Whether you're a man or a woman," he said, "it's all the same out there. The land calls for strong people, honest people, folks who want to build a future."

"But I thought you were a fur broker, working here in Saint Louis and bound to stay."

He gave me a sad, wry grin. "That was yesterday."

"What happened?"

"To be frank, I've run into some trouble. I had an agreement with Astor's American Fur, and they've let me down. I was to provide them with a certain number of pelts

23

at a given price. I already paid the trappers, and now American Fur has found a cheaper deal and left me without a buyer."

"Can't you do anything?"

"I've been fighting this for two weeks, and now I'm going to have to dump the pelts for less than what I paid for them."

"Maybe Father would buy them."

He grinned again, this time in irony. "Seems to me that's what brought us together—my visit to your father's office on that very mission and our subsequent conversation about events back home."

"You're from Mecklenburg County?"

"From near Lexington. Davidson County." His eyes searched mine for something I didn't understand.

"It was named for my grandfather, William Lee Davidson," I said, as if to answer a question. I fiddled with my lace hankie, suddenly uncomfortable.

He nodded. "I know. My grandfather fought in that same battle, though he wasn't so fortunate as to get himself killed in a heroic manner. He just lost a toe or two."

I felt myself flush as if I'd been personally insulted. "It wasn't something my family planned."

He suddenly smiled again, warmly. "Reckon I just wanted to examine your attitude about your family name," he said. "And I reckon you've passed muster just fine."

I gave him a hot, angry glare. "So you had me pegged as pretentious?"

He laughed. "You do seem saucy now and again."

I tossed my head. "I am nothing of the sort. Though people do tell me I am full of high spirits, and I fail to see a thing wrong with that."

He nodded. "Reckon if that's all it is, you'll pass muster."

I gave him an angry look. "I'm not sure I can say the same for you."

"So I don't pass muster?"

"Not until you become more polite."

He grinned again. "No offense. I just wanted to know more about you. Some folks of your station do tend to put on airs."

"I suppose that means you come from a poor family?"

His face went empty, as if he'd just flushed it of any expression that might give him away. His square jaw jutted out a bit. "I'm afraid that means I come from a family I don't talk about much."

"But are they paupers?" The thought made me curious and not at all displeased. And though Father had said Corrin came from a good family, that did not always equal wealth.

He shot me a puzzled look. "Not necessarily."

I started to ask another question, but from the sour expression that had come to his face, I knew he really wasn't eager to talk about family. I could ask Father about them later.

Corrin McCannon must have read my mind, for he said, "Your father is a decent gentleman. I met him once when I was a boy, and he remembered. He's agreed to purchase the pelts I can't sell otherwise, but his going rate is far less than I paid for them, and I'm certainly not asking him for handouts."

"But...there will be other traders..."

"Not who'll pay what I need."

"Maybe you could ship the bulk of them to Europe, like Mr. Astor does."

"Astor nearly has that market sewed up, and there's no way to get past the few other middlemen. No, it seems I've invested most of what I had and made a bad bargain. I've lost the bundle." He cocked an eyebrow and managed to look morose, though there was a certain devil-may-care attitude behind it. "I've run aground, Miss Davidson."

"Can't your family help?" I had to send out just one more probe.

His scowl quenched my speculation. "I'd chop cotton before I'd ask them."

I changed the subject. "You can start over. Father might help you in some other way. Maybe he has a place for you in the warehouses."

He frowned, his dark copper eyebrows dipping low between eyes suddenly lit with pride. "Where I come from, a man stands alone when it comes to his business dealings. Problem is, I'm still used to doing business with an honest word and a handshake, and there are too many bottom-feeders in these Mississippi River waters. I am frankly fed up with being a businessman."

"So you're going back to trapping?" I didn't know whether to be desolate for myself or happy for him.

"That's my intention."

"But I hear that's getting cutthroat too. That there is more and more competition for the pelts."

"Only amongst those who sign on with the big companies. Independent trappers still have a free hand, if they're willing to go out on their own. And even if a man signs on with a company, so long as it's a reputable one it's possible to make your bacon."

"Well, I'm sure the trapper's life is perfect for you," I said, hiding my disappointment behind feigned indifference.

"It could be, if it wasn't so lonely."

His gaze suddenly pierced through me, as if he were yearning for something he'd never have.

I sat back some, startled, though it hadn't been a predatory look.

He saw that he had alarmed me, and he swiftly looked away.

We were still alone. Fiddle and pianoforte music drifted out from the Great Room where a reel was in full tilt. He stepped over and shut the door, and the sound became a faint hum.

"Too confounded noisy here in the city," he said, as he sat back down, a little closer to me this time. He hunched down a bit, so that his eyes met mine.

"Yes," I said. "I suppose it's very silent out in the mountains at night."

"Daytime too." He grinned. "So quiet you can hear your heart beat at the beauty of it all."

"I imagine it's wonderful."

"It is. You've never seen beauty till you've seen an aspen grove in autumn or a bluebird in flight against a fleecy sky. There are herds of elk and antelope, thousands deep, that thunder across the meadows, and pheasant—birds in colors you've never seen. Belly-deep grass for a horse to feed on. And then there's winter. Have you ever wintered where it really snows?"

"Hardly."

His poetic talk was making me hunger for something too. An ache had opened up within me that I didn't understand. I expect that's why I masked the odd feeling with disdain.

"Have you ever even seen paintings of the Rockies?"

"I've seen both drawings and paintings. In school we read the diaries of Lewis and Clark from their expedition of 1807. Are the mountains really that vast?"

"So big they'd swallow you whole."

"Bigger than the Blue Ridge or the Smokies?"

"Different. Wilder, higher. There are jagged peaks that are unpassable, spires that pierce the sky. And the whole region is filled with streams and rivers and lakes like something out of a storybook."

I was awestruck at the thought of it all.

"And you should see the mountain sky at night," he went on. "It's huge and deep and black. The stars twinkle as if God spun them from light itself, far better than those fancy rings on your fingers."

He glanced at my jewelry.

27

I shifted, uncomfortable at the warmth of his body next to me. I looked down at my hands. People said they were elegant, even beautiful. I expect that their long, slender shape came from so many years of pianoforte lessons.

The clustered diamond on my right hand had been my parents' gift for my eighteenth birthday. Mother had insisted I also borrow her two dress rings for the party tonight, diamonds and rubies as well as the pearls, to set off the pale pink dress. Suddenly I was embarrassed by all the finery.

I fell silent.

Someone opened a door somewhere, and the music played through the huge old house again.

It was the beginning of fur trading season in St. Louis, and there were always a goodly number of parties in the few finer houses. In spite of the scruffy nature of some of the newfound denizens who came down the rivers and over the mountains and into our lives, we used any excuse we could to brighten up the hardworking river town, and a Davidson family birthday was really special. Folks would be here till nigh unto midnight.

As for me, I thought early spring with its revelry was the best time of year. But only a few of the fur-trading renegades, as Father called them, were ever invited to our home. Corrin Brevard McCannon was certainly an exception in every way.

He started talking again, and there was a longing in his voice that captivated me. He said he wanted to go back to the Rockies some day.

"In fact," he said, "the fellows I trapped with plan to build a trading post right there on the Sheets-Kadee, where the trappers can winter. Ought to be working on it now. One of them wants to call the place Fort Davy Crockett." He paused and grinned. "Another of them—a Frenchman— thinks we ought to call it Fort de Misère."

"Fort Misery. Why call it that?"

"Because Davy Crockett has never even seen the region, whereas misery seems to move in and out on a regular basis."

"If it's so miserable, why are you going back?"

He turned and looked me full in the eyes. "Because I can earn ten times more in a year there than I can earn here in Saint Louis, even if I was to become a crook like most of the other fur merchants moving in on the trade. Free trappers are getting rich these days—if they have enough sense not to drink up their profit or get it stolen. Emily, I can take in a hundred thousand a year, if I work at it. A few years like that, and I'd be set for life."

And in that moment, out of the clear blue, I suddenly knew that I had to find a way to make him stay in St. Louis. No decent woman ever gallivanted off to the mountains with a trapper—not unless you count the Widow Keeney, who had married that thorny old renegade Manuel Lisa years ago and gone upriver to his fort to live. And even that was a far cry from the wilderness Mr. McCannon was talking about, that place he called McCannon's Country.

"I have a cabin already built," he said.

"Where?"

"Right near where the fort will be. It's well sheltered from the worst of the winter in a place called Brown's Hole. A few trappers already rendezvous there. A man can find water there, plenty of wood for fuel. There's good rangeland for a man's horse and plenty of wild game. And a river filled with the plumpest trout you ever tasted. A man could live his life there and never leave."

I felt my throat close up. I waited a moment, then said, "Is that what you plan to do?"

"I wouldn't mind, me and my wife."

"You're married?" I drew myself up, horrified.

He laughed, then laughed some more, until I felt the color rush to my cheeks.

I said, "I fail to see what's so amusing."

29

"You. I'm asking you to marry me, Emily Anne Davidson. Marry me and go with me to live as a trapper's wife."

I physically recoiled at the very thought of it. I managed to hold my tongue but only because he'd left me speechless.

I thought about the gossip when Manuel Lisa took the Widow Keeney upriver. It was commonly agreed that no sane woman would do such a thing, nor would any decent man ask her to. I shuddered.

Mr. McCannon saw my reaction. "You have two red spots in your cheeks. You should see yourself."

I was angry, and I parroted the common opinion on the subject. "What do you expect? No decent woman should be asked to live as a trapper's wife."

He tilted his head. "Does that mean I'll have to turn you into an indecent one?"

"I mean no such thing. I mean only that—"

But he choked off my words with his mouth. His arms were around me, he was kissing me gently but firmly, and the feeling was so sweet and tender and filled me with such pure love that I felt my anger—even the memory of why I was angry—melt away.

It was a short and respectful kiss. He pulled away, sat back, bowed formally, and said, "I beg your pardon, Miss Davidson. But from your reaction to my proposal, I fear that may be the only one of your kisses I ever manage to steal."

"That was really a proposal of marriage?"

He nodded. "And a serious one. I'm going back to the mountains—at least for a year. My cabin is simple, but the area where it sits is a pinch of heaven itself. Only thing that would make it better is to share it with the woman I love."

I felt myself color up again, and I looked away so he wouldn't see the confusion in my eyes and sense the leap in my heart.

But he saw it anyway. He moved down so that he was on one knee. He took my hand again, looked up with those warm hazel eyes, and said, "I'm asking you once more. Marry me, Emily. You're the one woman that God made for me. I knew it the minute I first laid eyes on you."

My head was whirling. I said, "I'm sorry, but this is more than I can deal with right now. I—I think you'd better go."

He nodded. Then he stood up and politely led me out to the main room as if he were suddenly a stranger. He took me to where Sally and her beau were standing beside the punch bowl, bowed, went over and made his excuses to my parents, then left the party, smiling as he went out the door and giving me a broad wink that left me feeling puzzled and desolate.

3

Corrin Brevard McCannon surprised me by return-ing the very next night. A true wonder. After he'd left my party so abruptly, I feared I might never see him again.

He courted me every single night after that, staying exactly two hours each time. Father and Mother were delighted until I told them that he'd resigned his position as a broker and was going back to trapping and had asked me to marry him. In fact, he continued to ask me every time we saw one another.

At that news, my father was fit to be tied.

"I'll tell him he can't come to see me anymore," I said, trying to dampen the choleric color in Father's face.

"Please," said Mother, holding a scented hankie to her nose. "I can't bear even the thought of you gallivanting off into the mountains with a perfect stranger."

"He's smitten by you," Father said darkly. "He's not going to leave easy. I may have to drive him off with a rifle."

"Oh, Father, just yesterday you thought he was per-fect."

"Not if he's a trapper. Not for any daughter of mine."

"He's a good man."

"He's no good for you," Father said. "He'd take you out into the wilderness and use you up in a year. You'd be an old woman before you ever had a chance to see what life is all about."

"Oh, Father, don't be silly. He'd do nothing of the sort. He's just . . . well, interesting."

Mother said hopefully, "More interesting than William?"

William Baxter was my last suitor. He had more or less courted me until I'd recently refused him. At the moment, William was back East in Boston, going to medical school.

"When William comes back, maybe you'll be ready to settle down," Mother said. "In the meantime, why don't you just tell Mr. McCannon that you're already engaged?"

I felt my stubbornness well up as she once again set about trying to arrange my life. I said, "Corrin is far more interesting than William any day."

But I said it only to get her goat. At that moment I had no intention whatsoever of traipsing off after some wild mountain man. Why, folks said some trappers even married into the savage tribes and had families with them.

I thought about that some and didn't like the way it felt. The next time Corrin came calling, I asked him.

"That time I asked if you were married..."

He grinned again at the memory of it. That was one of the best things about him, his constant good humor. "What about it?"

"You never came right out and answered me. Are you?"

"Am I what?"

"Married to anyone."

"What on earth are you talking about? Would I ask you to marry me if I were?"

"See? You're evading me again. You never give me a direct answer. Yes or no?"

"I don't even see why you're asking." He shook his head back and forth.

"I hear rumors," I said, "that most mountain men have Indian wives. Have you ever done that?"

A dark cloud crossed his face. He said, "A lot of people should keep their tongues in their heads."

"Why? Do you have an Indian wife somewhere?"

"I most certainly do not."

"Are there Indians near your mountain cabin?"

He shot me a puzzled look, as if the scope of my naiveté had never crossed his mind. "Of course."

33

"I mean, I know there are Indians. They're everywhere. We have plenty right here in Saint Louis. What I mean is, what kind?"

"You run into the Pawnees, Otoes, and Missouris as you cross into the West. Mostly Kiowa, Cheyenne, and Arapahoes once you hit the great prairies and foothills. The Arapahoes live on the prairies to the east side of the Rockies. They move into the mountains in the summer from time to time."

"What about the Blackfoot?"

I'd heard they were an especially savage tribe, known to kill on sight. They were encouraged by the British up in Canada to kill all American trappers and get them out of the competition. The Blackfeet had attacked more than one fur party in recent years.

"No need to worry about them. They're way farther north. But we've got some ferocious braves in our part of the world too."

"Oh, Corrin. It sounds dreadful." But I knew there was excitement in my eyes.

"Once you get into the middle Rockies there are Shoshone, and the Crow ride there too. But like the Blackfeet, they're far north of where I'll be going. Some Navajo and Bannocks ride into the high mountains from time to time, mostly when drought hits the lowlands and they're following game. The Arapaho come now and again on raiding parties, though there hasn't been any trouble like that in Brown's Hole for a long time."

"What about the Indians at Brown's Hole itself?"

"Several kinds. They were using the region for winter shelter long before any trapper showed up. But mostly they're known as Shoshone or Snakes—"

"Ugh," I said. "What a terrible name."

"Don't mean much. They're called that because they hail from round the northern Sheets-Kadee and the Little Snake River. And then we have a goodly number of another breed of Shoshone known as Yutahs. What some folks just call plain Ute. You ought to see them in winter! What a sight to behold, all wrapped in fur robes and fur moccasins."

"Are they civilized?"

"Not in the way you mean. But they more or less run things in that region. They call the area 'The Land of Shining Mountains.'"

"They sound poetic."

He laughed. "Reckon some are, some aren't. They're nomadic. They live in bands of a few families each, and they're usually at war with the Pawnee or Snakes, when they're not fighting with the Arapahoes. Those three tribes are bitter enemies. But like I said, we don't see much of the trouble on our side of the Rockies."

"You talk like you still belong there."

He grinned, and it made him all the more handsome. "In a way I feel that I still do. After all, the western Rockies are not only God's Country, they're McCannon's Country."

"Why do you call it that?"

"Because I've known since the first time I laid eyes on that region that my future lies there."

That gave me a little pang of doubt about him, but I swiftly pushed it aside.

"Do the Ute attack white folk?"

"Not so's you'd notice. There have been some incidents—but I reckon most of the trouble is because the white folk are getting in the middle of the ruckuses between the Ute and Arapaho."

"They sound fearsome."

"They can be. The Utes are fierce warriors. The best horse racers I've ever seen. And they have a mean streak when it comes to anyone crossing them."

"They sound dangerous, Corrin."

"Life is dangerous. Just yesterday two men were shot dead over a card game down on the waterfront. I'd venture to say that's two more than were killed at Brown's Hole by Ute."

"So you're telling me there are good Ute and bad Ute. How do you tell the difference?"

He grinned again. "Same way as you tell a good white man from a bad one. You learn to size them up, then you just wait and see."

"Isn't the trip west dangerous?"

"Not if you know what you're doing. I've been out and back, remember, and with good company. You have to be careful of the Ute as you're entering the mountains—and you always have to be careful of the Arapaho. And when you're passing through the territory of the Utes' other enemies, it pays to ride low and keep an eye open. Like I said, the Utes are at war with the Pawnee, the Arapaho, the Kiowa—"

"Why are they so violent?"

"Why are we? Why do both you and I have ancestors lying in the ground who were shot and killed by other white men?"

I nodded, acknowledging his point.

He said, "You ride into a war party, you're likely to get shot just for being in the wrong place at the wrong time. But when it comes to the high mountains, those bands of Ute more or less stay to themselves so long as they're left alone. Aren't too many white folk in that region yet, and the Indians are more curious about us than anything—though I'd never be so foolish as to take them for granted."

"My great-uncle Samuel Davidson was killed by Indians."

"I've heard the name."

"He was the first white settler west of the Blue Ridge Mountains in North Carolina," I said proudly. "But the Cherokees murdered him in 1784."

"That sort of thing happens."

"But aren't you ever afraid?"

I was being coy now. There was always talk of Indians attacking and raiding settlements all across the frontier. And nobody had any idea how many white folk had lost their lives to Indians during the movement to explore the Far West, though it wasn't all-out war yet.

Corrin was bound to be afraid at times. But I had no real business batting my eyes at him and cozying up, the way the flirtatious girls liked to do. It just sort of came upon me, and I found myself doing it without thinking, while using the pretext of talking about danger and all.

Corrin shifted, uncomfortable. "Seems like the places where a goodly number of white folks are settling have more'n their share of Indian trouble. Reckon the Indians don't like all that crowding. Where there's just a few of us, they more or less leave us alone so long as we return the favor. I've traded with the Ute and the Snake alike. They even set up camp and watched a spell when old Thompson and Saint Claire started putting up their chink-wood cabin in Brown's Hole. Most of them were right friendly."

"Those men have a cabin there too?"

"It was intended to more or less be the first stage of their fort. I expect they're still building on it. Leastwise, that's what they meant to do."

"Did you meet them in Saint Louis?"

"Nah. I'd been with an old French trapper name of Jake Roubideaux. I hooked up with him when I was going West. We went up the Missouri, then trekked back south. We'd been trapping in the Tetons way north of Brown's Hole when we heard about the folks building down in the Hole and went to have a look."

"You stayed at Brown's Hole after that?"

"Off and on. Trapping, you have to move around some, but it was a good place to winter those two years. They were clearing land, building drying racks for elk and bear meat, more or less turning it into a future rendezvous for the big companies, should they ever find their way to the real wilderness."

"I thought the fort's owners would be named Brown."

He laughed. "The Hole was named for some long-gone explorer—nobody is sure who."

"But Thompson and Saint Claire are going to create a settlement?"

"Last I heard they'd already started."

"Do other white people still live there? Are there any other settlements nearby?"

He laughed again. "Not unless you count a thousand miles away as 'nearby.'"

"Then what's out there?"

"Mountains, Indians, empty sky, twinkling stars, and a handful of peculiar mountain folk," he said with a grin. "Trappers mostly."

"Are there any women?"

"Squaws."

"No white women?"

He got uncomfortable, looked away. Then he looked at me imploringly. "Reckon you'd get a spell lonely out there."

"So you really don't have an Indian wife?"

His look turned to irritation. "Look at my head, woman."

He tipped his head so that his nose almost touched his vest, and I examined his fine thick shock of rust-red hair.

He looked up at me again. "Is it all there?"

"I guess so."

"Then I haven't been scalped yet, right?"

I was puzzled. "I guess not."

He said, "Point is, the Utes value their squaws more than most other Indians do. Most of them would drive a stake through my heart if I so much as looked at one of their women, and there's no way I'd walk away with my hair."

"They hate white people?"

"No. That's not it. It's just that they're different. Prideful. They think different, keep to themselves, do things different—it's hard to explain."

"Are they Flatheads?" This term was supposed to encompass any number of Indian tribes, for it was a practice rather than a tribal identity.

"Some folks say they are. I can't see it myself."

"But why can't you see it? Isn't it true that the Flatheads have heads which are only a few inches thick and flat as pancakes?"

He gave me a shocked look, then guffawed.

I huffed up. "I have been told that their heads form a straight line from the nose to the top of the forehead. They are made that way by their mothers, who bind them in compressing machines right after birth, which make their eyes pop forward while their heads are flattened like pancakes. I have been told that they believe this is a sign of great beauty or handsomeness."

"Where did you get such ideas?" He was staring at me now, as if just realizing that I was serious.

"From a traveler who went West and came to visit Father on his way back to North Carolina. He is considered to be a very good authority."

"He's a fool. Probably made it as far as the mouth of the Missouri, wintered up there, then came back telling tall tales the real trappers had spun for him in front of a fireplace."

I went wide-eyed, sort of flirting but partway curious. "Do you think so?"

"I know so. I've seen the Ute. You might say they have broad noses and flat, blunt foreheads. Some are muscular, thickset people who are strong as buffalo. But I ain't ever seen one yet with a head you'd mistake for a flapjack."

"But isn't it true that the flat head is the savage idea of beauty?"

"Reckon some tribes still bind their papooses in cradles that cause the back of their heads to be somewhat flat. But that's mostly the tribes up along the Columbia River, a good deal farther west than where we'll be going."

"What about the Pointheads, then?"

He laughed. "You've listened to every silly rumor afoot, haven't you?"

That irritated me. I said, "At least I don't believe that a lost tribe of Welshmen live out in the far mountains like some geographers say."

He frowned, thinking. "I've heard that tall tale too. Reckon those rumors did make it into some of the Eastern papers not too long back."

"They did. And Father said that Thomas Jefferson himself believed that the Paca of Peru could be found in settlements out West."

"In huge cities of gold, I expect."

"Oh, Corrin, you do carry on. I'm only recounting what I've heard."

"Well, I doubt if that's true. Though I have heard rumors that there's plenty of color in some of the Rocky Mountain streams."

"Gold, you mean?"

"Yes, indeed. I've traded with Indians whose tribes were visited by the Spanish a hundred years ago, when they were looking for their Seven Cities of Gold. Had one fellow pay me for grub with a solid gold nugget year before last."

"Then the Spanish were right!"

"I'd say so, but who knows to what extent?"

I felt my eyes shine as if I were a child again, and that a fairy-tale book had just opened up before me. "Do you think there might actually be golden cities?"

He shot me a disbelieving look. "I'd say not." Then his expression turned contemplative. "But I haven't seen all the West by a far shot. There's thousands and thousands of miles where no white man has even trod. Who knows what might lie out there? Why, I've heard tales of great lizards trapped in the stone cliff walls. Elephants with tusks big as a house buried under the ground—"

I rolled my eyes. I'd had enough of his funning me. I said, "Will there be a church in Brown's Hole?"

"Reckon you can make a church anywhere. That's up to you."

"I've heard that the Indians believe the beaver is a fallen race of Indians who have been condemned to be brutes because of their evil ways. Do you think that's true?"

"Can't say. That's the first time I heard of it. There are all sorts of Indians out there with all sorts of beliefs."

"The Indians are heathens," I said. "Our minister said so."

"That's his opinion. In my Bible, the good Lord admonishes us to love everyone and show them His grace."

"Do they worship idols?"

He frowned and thought. "It's more that they're tuned into the natural world. They talk to the earth, the wind, the sky, and some folks think that's worship. But they have the Great Spirit too, who is supposed to be the source of it all. A Being that seems a lot to me like God, though the rest of their beliefs confuse me some."

"Do they believe in a heaven and hell?"

"Not in exactly the same way we do. But they believe in a good spirit and an evil one. They believe that after death, if you've lived a good life, you go to a Happy Hunting Grounds where it's always summer and there is plenty of easy-to-hunt game. Those folks who live an evil life will go to the other place, the Land of Eternal Snows, where there's fire just out of reach and the game always gets away just before you can catch it, so you're constantly aching with hunger."

"Then they don't know about our heaven or about the streets of gold."

"Might be hard to explain streets of gold to folks who've never even seen streets."

I thought about that after he left. And then I started thinking that maybe I'd give up on teaching and go out West to be a missionary to the Indians instead.

41

When Corrin came back the next night, there was something different about him. A faraway look in his eyes, as if he'd already left me, and suddenly I felt a dark, lonely wind blow off the river, and a painful lump came into my throat.

He sat down and didn't say a word—just handed me a piece of paper, a well-handled clipping from the *Missouri Republican* dated some fifteen days before. It said:

> TO ENTERPRISING YOUNG MEN. The subscriber wishes to engage one hundred young men to ascend the Missouri River to its source, there to be employed for one, two, or three years. For particulars inquire of Major Andrew Henry, near the lead mines in the county of Washington, who will ascend with, and command, the party; or of the sub-scriber near St. Louis.

It was signed "William H. Ashley." I knew him because of Father's business. He was a wealthy Virginian who had taken to the mountains long ago, enchanted by the wildlife. He had been back in St. Louis for some time now, talking of forming such a company, and now here it was.

He and his partner, Major Henry, were old hands at the fur trade. Father dealt with them often. They were try-ing to put together a team of roving trappers who would comb the land, bringing in furs. That way they could under-cut American Fur, with its overhead of dozens of forts and trading posts.

"Are you going?" I felt tears well up in my eyes.

"I figure I might as well."

"But—couldn't you stay here a while longer?"

He shook his head. "Reckon not."

"Can't you find some other way to make money?"

"Nothing that I want to do."

"I thought you were going back to Brown's Hole."

42

"Thought about it. You see, with a wife I'd pretty much have to go back there and set up housekeeping so we'd have a roof over our heads. But as a young bachelor who's been abandoned by his one true love, I can pretty much go anywhere I want." He tried to say it lightly, but I could see it hurt him.

"I think you should go back to Brown's Hole. It sounds so wonderful."

"It is, but maybe not right now. I built my cabin with the feeling that I'd bring back a bride if I ever went back." He gave me a long, searching look.

I quickly looked away.

He nodded, as if reassured of something he'd been pondering. He said, "Reckon I'd best wait awhile before I go back alone. It might seem especially lonesome there now."

I felt cold, icy. Still, my voice was clear, and I sensed a stubbornness well up in me that kept me from saying what was really on my mind. I sounded downright haughty to myself as I said, "When will you leave?"

"Tomorrow morning. Early."

And suddenly Corrin was looking past me, and his eyes were lit with a fire of adventure that made my heart twinge with envy.

The whole thing sent a little shiver through me—the thought of leaving the city, of traveling out into all that wildness, of the things that could happen out there.

I almost told him I'd changed my mind, that I was going with him after all and we'd have to go to Brown's Hole. But something stopped me. More stubbornness, I expect. Or maybe I wanted him down on his knees again, begging, though I knew that at this point I'd rejected him often enough that such behavior would be akin to breaking his spirit, and I wanted no such thing.

He left finally, with me acting stiff and indifferent in spite of myself, and he with shoulders slumped but still giving the impression that he'd done with an impossible situation and was ready to move on.

43

I sat in my room that night listening to the rain blowing in from across the river. I felt a lonesomeness I'd never known before. I kept thinking about that clipping, about how it had said "one, two, or three years." I prayed some and read my Bible, and I wondered what to do.

Finally, around three in the morning, I was so tangled up inside that I just had to do something, so I pulled on my garments and my darkest cape, tied on my black bonnet, and tiptoed out the kitchen door.

I rode my horse down to the boarding house where Corrin was staying, rapped on the door, and asked for him.

Mrs. Livingston, his landlady, gave me such a look of disapproval that I almost wilted from the heat of it. Then she told me in no uncertain terms that he was already gone and no decent young lady had any business coming there in the middle of the night.

You'd think I'd have gone home then. But that's when the madness overtook me, and I still can't tell why.

I stood there on the dark, empty street corner, looking out over the wide, spring-muddied river. Two steamboats were tied up at the wharf. I wondered which of them would bear William Ashley's company of young men up the river and away from me. The waterfront seemed different now. Dark and forbidding and frightening. I looked around, perhaps thinking I'd see Corrin, that he'd return to rescue me from the flood of strange feelings that were washing through me. And that's when temptation stepped in, because at that very moment I spotted a shadow that moved. I froze, expecting a robber or worse. But the moon slid from behind a cloud, and the shadow became a young lad—perhaps an orphan from the scruffy looks of him—a boy about my own small size.

The lad was sitting beside a heap of trash behind one of the liquor emporiums, and on an impulse I fished in my pocket. I found a few coins and even a whole silver dollar. I marched straight over to him.

A funny look appeared on his pinched-up face as he saw me approaching, but he didn't seem to have the gumption to get up and run away.

I said, "Good evening, young man. I have need of some clothing in your size, if you have anything to spare."

He gave me a fearful look, as if he'd already figured out that I was a little peculiar.

He said, "Don't have nothin' much but the rags on my back, ma'am, and I reckon I'd best keep them."

I looked more closely at his clothes. Though they were ragged, they seemed to be fairly clean.

I said, "Where do you live?"

He pointed toward a shabby little boarding house beyond a roughhewn fence. "My ma and me live there, since Pa got killed on the river."

"Where's your mother now?"

"She be a barmaid, workin' inside that saloon. They's a bunch of fellers celebratin' late as they're to go upriver tomorrow."

I suddenly wondered if Corrin might be among them.

I said, "Are you familiar with the Ashley expedition?"

His eyes lit up. "Am I! I'd go in a second if I was old enough."

"Are those the fellows getting liquored up?"

"I reckon some of them are."

"What are you doing here?"

"I be waitin' for Ma to come out so's I can take her home. She be drunk a good deal of the time."

"Can you run and look in and tell me if there's a tall fellow with rust-red hair inside?" I didn't want to risk Corrin's seeing me peer through the doorway.

"Yes'm."

He hiked over to the makeshift wooden hovel and peered in, apparently scanning the room. Then he came back, shaking his head. "There's most every other kind of gent you could imagine, but none with rusty hair."

45

"Are you sure? Might he have been wearing a hat?"

"Didn't see nobody with hats, though there be a couple of trappers wearing coonskins."

"Very well." I pursed my lips and thought. Then I said, "Do you have any other clothes at all in your room?"

"Jest another pair of pants and a raggedy shirt, and my pa's old suit jacket."

"Look," I said, falling deeper into my madness. "Run over there and bring me your extra set of clothes—shoes included, if you have any—and I'll give you this silver dollar and all of these smaller coins besides."

His eyes went wide with speculation. The coins would buy him at least one brand-spanking-new outfit, and I could see that he thought I was a madwoman for sure.

I tried to explain. "I need to get on a riverboat, and they'd never let a woman aboard—especially this time of night. I have to disguise myself. Please."

"What you want on the boat for?"

"I must speak with someone."

"The copper-haired feller you're lookin' for?"

"Yes. It's a matter of utmost urgency."

Apparently my words sounded important enough, for he looked me over again, then wheeled and took off at a sprint.

I stood waiting in the darkness, while the sounds of rowdy music floated on the chilly air. I wondered if the boy planned to come back. I stepped back, startled, as a loud burst of drunken laughter came from inside the barroom, but I quickly regained my courage. Nothing else happened to send me skedaddling for home.

The boy quickly returned with a neatly folded pair of twill pants with suspenders and a boiled homespun shirt. Atop them was a pair of what I took to be his old boots, for they were about my size and had a silver-dollar-sized hole in one sole. He also brought his father's jacket, which was a bit large but in somewhat decent shape, and he had added an old, battered man's hat to the display.

I handed over the money and took the lot.

Then I said, "I need to change my clothes."

"You ought to go on home to do that," he said, looking at the toe of his boot. "No lady ought to be out here this time of night anyways, and certainly not nekked, beg your pardon."

I bit back the sharp retort that came to my tongue. I might need more of this young man's help. I didn't want him angry, even if I had to ignore his rudeness in mentioning such as thing as nudity before a lady. But then, on the other hand, no lady would be out and about at this time of night.

"Surely there's someplace nearby where I can find privacy," I insisted.

But there wasn't. At least, not enough privacy to suit me. I bundled up the clothes and carried them, saving them for later. The boy walked alongside, looking at me curiously from time to time, as we approached the wharves.

"Do you know which steamboat is Ashley's?"

He tilted his head and gazed at me as if I were soft-witted, then he said, "Ashley ain't going nowhere on a steamboat. Heaven have mercy, lady. They're trappers—that's why they be calling that outfit the Rocky Mountain Fur Company. They're traveling upriver on special-made keelboats, going all the way up to the Three Forks of the Missouri and maybe even on to the mouth of the Yellowstone. They tells me that's some sixteen hundred whole miles." He said it with awe.

I swallowed hard at the thought of so much distance between me and Corrin.

The boy said, "They're goin' for three whole years, trappin' and adventurin' and sech."

But I was full atilt now, and nothing was going to stop me.

"Point me in the direction of the keelboats," I said.

He did. He went so far as to walk me right down to the levee and up to the pier.

There, tied up, were two riverboats more than a hundred feet long apiece. Giant boats, they appeared to have a draught of only some three feet. Father had explained keelboats to me when I was younger. The river was shallow in places and treacherous, he said. The boats were built shallow since it was important that they not run aground on the sandbars and snags and flood-drowned trees that made that old muddy river so downright dangerous in places.

The keelboats had both poles and oars, and the Mississippi could be traveled most of the way, so that the boats tended to go from the topmost settlement, which was nigh unto Canada, down to New Orleans. They'd float down with one form of cargo, usually furs, and ofttimes they'd just break up the boat for lumber rather than face the job of getting it back upriver. But sometimes, if the boat was a good one and the crew was dedicated, they'd pole and pull the vessel back up with a new cargo aboard. Some journeys took as long as nine full months.

At the best of times, when the boats reached the fork of the Missouri River, the current became too strong to row against. That's when the poles came out for sure, and men built like oxen went to work. They hitched their rope to the stout, tall mast, sails furled unless the wind decided to lend a hand—which was seldom.

The going was perilous, and the men were forced to scramble, wade, and otherwise labor upstream, sometimes poling, sometimes pulling, making their way through the rough terrain alongside the river.

Around each boat's periphery was a walkway for the polemen. And within that was the cargo box, an eighty-or-more-foot oblong storage and sleeping shed, sometimes separated into bunkrooms, and tall enough for a man to walk within. Forward was the galley, astern was the rudder and the pilot's station.

Against the faintly moonlit sky I could see bundled up shapes atop the cargo box. I figured men were sleeping there, so many going upstream and all. It looked like a harsh way to live, and I was suddenly determined to save Corrin from his foolishness. I would convince him to stay safe and sound right here in St. Louis. We would be married, and I would insist that Father give him a safe and decent job.

The boats were dark against the water. Their heavy timber keels creaked with the river's motion, and the night smelled of dampness and wood rot. The oilskin windows in the cargo box were dark, and along the sides and on nearly every part of the deck, oilskin-covered piles of supplies lay heaped sky high, ready for the journey. Long poles also lay ready for when the river turned dangerous on the way upstream.

"Which of the two boats carries the consignees?" I asked.

The boy frowned hard and shrugged. "I'd expect both of them. What you going to do, anyway?"

"I would like to make a request of you," I said. "Wait here for a moment."

He nodded, as if he took such a mission seriously, and even that encouraged me. Perhaps if he'd acted flippant, I'd have just gone on home.

I had spotted a coal shed, and now I stepped into the suffocating darkness and quickly changed my clothes. I tucked all my hair inside the tattered old hat and dabbed some coal dust on my cheeks and chin. Then I went back out and handed the boy my bundle of clothes—a dress, the cloak. I had traveled light, not carrying even my little draw-string purse, and the clothing was dispensable.

"Give these to your mother," I said, "and tell her she has a fine son."

"Yes'm."

"And please check back here at eight A.M. If I return, I'll leave your jacket and hat alongside that dinghy over there. If it's not there, that means I have gone with the boat. In that event, you are to go to where a small bay mare is tied up at the hitching post just behind where I met you."

"Yes'm."

49

"Lead the mare to the offices of the Far West Fur Company and ask for Mr. Arthur Davidson."

"Yes'm."

"Tell him, please, that Emily Anne is conversing with Mr. Corrin Brevard McCannon, and he is not to worry. Tell him I shall be back at my earliest convenience."

His eyes went wide, and he stared at me. "Don't know as I want to do that, ma'am. Why, if you're seriously goin' aboard—"

"Tell him also that I requested he give you five silver dollars for your trouble, so you can buy some new suits of clothes. He'll be sure to comply."

"What if he asks about you sellin' your clothes and sech?"

"Tell him the truth, but you needn't worry. I should be back on shore well before then. I only need to find my party and deliver a message that might well save him from terrible hardship."

It sounded mighty noble when I said it like that. And as I scrambled aboard the first of the keelboats, I felt adventurous and downright daring.

I considered climbing up the ladder to where the men were sleeping. I considered confronting them and demanding to speak with Corrin.

But just as I was about to step onto the ladder, a fearsome snarling snore came from topside, startling me. That made me think about the cantankerous nature of most riverboatmen, and I decided to wait until daylight, which was due to set upon us in about an hour. Then, just before the boat cast off, I'd confront Corrin under more comfortable circumstances. I had no doubt that he'd be so happy to see me he would abandon his plans forthwith.

I hadn't parceled in my own fatigue, though. I walked slowly around deck for a while, careful to avoid the ropes and such that were holding down the supplies—and at one point almost stumbled over a pile of what seemed to be clothing but which rolled over and snored.

Then I heard some rough swearing. Someone was coming toward me, and I quickly ducked backward into one of the storage bins of the large central storage area, the cargo box.

Enough moonlight filtered through the oilskin window so that I could see to creep in amid a heap of flour barrels and sugar sacks. I found a little place to sit right alongside a window that looked out over the dock, where anybody coming aboard would be visible, at least in outline. The whole night was uncommonly dark.

I looked around, then used my hands to feel the terrain. I was sitting beside a ceiling-high stack of wooden crates. I positioned a sugar sack to support my back, then leaned back and breathed deeply, trying to make my heart stop beating so fast.

But it was a wonderful feeling too. The adventure of the night had my heart singing like a bird set free for the very first time. I was going to surprise Corrin and take up his offer of marriage after all—and just in time to save him from the wilderness.

I must have nodded off for a bit. I suddenly awakened to the sound of voices, liquor-sodden from the rough sound of them. Men were coming aboard. I shivered a little and hunkered lower in my hiding spot. But I listened closely, hoping that one of the voices might be Corrin's.

Just then something slammed through the darkened doorway. I was at the far side of the shed and unable to see anything but hulking black outlines. Someone had pitched an object in—it might have been a buffalo from the size of it—and it almost landed on me. Then something else was thrown in, and I was just beginning to worry when I heard more voices and more thudding, and suddenly everything caved in above me. Sugar, sack after sack, bolts of cloth, barrels, crates were collapsing in an avalanche from the weight of whatever had been thrown in atop it all.

I was shouting—or trying to, for a barrel of flour broke open just then and I was half buried in thick powder,

51

strangling. The flour muffled my shouts. I could taste it—
that's how I knew for sure what it was—and I began flailing
about in a white cloud, still not doubting that my yelling
would be heard. But lo and behold, at that very moment the
entire boat listed with a sudden wave and the stacks of flour
and the crates shifted position. Boxes tumbled down around
my head, with me crying and spitting flour out of my mouth
and pinned tight against the wall now so that I couldn't even
see the window, much less what was beyond it.

Nobody was hearing me.

4

It took me a minute to get hold of my anger at who-ever threw in that baggage and caused the cargo to shift. I might have been buried alive. But as soon as I had hold of myself, I realized what a pickle I'd put myself in. And that's when I got downright ferociously scared.

I was indeed pinned tight. I tried again to shout, but the sacks and barrels and boxes surrounding me made it nigh unto impossible for me to even hear myself. I sat there with legs akimbo, elbows sprawled out like a hen's wings, and my heart beating even harder now. There was a gun-metal taste of true fear in my mouth.

I thought about Daniel in the lions' den, and I prayed that the Lord would deliver me from my folly and my pride.

About then the flour began to settle, and a dim square of daylight leaked through the oilskin window. Now I could see that I was in an even worse predicament than I'd thought. The little aisle that I'd traveled from the door to my perch was filled solid with fallen crates and sugar sacks.

My only hope was that I might tunnel through the supplies to the window, where I might break through the heavy oilskin. I set to praying and thrashing and angling, fighting with nail and tooth, and finally I forced my way to the nearest window.

But I had nothing sharp enough to penetrate the heavy oilskin. And though I tried to use my nails and broke every last one of them down to the quick, I was still trapped, made part of the baggage destined to go upriver with the Ashley Expedition, freight on its way up the Mississippi, then the Missouri, and all the way to the Yellowstone.

I broke down and cried for a while, partly from pure orneriness, partly from self-pity. I was sure by then that I was bound to suffocate. The keelboatmen would get up to the Three Forks on the Missouri, the full sixteen hundred miles from here, and finally unload their supplies, only to find a white-coated skeleton in men's garments stuck between the flour and the bolts of cloth, a mystery to one and all forevermore.

I cried again at the thought of it. And finally, after crying till I was cried out, I must have fallen into a light sleep because I shot awake, stiff and sore, to the sound of folks shouting and cheering and a volley of musket shot, then another.

I heard a lusty voice cry, "Set poles for the Three Forks of the Missouri!"

A boat horn blew several loud blasts, and I felt the boat lurch left. I could almost see the polemen heaving against their long poles, pushing and straining to move us out of the dock, circling slowly to get midstream, and then poling on upriver until, with luck, the sails might catch a breeze and move the boat on its own.

As soon as I felt the motion of the boat, I knew for a fact that madness had indeed taken me during the night and dragged me into this fix. And now I was all the way at the bottom of the pickle barrel, because daylight allowed me to see the dim surroundings of the full storeroom.

But there was no use shouting about it. The crowds ashore were seeing us off, shouting themselves. I remembered that the festivities had been in the works for days. I could feel more motion in the vessel as the great shallow boat slowly battled the current, then gathered speed. We were starting upriver.

Panic took me, and I yelled and kicked and tried to strike a bargain with God that if He'd get me out of this I'd never again disobey anybody, much less Mother and Father; that I'd never so much as have a strong thought against anyone in the world; and that I would most definitely never chase after another man, even if it seemed like the right thing at the time.

And then, after a while, when nothing changed and a soreness began to set into my throat from all the hollering, I managed to peer through the murky window again. The morning light allowed me more visibility now, and I could tell, with a sinking heart, that not a wisp of St. Louis was visible on the shore.

We were already upriver, well afloat. As for me, I was hungry, disgruntled, and suddenly angry at Corrin Brevard McCannon. I now blamed him for what I saw as my imminent death. He was at fault for tempting me into this. I wanted him to pay.

And at the same time I wanted to see him. I wanted to look into his warm hazel eyes and explain how I'd acted on a foolish instinct, and I wanted him to save my skin and take me back to St. Louis and stay there with me and work for Father. I wanted him to marry me and settle down in the city and act like a decent husband for all our born days so that I never again had an excuse to go gallivanting, as Mother called it, and get into trouble. And I was sure that once Father understood, he'd forgive me and everything could go back to being exactly the same as it was, though with Corrin in the picture, of course.

What a bunch of humbug that was. After what was to come next, Mr. Corrin Brevard McCannon was bound to be horsewhipped by my father if he so much as came near St. Louis.

That hour or so after we first shoved off was long and dreary, and I had all but given up on getting free. After a while, I managed to drift off again, figuring that I'd maybe die in my sleep and then the ordeal would be done with.

But after a bit I awakened to see that the sun had grown even brighter through the oilskin. My nose twitched at the smell of fresh-brewed coffee, frying bacon, and flapjacks. I was starved.

I dusted myself off some, and flour fell like snow from the narrow brim of my battered hat. I repinned my hair, put it tightly under the hat, pulled the hat down, and sat there, scowling.

Then I decided to try to struggle free once more. I was just shifting positions when the plank door suddenly swung wide open and a giant of a red-faced, liquor-soured keelboatman hove into view.

I managed a feeble cry for help that sounded more like a sob.

The man's head jerked around, and he stared at me, his red-rimmed eyes widening with astonishment. Then he rubbed his eyes with the heels of his hands, looked at me again, and said, "Wal, I'll be a ring-tailed vinegarroon."

He leaned back out the doorway and bellowed as loud as a boat horn. "Hey! Eh! Git in here, Mike Fink! We got a half-drowned river rat gnawing through our sacks and barrels!"

He would have stormed in then and yanked me up by the collar—I could see it in his eyes—but he couldn't get past the fallen barrels and crates and sacks either. He started toward me—first one way, then another. But then he gave up, so he was left on the far side of the landslide, glaring at me with nostrils twitching and fingers flexing, all but growling aloud in frustration.

I was glad to see even him. That is, I was glad to see him at first.

As if sensing my mood, the man relaxed some, probably figuring from my size that I wasn't much of a threat. He just stood framed in the doorway, a black-bearded man wearing a coonskin hat, scruffy clothing, and rough manners, his head tilted, looking me over and stroking his chin as if trying to decide what in fact I might be.

I started to tell him.

But just as the words came to my throat, I thought better of it. I suddenly realized that I was alone amid a boatload of some of the most depraved varmints that ever plied the Mississippi. Keelboatmen. Ever since we'd come to St. Louis, I'd heard stories of their coarseness and fighting, of their foul-witted lack of respect for womenfolk. All of a sudden all those memories boiled up, and I wasn't eager to admit that I was alone and at their mercy.

I forced my voice as deep as it would go and said, "Please, mister. My name is David McCannon. I've come for my brother, Corrin Brevard McCannon. Can you fetch him for me?"

Someone roared, "Fetch who, do ya say?"

The bellow came from another shaggy man, who loomed in the doorway behind the first one.

Blackbeard pointed at me. "There it is, Mike. A stowaway rat or a half-drowned vinegarroon, sure as your Auntie Mabel's gizzard."

Mike Fink whomped the fellow on the back of the head, hard enough to lurch him forward and knock his coonskin hat askew. "Watch your tongue about my Auntie Mabel," he said. "She's as fine a lass as ever wore a wooden leg."

I swallowed hard. I had heard about the legendary Mike Fink, and here he was in the flesh. He was dressed in a mud-stained buckskin shirt with fringes, and a pair of leather britches that seemed half threadbare and half stained. He had a full brown beard with hints of gray. He was tanned to nut brown, his face round and pleasant. But his pinched-up little blue eyes held fire, and they rested beneath furry eyebrows that darted around like caterpillars as he considered what he was seeing.

Fink was reputed to be the most rough-and-tumble fighter on the Mississippi, a riverboatman with no scruples and little sense, a man who might beat you to within an inch of your life for refusing to laugh at his constant jokes, a man who had once shot off a young slave's heel so that he'd be better able to fit into fancy shoes.

My fortunes had not improved.

As if to prove my thoughts correct, Fink hopped up and down, flapping his thick arms as if he were a chicken.

Sure enough, he crowed at the top of his lungs and shouted, "Cock-a-doodle-doo! A vinegarroo!"

Then he stopped short and cocked his head, craning it forward to peer evilly at me. He bellowed, "I'm half scorpion and half alligator, and I eat drowned rats and lizards for my breakfast. I can spit your bones out on a six-sided hurricane; I can eat your liver whole! Get up here, and I'll give ya a taste of old Mike Fink's thunder, you spawn of rabid skunks! I'm a saltwater roarer, and I'm chock-full of fight!"

"That critter ain't big enough to have no fight in it," Blackbeard muttered.

Mike Fink cuffed him again.

The man said, "Ouch!" and stepped back out of the way.

Fink then grinned darkly like a man about to gig a frog with a stick.

I shut my eyes and sent up yet another prayer. And then I looked back at Mike Fink, who still stood there grinning.

Suddenly he lunged forward, tried to get to me, couldn't get past the flour barrels, shoved in another direction till some barrels tumbled, and then he stopped, roared in anger, and bellowed, "Blast it all, I can eat an alligator and spit out the tail awalkin', I can smash a rock with my spit, I was sired by a hurricane and spawned by the thunder, but I can't get my hands on some ignorant, half-drowned stowaway whelp!"

He turned to Blackbeard and whomped him again alongside the head. "Get in there and get them barrels and sacks out of my way."

Blackbeard shot him a baleful glare. "The critter says he's the brother of that red-haired consignee, Corrin McCannon. Ought to let the brother move all them sacks, I say."

Mike Fink roared again, this time at Blackbeard. "By thunder, you're lookin' at a man who can eat a bushel of rattlesnakes for breakfast and polish it off with a barrel o' whiskey. I can split the earth with a stomp of my boot. Don't be tellin' me what needs done, you worthless mud-wog. Go git the feller yourself, or I'll have your hide for a new pair of boots."

I was wide-eyed. Trembling. Scared half out of my wits. And praying—silently. I was afraid now to let these reprobates so much as see me shut my eyes to send up a proper prayer.

Blackbeard hove out of view, and Mike Fink just stood there, filling the doorway, larger than the man who had preceded him. He appeared to be studying me anew.

"How'd you get aboard?" he growled.

I forced my voice into the low registers and said, "Please, sir, I didn't mean any harm. There's trouble at home"—that much at least would be true—"and I needed to get my brother."

"You're kin to that rust-headed young Scot?"

"Yessir, he's my brother." And thus I chalked up another lie.

"He sneak you past the guard?"

"No, sir, I just came aboard. No one was standing guard."

Mike Fink looked skeptical. "Had a guard on all night," he said. "You're a lyin' fool."

"Sir—"

"Aside from that, you're too feeble to be a boy." He inclined his head at another angle. "Pitiful, scrawny little runt of a specimen you is. Reckon we ought to just drop you overboard and have done with you—or use you as catfish bait."

"I'm sorry, sir, I—"

"Why, you're scrawny as a girl. Pitiful."

I felt anger rise up in me, but I bit it back. I said, "If you'll just get my brother, he'll explain everything."

"Reckon I'd best just drop the two of you overboard, if the McCannon blood has got so thin they's hatchin' out sech as you. Why, I've seen drowned kittens look a whole sight better."

59

I had to breathe hard before I replied. "I'm sorry, sir. I do the best I can."

He grinned. Then the grin grew broader and showed a wide gap in his teeth. He said, "Somethin' wrong here, if you was to ask me."

I bit my tongue and didn't say a word.

"Look at you. You're a mite too peaked. What you been havin'—a spell of the tizzicks?"

"My family has seen hard times. We had a spell without enough to eat." Yet another lie.

"I seen you before somewhere anyway. Don't know why, but you put me in mind of them fine, fancy fur traders. Heh. You been spendin' time on the riverfront?"

"Nossir, I—"

"What's going on?" Corrin said as he hove into view. He was speaking to someone behind him, and then I saw Blackbeard standing there. With irritation, Corrin said, "I don't have a brother," just as Blackbeard stepped up beside him and pointed. Corrin's eyes followed the gesture, his gaze lit on me, and he exploded in an exclamation of surprise and anger that does not bear repeating in decent company.

I looked at him, surprised.

"Beg pardon," he said to me, "but you can hardly blame me for being surprised. What in thunder are you doing here?"

Mike Fink wasn't about to relinquish his torment yet. He said, "Squishy little thing says it's your brother. Reckon you might be related to a bedbug?"

I saw Corrin stiffen. He turned partway toward Mike Fink, who grinned like an ape at the prospect of a fight.

Fortunately Corrin saw through him, swallowed his anger, and said, "Did sh—ahem—did he, well, did he really say he was my brother?"

"Slipped right off his tongue like molasses, and there's somethin' funny goin' on here."

"He's my younger brother all right," Corrin said quickly. "Though I hate to admit it. I beg your pardon for him. The boy's a little teched in the head. No harm intended, Mike. I'll take responsibility for him."

"And how do ya expect to do that, what with us going upriver? We ain't taking no sicklings along."

"I'll find a boat to take him back home."

I started to say, "No, you won't," but before I even had it out, Corrin flashed me a look that shut me up fast.

Mike Fink stepped back some, and I could all but see dollar signs rolling into his eyes. He said, "The lame-brained critter ruined some of our flour and sugar."

"I'll pay to replace it." Corrin quickly said.

Mike Fink looked around for anything else he might add to the tab.

I lowered my voice some more. "Can't some of you help me out of here? My whole body's been numb for an hour or more."

Corrin's lips pursed, and I wasn't sure right then if he really was glad to see me and was pretending otherwise or if he was so angry that he might drop me overboard himself. But he set to hauling barrels and sacks out on deck.

As soon as the work started, both Mike Fink and Blackbeard uttered a few curses, then vanished.

When they were out of earshot, Corrin stopped work and glared at me. "What in the name of all that's holy are you up to, Emily? You almost stopped my heart when I saw you. How did you get aboard?"

And that's when I started crying for real, just blubbering, making a total fool of myself.

"Hush. Hush up now. If those keelboaters hear you blubbering, they'll figure you for a female for sure. Just hush up." And he fell to work, throwing the rest of the sugar sacks out of the way.

By the time I was freed from my prison, I'd cried myself out.

Corrin wiped my face some, helped me tuck some stray strands of hair back under my hat, and then took me on deck.

A gnarly assortment of men lined up to take a gander at me—me feeling shamed now by the spectacle I was making of myself—and in front of Corrin at that.

He made me stand—hat on, of course—while he poured buckets of river water over me to wash off the flour. He poured a last bucket of fresh water to clean me off good. Then he stepped up and grabbed me by the ear and started steering me toward the galley.

"Give 'im what for," shouted one of the men.

"You need any help tannin' the runt's hide, I be willin'," said another.

From the looks of things, they were getting past their hangovers from the night before and working themselves up to some fresh revelry.

I tried to yank my head free, saying, "Ouch. Stop. You're hurting me," but Corrin just held on harder than ever and mumbled, "You'd best go along with whatever I do, or they may still figure out that you're not even a boy."

"So what if they do?" I said, trying to toss my shoulder.

"No telling," he said. "These men are used to painted women and squaws. They could do most anything and not even see the harm in it."

I shivered, sickened, and let him lead me forward by the ear.

He took me around to the other side of the deck, then shoved me back into the storage shed, handed me a broom, a mop, and a bucket, and said—loud enough for everyone to hear—"Now get hopping to clean up that mess, or I'll throw you overboard myself."

I worked till the storeroom was tidy again, though I have to admit I was muttering under my breath and my already stiffened muscles were soon sore as all get out.

When I was done, I stacked my implements in the corner and started to leave, but the door was shut and latched from outside. And so I went back by the oilskin window and tried to see out but couldn't see much. Then I sat down in a corner and worked myself into a brown funk, thinking about all the bad things that had ever happened to me, and how I tried so hard to do the right thing and nothing ever turned out, and about the way that Corrin had talked, and how he'd treated me with such disrespect.

After about half an hour he opened the door and handed me a tin plate with some flapjacks and eggs on it, and a tin mug of hot coffee.

I was mighty glad to get it. All the fight had gone out of me by then, what with the night's troubles and the last hour's work. I hung my head and said, "I'm sorry."

"You'd best be sorry indeed. What in thunder made you do it?"

"You," I said. "I didn't want you to leave."

I expected him to be pleased, but he shot me a dark look. "You sure have a knack for doing things at just the wrong time."

"I said I'm sorry."

"I'll have to give up the expedition."

"I had hoped you would."

"I'm going to have to take you back to Saint Louis, and there'll be no way to catch up with them again."

I didn't say a thing.

He gave me an almost pitying look. "I know what you've been thinking, but I'm not going to stay in Saint Louis, Emily. There is nothing there for me."

"I didn't expect you to stay," I lied sadly. In truth, I was convinced that the moment I got him back to the city I could make him stay after all, if only I'd agree to marry him.

But I still had a great deal to learn about Mr. Corrin Brevard McCannon, and I was bound to learn it all in the hardest possible way.

5

Corrin made me stay in the storeroom. He told the others he was punishing me, but he told me that he was doing it for my own safety, so that they wouldn't discover the truth.

I stayed in there all day, moping and feeling sorry for myself and plotting my revenge against the world for the way my quest had turned out.

It was well after dark when Corrin appeared again. He said, "You can come out for a while now. We're eating, and then the boys will start drinking and such. We'll go on upriver a ways, then put in to shore to sleep overnight on land. I'll put you back in here before the revelry turns rough."

I just turned up my nose and wouldn't say a thing to him, hoping to bring him to heel. It didn't do a lick of good.

He looked disgusted as he led me forward to near the cook's shack. Wooden tables had been set up, and iron pots filled with venison stew were sitting here and there. The men were dipping it out onto wooden plates. A huge pot of coffee rested atop an iron stove just inside the cookshack, where the potbellied Frenchman who apparently did the cooking had to pour it for you.

"Keeps the boys from throwing it when they get mad," Corrin explained.

There wasn't room enough at our plank table for everyone, so I sat on a barrel, tucked in behind Corrin, and gulped down my stew and coffee while he sat positioned between me and the others, halfway protecting me but halfway mad too. I could tell he'd really rather not have me on his hands.

After a while they finished their meal and started passing around a brown whiskey jug. Corrin took a swallow, even though I jabbed him with my elbow so hard I made him wince.

Then one rough-spun young man said, "Give the boy a swaller."

I seemed to recognize the voice.

I looked up, and the man's face loomed into the firelight. He had a broad nose and a square jawline, dark eyebrows, and a friendly slit of a mouth. He was wearing a buffalohide hat that mostly hid his brown hair, and a brand-new buckskin jacket decorated with porcupine quills. The knife strapped to his hide belt was so big that it made me cringe. He was familiar all right, but for some reason I couldn't place him.

"No, thankee," I said, trying to sound coarse, male, and unafraid. Why did this man look so familiar?

"Go on, give him a little taste. Warms a body up," the man insisted.

"Mind your own business, Bridger," Corrin said.

And in that instant I realized who he was.

Jim Bridger! But he seemed a man now instead of the boy who worked in the St. Louis blacksmith shop. Reckon I'd never really looked at him to see how much he'd grown that day he came to church.

I'd had no idea that he'd signed on to this expedition. I huddled deeper into the shadows, worried that he was going to recognize me and give me away.

At that moment, Bridger seemed as rough and as coarse as any of them. He was bound that Corrin should pass me the jug. "Go on," he said. "Give the boy a little nip. Warm up them skinny bones."

Finally Corrin turned steely-jawed stubborn, and Bridger stepped over and handed me the jug himself. He glared down at me, saying, "I don't mind that you're a half-wit. I'm bound to drink with any man who rides aboard the same riverboat, teched in the head or no. I said drink, boy. I don't like the way Mike Fink here is treatin' you. Drink, and drown the lot of them if they don't like it."

I leaned forward, accepted the jug, and put it to my lips—partly because Bridger surprised me so much by standing up to them all. Besides, if I had another choice, I couldn't think of it at the moment.

I turned the jug up and let just a tiny bit of the poison trickle down my throat. I all but gagged before I could swallow, never having tasted liquor before. That was the nastiest mouthful I ever had in my life.

I handed the jug back, wiped my mouth with the back of my hand as the rest of them were doing, and said, "Thankee, Mr. Bridger," trying to sound like the half-wit they said I was.

Several of the men were peering darkly at me from beneath beetled brows now, as if in speculation, and I was not at all comfortable with the harshness of that brigade.

Bridger looked around at all the men sitting there, trying to see if anyone wanted trouble over his friendly gesture toward me, I suppose. Nobody did much of anything, not even Corrin, so Bridger gave me a big friendly wink and went back and hunkered down. I wondered for a second if he had recognized me. But he looked away into the blackness upriver, as if looking toward his future. He took another swig, brought a lick of tobacco out of his trap sack, lit up a pipe, then passed the jug along and the tobacco pouch right behind it.

They had a boatload of explorers and trappers aboard, many of whom were bound to become famous one day. There was Jim Bridger himself, who would become the king of all the mountain men. Thomas Fitzpatrick was aboard, and Jedediah Smith, that strong Christian man whose morals never wavered though his path was to be a hard one. He was finally shot down at a watering hole by angry Creek Indians, or so I would learn from mutual friends.

David P. Beckworth was there too, going upriver for the first time, and Etienne Provost had come along for the

66

adventure. The brothers Hamilton and William Sublette and another man named Robert Campbell were three more names that would become legends in their own lifetimes, and later those names would appear on valleys and mountain passes, forts and holes throughout the West. Henry Fraeb was on board, and years later he would open a trading fort above Brown's Hole on the upper Elkhead Creek.

Before that night was done, I was to watch the besotted antics of the lot of them and develop an image of mountain men that I have yet to repair—though I certainly would come to see another side of them, and you'd think the two would even each other out.

But youth is impressionable, and those hooligans were a caution, all young men and most of them off to see the world for the very first time.

After the whiskey jug was empty and another broken open, most of them set to trying to outbrag Mike Fink himself, all of them growling about how they could outfight and outtrap and outdrink one another—and Fink roaring about how he was half man, half hoss, and half alligator.

And then he said he was a saltwater roarer who loved the women, and he was chock-full of fight again. He said he could peel a coiled-up rattlesnake with his breath, and drink the river dry with one big gulp, and break the boat in half by a stomp of his foot. And all the other men were getting in the spirit of things and trying harder to outbrag him. He was still treating me as if I were dirt beneath his feet, making nasty comments about my puniness until I was nigh unto convinced that he suspected the truth and was just too blamed mean to come right out and say it.

Mike had brought a close friend along for the ride, a man by the name of Carpenter. When the men were liquored up, Fink and Carpenter started pacing one another off, from one end of the keelboat to the other. The men set up a roar, standing back then, hooting and placing bets, and I had no idea what chicanery was afoot until Bridger came over to Corrin and said, "My money's on Mike Fink. You want to place a bet on Carpenter?"

"What are they doing?"

"They got them a habit of shooting tin cups full of whiskey off one another's heads," Bridger explained. "They try to back off at least seventy yards afore they commence, but this boat ain't going to allow for such a distance as that and so they're figuring to up the ante by doing it in the dark."

"Seems foolish to me, not to mention dangerous," Corrin replied.

Bridger said, "I once seen Fink take the tails off six pigs at thirty paces—and never put another mark on them."

"Yes," said Corrin, "and I've heard about his escapade with the slave boy downriver too—about how he shot off his misformed heel just to provide the foot some symmetry. I don't need to tell you what I think of Fink's shooting. But what he has in skill he sorely lacks in brains."

Bridger gave us a grin. "Fink shoots better close up, whereas Carpenter has it all over him when it comes to a really long distance. That's why my money is on Fink."

Indignantly I said, "The Reverend Farnsworth would not approve of gambling."

Bridger stared at me as if I'd turned bright green.

Corrin said, "I'll put a silver dollar on Carpenter then."

"Heh," said Bridger, looking sideways at me. "That ain't enough to bother bettin'. I'll catch you after you've trapped a year, and we'll commence to try this whole thing again."

He returned his level gaze to me then and said, "Hello, Miss Davidson."

I swallowed hard and had a hard time speaking. I finally mumbled, "You know who I am?"

"If I hadn't, you sure would have given it away just now, wouldn't you?"

I realized my slipup and was too embarrassed to say anything else.

"But yes, I knew you. I seldom forget a face—and especially not one so prominent as yours."

Anxiously Corrin said, "Does anyone else know?"

"'Spect not, at least not yet. I been covering for her as best I can, though I can't for the life of me figger what she's doing aboard."

"Stowed away," Corrin said and shot me an angry, sideways glare.

Bridger gave him a strange, almost accusing look, then shrugged his shoulders and said to me, "Some of the others are getting mighty suspicious, though. I'd skedaddle overboard first chance I get, if I was you. I know some of these rowdies. They find out you're a woman, ain't no tellin' what to expect."

I said, "Thank you, Jim. I shall owe you a debt of gratitude all my life." I looked up at Corrin. I was afraid, and I didn't try to hide it.

He said to Bridger, "It could come to bloodshed, if Fink figures out who she is."

Bridger nodded. "Your father has an enemy in Mike Fink," he explained to me. "Seems that Fink was giving some slaves the what for down in Saint Looey a while back, when your father sent him skedaddling. Fink would likely stop at nothing for a chance to get even with him."

"That seems unfair—" I said, but just then the shooting started.

Corrin and I ducked back along the cargo house with the others—I was holding my hands over my ears. The shooting was over just as fast as it started, and the keelboatmen roared and clapped and shouted. It seems that both men had drilled each other's cup at the very same moment, neither one harming so much as a hair of the other's head.

"Wal, if that don't take all," Mike Fink shouted. "Break out another of them jugs and let's celebrate!"

At that, the whole lot fell to whooping and hollering even louder, and Corrin wasn't a whole sight better than the rest.

I had taken a closer look at Corrin by now and saw that he was dressed no better than the rest of them. With every passing moment, he seemed more like one of these rough-hewn trappers and less like the gentleman I had known in St. Louis.

He wore a black felt hat and a buckskin shirt over a flannel undershirt. He had a long knife in a buffalohide sheath at his waist and a stubble of rusty beard was already beginning to grow on his handsome square-jawed face. I had some second thoughts about him. I was beginning to see a side of him I'd never suspected. And I was beginning to rue my actions in coming upriver all the more.

Finally we started putting in toward shore, where the men would camp out on land for the night. It was a gradual process; we were headed for a point upriver, just barely visible in the moonlight.

I leaned back into a sort of alcove and let my gaze wander upward to the sky and its canopy of stars. The trees hung like black feathers over the riverbanks, and the river sounds were a gentle, soothing murmur. Behind the snarly bragging of the keelboatmen, I could hear the hum of crickets. The smell of mud and foul water and river foliage was strong in my nose. The moon was a pale gold quarter disk, reflected and wrinkled in the water.

After a while I started feeling more or less content to be just floating along as the polemen and oarsmen moved us forward. I must have fallen asleep, for I came awake with Corrin nudging me, then shaking my shoulder.

I heard it then. A ghostly voice, drifting across the dark water and through the night. "Halloo...halloo..."

The men were all listening too, sort of hunkered together, and it was deathly silent except for the night noises and that eerie hollering.

And then a smaller keelboat washed around the bend up ahead, a thirty-foot vessel. They had a lantern in the prow, and the voice was now joined to the man holding the lantern. "Halloo...halloo, there. Who's aboard? What craft are you?"

Apparently they had spotted us in the moonlight through a break in the trees while still on the far side of the bend, whereas we'd only heard the spooky voice coming out of the blackness.

The men all grinned sheepishly, and then Mike Fink stepped up to our prow and hollered back, "Ashley expedition, Captain Mike Fink, patroon of the flotilla. We's headed for the Three Forks of the Missouri, and we're fresh out of St. Loo."

Jim Bridger moved up beside him and shouted, "We have need for you to pull aprow."

"You have goods for downstream?" the voice echoed back.

"More or less," Jim said.

As the boat began to change course and make for us, Fink came over to Corrin. "I was of a mind to let your little vinegarroon go on upstream—maybe trade him to the Injuns for a good dog or two. But Bridger's got his wind up, so I reckon now's the time if ever there was one to send that half-wit brother of yours back downstream."

Corrin's shoulders slumped, but he stood and helped me up. Then he went into the storeroom. When he came back out carrying powder horn and rifle, bullet pouch, and other deerskin bags, I suddenly felt ashamed.

I said, "You don't have to come back. Just put me aboard, and I'll go by myself. I'm really sorry for what I've done."

"There's no other way for it, Emily," he said softly. "No telling what sort of varmints are aboard that keelboat. They may be decent men or killers. If I put you aboard by yourself, we may never see nor hear from you again."

I hung my head. "I expect you'd be pleased by that."

71

"Don't talk nonsense. Look. Here they are now. Step careful—come on—there you go."

With that, he helped me over the side, and I tumbled down and was grabbed by other hands and set on the deck of the smaller keelboat.

Corrin threw down his bags, then jumped down beside me.

"What's this?" said the man with the lantern.

"A half-wit stowaway and his fool of an older brother," Mike Fink called back, then he laughed like the drunkard he was. "They're bound back for Saint Loo, and you can set them down at the docks. Charge them any size fare you like, and pray that you'll get it!"

And then the larger keelboat was pulling away, the men outdoing themselves to put distance between us, and I knew who was behind that too. Jim Bridger meant only the best. He really was trying to save my skin.

The captain of the smaller vessel was a man by the name of Three-Toes Adams, who said he hailed from New Orleans. He explained that he'd received the name because of an accident, then asked us what we were doing on the river.

I more or less stayed silent while Corrin tried to explain things as best he could. But the only thing the captain seemed to care about was whether or not we had the ability to pay.

Suddenly Corrin said, "Where's your crew?"

"My polemen got a better offer and stayed upstream," Three-Toes said. "My oarsmen, the same."

"You going to be able to navigate without them?"

"Reckon so. Ain't had no trouble so far."

"I'm happy to help if I can," Corrin said.

I said, "It seems to me that we're floating along just fine."

"That's a fact," Three-Toes said.

"Who are the other passengers?"

The captain eyed Corrin carefully, then said, "Got three trappers aboard who are bringing beaver plew downstream. Say they had a scurvy season—they're barely paying for their grub. Skinny trip for me, I'll tell ya. I don't cotton to free passengers."

"We intend to pay," Corrin said.

"Ya shore as skunks will. I'll take ya downstream if you got the fare, but otherwise I'm bound to put you back aboard that ugly boat you got throwed off of."

"It's too late," I piped up.

"Ain't too late to throw ya overboard," Three-Toes said.

"We can pay when we get to Saint Louis," I quickly replied. I was still using my deepest voice.

"Feared that won't be soon enough."

"How much?" Corrin said, sighing in exasperation.

"What ya got in that pouch there?"

"Buckshot. But I have this new rifle and other negotiable goods that would interest a trapper, all brand-new and unused."

"Then I'll take the lot for the trip."

"But—that's robbery! These things are worth a dozen trips downriver."

"Worth is as worth does. And you'll be thanking me too, afore the night's done. Giving up them goods will keep the others from robbin' you of it in your sleep and droppin' you overboard to drown in your dreams, so you might as well say I've jest saved your worthless hide."

Corrin glumly handed his goods over to the man, who grinned toothlessly, took them away, stowed them somewhere, then came back to steer the boat, not bothering to say another word.

Corrin and I settled against the steerhouse wall, he not speaking to me, his shoulders still slumped in defeat. In the distance, we could still see the black hulk of Mike Fink's keelboat laboring upriver in the cloud-shrouded moonlight. The polemen and oarsmen ground away against the choppy

73

water, apparently having decided to make more distance before putting in for the night. We could hear the men's reveling voices drifting on the wind. They were singing now, probably celebrating the fact that they'd seen the end of us.

I felt beside myself as I saw the hopeless look on Corrin's face.

It would be some time before we learned we had been blessed by the Lord to be rid of Mike Fink's keelboat. Fink and his boys made it only as far as Fort Osage before their boat ran aground on a sandbar and sank to the tune of $10,000 loss for the Ashley Expedition. All the survivors piled aboard the remaining boat, and the expedition forged on, finally making the mouth of the Yellowstone, where Mike Fink and Carpenter built a fort.

It seems Fink and Carpenter kept to their old habit of shooting tin cups filled with whiskey off one another's head. When they got into a howdy-do over a squaw, Mike Fink talked Carpenter into settling things as usual—by "shooting cups."

But Fink tricked Carpenter. He drilled him through the forehead at sixty paces, then wept and claimed it was all an accident. A third party decided that there had to be some law afoot, even at the mouth of the Yellowstone. He shot Mike Fink, then was in turn mysteriously drowned the following summer, and that was the end of the lot of them. I shudder to think where Corrin might have ended up had he been in on that foofaraw.

When we later learned the truth about what happened, Mr. Corrin Brevard McCannon and I were both pleased that we had missed that party. I even ended up with the satisfaction of knowing that I had saved Corrin from a bad fate after all. Corrin himself admitted it, though I was careful not to let myself crow.

Nevertheless, I was to pay a high price for my tomfoolery in stowing away on that keelboat. My own expedition on the mighty Mississippi had only begun.

74

6

I fully expected the boat ride back downstream to be a simple matter. After all, we were only fourteen or so hours out of St. Louis.

On Mike Fink's boat we had been oaring and poling upstream, and that was slow going. The mighty Mississippi was doing the pushing now. With the power of that big, muddy river behind us instead of fighting against us, we figured we'd be back in the city in under six hours.

The trappers also seemed eager to get to St. Louis. They acted furtive and edgy and kept looking upstream. I decided it was because they'd been in the wilderness for such a long time that they were anxious to finally reach the city and all its luxuries.

The few men on this pitiful excuse of a keelboat were a whole different tune from the twenty or more hard-backed men who had poled us upstream. There were only the captain and five trappers, two of these being skinny French woodsmen in coonskin hats. The latter were leaning back resting, watching the dark river and trees float past while they talked of the weather and furs.

I napped a bit.

Just past sunup, Corrin pulled out his pocket watch and calculated that we'd be in the city by mid-morning with no trouble at all.

After a while the sun got hotter. I got stiff and sore and tired of sitting beside Corrin, who just stared solemnly at the muddy water as the tree-lined shore rolled by. He refused to say more than an occasional harsh word that made my hide feel raw. And it seemed the closer we got to St. Louis, the worse his mood became.

I finally got up and stretched, then started exploring the boat. I spoke to the men, for I had them all thinking I was a boy and they scarcely paid me any mind at all.

I approached one of the French trappers. This grizzled old villain was down from Canada to work for what he could find. He called himself Louis, and he seemed a lonesome cuss. As I talked with him, he began jabbering as if he hadn't spoken with another soul for a year.

Once he started talking, he had a hard time quitting. His accent was amazing, so full was it of buzzes and hisses and soft little sighs. I had to listen closely, and sometimes translate the French, in order to stay on top of his flood of words.

I asked him where he'd been trapping, and he mumbled something about the Yellowstone. And then he started mean-mouthing his fellow travelers. He said the others were a mite rough for his taste, and he tended to keep his distance. Once they'd sold their pelts in St. Louis, he was going to be rid of the bunch of them and go on down to New Orleans by himself.

He was kind enough to take me on a tour of the boat, and he started by talking about the beaver packets that lined the decks and filled the storage spaces. After cleaning, dressing, and curing the hides, the trappers then had bundled them into hundred-pound stacks of beaver plew, each one holding some eighty pelts. These were worth some $300 to $500 in the mountains and three times that much in the city. There were dozens of such packets aboard.

And yet Louis, too, told me that he and the others had had a poor trapping season. I thought that peculiar but didn't bother to call him on it.

I suppose I did give him a strange look, because out of the clear blue he shifted stories and told me how they would have had the best year ever, but some unscrupulous trappers found their cache in the woods and stole it. Cost them most of their profit for the full year, and though it looked as if they had quite a stack of property, every remaining beaver pelt was dear to them. The profits were to be their grubstake to let them start afresh, he said sadly. It was all that the six of them had in the world.

I said, "Why six?"

"Why, there's me and Pierre and Three-Toes—"

"Three-Toes? I thought he was captain of the keel-boat."

He frowned, looked angry for a moment, then said, as if it had just dawned on him, "Why, that he is. Wonder why I was adding him in? Reckon this trip is getting me a bit addlepated."

I was puzzled too but didn't make much of it. I wanted to tell him I knew how it all worked, that my father was Owner & Proprietor of the New West Fur Company and I'd been spoon-fed on such trappers' tribulations for most of my life. But I feared that he might either know my father—or know of him—or more likely might peg me as a bald-faced liar.

Worst of all, he might know that my father had sired two spunky daughters and nary a son. So I kept my mouth carefully shut on that subject and acted as if every word he spoke to me was freshly learned and cherished.

We were walking near the stern when I spotted a smaller-than-usual stack of pelts. "What's that?"

"Prime pelts," he said proudly. "There's some first-rate beaver but also some white fox and other fancy stuff. If we can sell it at a good price, we'll make our bacon for the year to come and then some."

Another lie! I called him on it this time. "Thought you said things were bound to be rough."

He looked angry again. He said, "A man is likely to say a whole passel of things when he's talking. Don't mean a fool needs to believe every one of them."

I ignored his attitude as I walked over to the packet to try to peer inside. It was wrapped in thick hide, skin side out. As we approached it, a bit of a swell rolled upriver and the packet rolled with it, up against the railing at the end of the stern.

We had a good wind behind us and were floating along fast enough to kick up a wake. Spray was flying, and I said, "Aren't those furs going to get wet?"

I stepped forward with all good intentions. I meant to roll the packet backward, to shelter it again beneath the lip of the deck. But at that moment I stepped into a tiny slick of water, and it set me off balance. I reached for the packet anyway. And just as I grabbed one end, another swell lifted the keelboat. It listed suddenly to one side. I slipped again, and my extra weight on the bundle of furs caused the whole blamed thing to tip end up.

Then the boat righted itself, and the whole packet slid, neat as a rattler into a hole, right over the side and into the deep, muddy water.

I leaped forward and tried to grab it, almost tumbling overboard myself, but it was too late. I could only stand there, blinking, and watch the wake swell up again and the plews sink to kingdom come.

And then I saw Louis's face register the shock of it. Suddenly he turned to glare at me, and he seemed to grow larger, looming up like a balloon being blown full of air. His eyes kept getting darker and meaner, and his furrowed white-flecked eyebrows kept dipping into a deeper and deeper scowl. And then he bellowed like a gator and lunged for me, his mouth all but frothing.

I ran.

He chased me, apparently bound to get his money's worth out of my hide since his other hides were long gone. I ran shrieking around the deck, yelling for help.

The others came to attention. Louis caught me. And then Corrin was in the fray, dragging the trapper off me, and the Frenchman shouted vile things I'd never heard before— some in French, but I could tell from his voice that he was cursing us both.

He went to pounding on Corrin, at the same time managing to tell the others that I'd pitched their good pelts overboard. He made it sound as if I'd done it on purpose, and then they were all coming for me. I felt as though I were in the middle of a pack of mad dogs.

I could see Corrin trying to defend me and getting pummeled in the process.

I had my arms up, sheltering my head, when somebody hit me with a left hook that sent me spinning. Somebody else grabbed me around the waist and lifted me up. My hat flew off.

I'd had it pinned on tight but not tight enough for this whoop-de-do.

And as my locks came flying loose, the whole bunch of them stopped short and stared. Louis shook his head, as though clearing it of cobwebs. Corrin was sitting on the deck beside him, holding his jaw, his eyes wary now and filling up with fear.

Louis shook his head again and swore. "It is a river wraith."

Three-Toes said disgustedly, "It's nothing of the sort. It's just a low-down scrawny girl."

"That's my wife-to-be," Corrin snarled, "and I'll thank you to watch what you say." Which surprised me no end, considering the way he'd been acting ever since Mike Fink set us aboard this craft.

Corrin tried to get up, but two trappers knocked him back down.

Louis gripped my elbow and turned me around in a little pirouette for the others to take a gander at.

"Skinny," he said. "And sickly. A puny leetle *blatte.*"

I had studied French in school, and of course the St. Louis waterfront was a school in itself when it came to French cursing and foul words. I knew full well that he had just called me a puny little cockroach.

I sputtered. "I most certainly am not—"

79

"Be quiet, or you'll make it worse," Corrin growled from the deck, and for a change I listened to him.

"Throw her overboard and let her dive for them pelts," one trapper snarled. "Don't matter if she's a girl or a mule."

Corrin clenched his teeth. "You harm her, and I'll live to shoot every last one of you dead."

The tallest trapper was a weasely-looking man with a thin face, who hadn't said much yet. He stepped up and kicked Corrin hard in the ribs. Corrin grabbed his side and grunted, then stayed quiet as two others leaned over him and dared him to stand up.

"My father owns the New West Fur Company," I shouted, trying to divert their attention from Corrin to me. Tears were streaming down my face, and I could see from their faces that I was in far more trouble than I knew how to get out of. "He'll replace your pelts or pay you the fair market value for them."

Louis cocked his head, and the hatred in his eyes was fierce. "You cost us plenty, and thieves are shot on thees river."

"I stole nothing."

"Ah, no, indeed. You just throw ze pelts overboard, and now you insult us weeth these lies?"

"I didn't mean to do it."

"Mean it or not, it's done," said the thin-faced man. "No backing out now."

"I say slit out her gizzard and send her after them pelts," said the third man, who was short and chunky as an iron safe.

But Louis was looking at me—thinking about something, I could tell. Then he turned to them. "What if she tells ze truth?"

"You crazy? You think old Arthur Davidson would let any daughter of his go gallivanting around on the river?"

That seemed to strike Louis's sense of humor, for he chuckled at the thought and fell silent.

"You goin' to fix her ticket?" asked the third trapper. "Or you leavin' it up to me?"

The tall one said, "What you expect me to do? I can't tan her hide—she's a girl, for crying out loud. Ain't the same as taking on a man."

"Girl or not, she's done for us."

"Tie her and her lovair up with that rawhide," said Louis, "while I consider thees."

"If you're going to do some thinking, you better hurry. We only got an hour or so till we hit Saint Loo," said the thin-faced trapper. "I say throw her and that fancy man of hers overboard right now and have done with it."

Louis cursed again. "It ees a hard decision," he said, stroking his chin. "Eef we kill theem, those who put theem aboard will remember us."

"'Twas dark enough that none of 'em really ever seen us."

"They'd remember the boat."

"Theen we would have to sink ze boat. Have you no sense?"

"We don't have to dock at Saint Loo," said the thin-faced man. "We could just toss the bodies and keep right on goin' down to New Orleans. We could sell the boat there."

As they were having this conversation, Corrin still lay on the deck.

Louis kept his eye on him and on me. Now he nodded, and the two men leaned over and pinned Corrin down. He struggled, but I could see that they'd hurt him bad. He was winded and bleeding. They started tying him with rawhide. He got a burst of energy and tried to fight back, but with four to one and him already down and bleeding, he didn't stand a chance.

While they tied him, Louis picked up a trap bag and pulled out a whiskey bottle. Then he sat down on a barrel and took a swig, acting as though he was thinking.

I didn't bother to squabble as the trappers bound my hands together too and then my feet. I knew I couldn't best

81

them and didn't plan to get hurt any worse than I already was.

They stepped back and admired their handiwork. And now that the trouble was more or less settled, Three-Toes came around the corner to see what was in the wind.

"What she done is ze same as stealing pelt," Louis explained. "Now we theenk we weel have to keel them."

Three-Toes agreed that we needed our medicine. "I says when I first laid eyes on them two that I was bringing trouble aboard. But we got them for a right fine rifle and trapping gear at that. Hee." Then he went back to wherever he'd been, while the others fell to plotting against us.

I had hoped that Three-Toes might be on our side, but now I knew that he was part of the conspiracy, and no help was going to be found from that cowardly bag of bones.

Louis and friends sat and glared at us for a while, and I could see all sorts of dark plans flit through their minds. They kept passing around the whiskey bottle. After the fourth or fifth round, they began to get more interested in the bottle than in us, and then they ignored our presence altogether and talked among themselves.

They kept lamenting the loss of their furs. Louis actually got teary-eyed as he talked about the hardship we'd caused them and the terrible time that lay ahead because of my inconsideration, talking just as if we weren't there to hear and as if I'd dropped those pelts overboard on purpose.

I butted in. "My father will reimburse you when we get to Saint Louis. I told you as much, and I'll see that it's done. I am genuinely sorry for what happened, but it was a pure accident, not—"

"Shuddup, girlie," said the man who resembled an iron safe.

"Stupid girls anyway," said the thin-faced one. He furrowed his thin eyebrows and shot me a baleful stare. "Women don't belong on the river no ways. What you doing on a riverboat?"

I wasn't about to go into it, so I kept my lip buttoned.

The man turned to Corrin. "What you doing bringin' a woman aboard a riverboat? What kinda man are you, anyways?"

Corrin's cheeks went dark with anger, and I thought for a moment he was going to explode. But he also managed to hold his tongue.

Louis said to me, "Why did you put our goods overboard? Have you no conscience, *ma fille?*"

"I am speaking the truth," I said, "and you know it. You saw what happened. You're just trying to make me feel worse about it."

Louis kept a pained look on his face as he took another swig.

"Yeah, and ain't that a caution," said the iron-safe man. "Your pa's so rich and all that you ain't even got a decent set of clothes. Look at you, all dressed up in rags and such." He guffawed, and the others joined in.

I fell silent, losing hope of communicating with them.

After a moment, a renewed look of mirth came into Louis's eyes. Well liquored up, he slurred his words as he said, "We best dress her up in ze fine clothes before we reach Saint Loo—for her oh-so-rich papa to see! Ah, *voilà!* That would be a proud day for ze family." He laughed again, so derisively that I cringed with shame.

"Scrawny as a runt pup, but ya take a look at her face, and it's right pretty," said the iron-safe man, peering at me. "Put her in somethin' frilly, and ya might get a penny or two for her in New Orleans—make up for some of our losses on them plews."

I felt my heart sink, Corrin looked alarmed, and the other men looked suddenly interested.

"Got to spruce her up some," said the thin-faced man. "Ain't nobody going to pay a red copper for her, way she is."

"And ain't no call to take her all ze way to New Orleans," said Louis. "There eez a bawdy house in Saint Loo that might just as well take her and save us ze trip downriver."

Corrin was flexing his bound-up hands. He said, "I am going to kill you all."

But they just chuckled and looked at him as if they were suddenly fond of him and appreciated his antics.

The iron-safe man told him, "Reckon I'm beginning to see what you was up to after all, feller. 'Spect you was up to pretty much the same thing as what we jest come up with."

Corrin ground his teeth and sealed his mouth shut, but I could see that he was quietly straining against the rawhide and going crazy from the frustration of having to listen to those river lizards crow and bellow and hoot and insult us both.

The thin-faced man took a long swig of whiskey. "Say, Clete—" and that was the first I'd heard the iron-safe man's name—"ain't you got that red petticoat you brought downriver for your lady friend in New Madrid?"

Clete's ugly face lit up, and a broad grin spread out upon it. He stood and wobbled toward the cargo shed.

The others kept sending the bottle back and forth, and by the time Clete came back with a parcel in his hands, Louis had bitten the cork out of yet another bottle, spit the cork overboard, and taken a long swizzle.

Clete brought out the petticoat, and it was a horror to behold. Bright shining red satin with a frill of net tulle like a ballet dress for the skirt, something designed to help puff out a dress like a fancy crinoline, though this was much shorter. It came to about the knees, and it was the ugliest garment I ever did see.

Clete came over and lifted me to my feet. "Let's see what you're worth when you're dressed up, girlie."

He untied my hands so he could get the awful thing over my head. I tried to get up enough wind to spit in his

84

face, as the heroines did in certain books I'd read. But when I tried, he punched me in the stomach, just hard enough to knock the wind out of my sails, then shoved me over and braced me against the mast.

"Let's tie her up here," he said. "Like she was a mast-head on some fine ship, good enough to carry her pappy's furs."

"Or like she's on a counter in a general store, cash on the barrel head," another added.

The men were so drunk now that they were all beginning to stagger. Their anger was turning into perniciousness of another kind.

I didn't want to be punched again, so I went along with them, not knowing what else to do. I prayed silently as they lashed me to the mast, and thanked the Lord that the worst they were up to—so far—was pulling on that silly-looking petticoat right over my shirt and pantaloons.

It looked all the more ridiculous for that. As soon as they saw me in it, they began to hoot and holler. Clete laughed so hard he bent double and had to hold his fat belly in his hands. And then they all shared another swig, and Clete yelled at one of the Frenchmen, "Bring your Jew's harp here, Pierre. I got me some wingdinging to tend to."

I glanced at Corrin then. The shocked look that came into his eyes as he got a gander at me was a sight to behold. I could tell by that look just what a sorry sight I had become.

Though I really didn't have to see his reaction to know how ridiculous I looked. I could tell that my hair stuck out like Medusa's snakes, my britches were ill-fitting, my old boiled shirt was stuffed into the petticoat so that the hideous garment frilled up around me and made me look like some half-witted ballet dancer fresh out of a hurricane.

Next, those varmints put the frosting on the cake. Pierre commenced playing the Jew's harp, twanging and thrumming such favorites as "Clementine," and they sang a few ditties with embarrassing words, sung only on the river,

I was sure. They set to clapping along with the music, then they began dancing a reel, arms twined together, first one direction then another, hopping and bellowing and roaring and thumping around so that I worried they'd pound clear through the deck. But no, the Jew's harp just kept on twanging. By that time old Three-Toes himself showed up, with—of all things—a fiddle.

I was stuck on the mast in the midst of them like a trussed chicken; Corrin was hunched up and tied, flat on the deck, looking so ashamed that I could have lain right down and died for him.

But I kept my chin up. I just stood there in that horrid red petticoat like the masthead on some bawdy ship. And as for that petticoat, no decent woman would even make mention of such a garment, much less wear one. Yet there I was, decked out in it for all of the keelboatmen—and all of St. Louis—to see.

St. Louis. I was floating along on the keelboat, tied to the mast in my unmentionables, when the city hove into view. The trappers had drunk themselves blind. None seemed even to consider cutting me down as we approached the wharves.

I started to shout, then caught Corrin's eye and realized that I didn't want to bring our approach to anyone's attention lest these river rats decide after all to take me downriver to New Orleans.

The current was swift once we rounded the last bend. We were pulling closer and closer to the busy wooden piers. Several fancy white riverboats were tied up farther down the waterfront, but up here were the keelboats—and not many of them. We were out in plain view.

This was St. Louis's busiest commercial region, and the throngs that always filled the area during the daytime began to stop and point as the sound of music and the bright red of my garment drew their attention to us.

I wanted to shrink inside my skin, but at the same time I didn't want to make a fuss lest the trappers put back

86

out to the center of the river. Perhaps Three-Toes was steering for the piers, not knowing of the trappers' indecision about where to put ashore.

In any case, we sailed right up into the midst of the crowd gathering on the docks, and in that moment I'd like to have died.

I was scarlet-faced, wanting to cover myself but unable to do so because my hands were tied. Corrin curled up and hid his face. The trappers kept on with their revelry, too drunk to realize where they were.

As the keelboat bumped against the pier, Louis finally looked up, bleary-eyed, and registered the crowd with some surprise. But then he hee-hawed and offered around the whiskey bottle again to his partners in crime.

That's when I spotted Father.

The noise had apparently brought him out of his office, which was at the front of his brick warehouse, right beside those particular piers. Of course. Considering my poor luck in nigh unto everything that had happened up to that point, where else would it be?

There was a buzz of delirium running through the crowd. I was crying, shouting now for someone to help me, trying to tell them all I'd been kidnapped. But the commotion was too great; nobody could hear a word I was saying. Corrin looked dazed, as if somebody had knocked him on the head with a club.

Father stood looking at us, his hand shielding his eyes from the sunlight. I couldn't see the expression on his face, but I could certainly imagine it.

He suddenly spun around and disappeared off the pier and into his office. He came immediately back out with a pistol in one hand and a horsewhip in the other.

I could hear the rowdies in the crowd getting into the spirit of things. They were jeering at me. Several bonneted ladies held handkerchiefs up to their faces, as if about to take on a case of the vapors at the very sight of me. And Father was shoving his way through the crowd, terrifying in his anger. He marched toward us with frightening purpose in his stride.

The trappers were still oblivious to the goings-on. They seemed to think they were at the center of one big party—come one and come all, the more the merrier.

Now the constable came running with several of his men, their dark blue, brass-buttoned uniforms visible in the colorful turmoil of the crowd. They rushed toward us as the keelboat docked.

One trapper jumped off onto the pier, as if to tie us up. But immediately he darted a guilty look around, then sprinted off into the crowd.

Father stormed aboard. His face was something awful to behold. I was afraid at first that he was coming to shoot or horsewhip me.

I yelled at him, trying to explain, but he couldn't hear me for the turmoil. He was shamefaced—for himself *and* for me, I was sure. He couldn't even look at me, and there was a fury about him that made my heart beat fast even though my flesh was cold.

He marched straight to where Corrin lay still tied up. He said something I couldn't hear, then he lifted that horsewhip and brought it down across Corrin's shoulders with a crack, once, twice. I started weeping, shouting for him to stop, telling him that it wasn't Corrin's fault at all.

And then he seemed to realize that Corrin was tied up, for the madness went out of his eyes, lucidity came back, and he turned toward the drunken trappers.

"It was them, Father! It was all their doing," I shouted, and he seemed to hear me this time. He nodded once, a quick snap of his neck. Then he was at the trappers like a windmill, whipping first one then the other, slicing skin. All of them danced about but howled now, trying to avoid the whip.

At the same time one of the constables reached me and cut the ropes that held me to the mast. I collapsed into his arms with a sob, so humiliated that I didn't want to live.

The man gently placed a blanket around my shoulders and rushed me off the boat. But not soon enough. Not by a long shot. The whole blamed city of St. Louis had already seen all it needed to see.

7

It turned out that those varmints had stolen the keel-boat. They'd pirated the whole thing, pelts included, up above the mouth of the Missouri, leaving all but one of the rightful owners in a watery grave.

The lone survivor had made it to the trading post upriver. Folks from there had already arrived in St. Louis, having ridden hard in order to catch up with the boat before the thieves got away downstream.

As soon as the constables explained why they'd arrived at the suspect keelboat so fast, Father and Mother and the others stood around fussing and fretting about how both Corrin and I had barely escaped with our lives.

Corrin was thin-lipped and grim, and the life had gone out of his hazel eyes. The constabulary doctor tended to his wounds. He applied a corn plaster to one cheek. Then he examined Corrin's right arm and tied a sling on it. While the doctor worked, Corrin stood stone-faced and stared into the distance, as if he couldn't bear the sight of the whole sorry lot of us.

I was fighting my own sense of shame. But as soon as the doctor finished, I went over to Corrin and said, "Are you hurt bad?"

"I already told the constables. I don't even need a doctor."

"We can take you to Dr. Payne. He's our family doctor—and just a few blocks away."

"No. Just leave me alone."

I hesitated, looking at my toes, then finally mustered up the courage to look him in the eye. I said, "That was a very stupid thing I did. I am really, really sorry."

"Wasn't your fault." But he wouldn't meet my eyes.

"I'll do anything I can to make it up to you."

"You don't owe me a thing." His voice was indifferent.

"Will you come calling tonight?"

His jawline set stubbornly, and he finally met my gaze full on. There was a deep and abiding anger in his eyes. "Most likely not."

"Then tomorrow?"

"Don't know as how I'd like to visit with your father just now."

"I know he's sorry, Corrin. He just flew off the handle and jumped to conclusions when he saw me like that and you there. As soon as he can break free, he'll apologize."

"Don't know as how I could be around a man who could so much as think something like that about me."

"Give him a chance. I know he's truly sorry."

I went back and pestered Father to try to make things right with Corrin right away.

But by the time Father extracted himself from the excited crowd and went to talk to him, Corrin had disappeared.

The owner of the *Missouri Republic* newspaper was a friend of Father's. He made it a point to let St. Louis know what had happened by printing it up in the boldest of headlines. Mother brought me the clipping from the morning paper:

FUR TRADER'S DAUGHTER BECOMES HEROINE! HELPS FOIL DEADLY RIVER PIRATES WHO TOOK FUR TRAPPERS' PELTS AND LIVES.

The paper said I had been put aboard the keelboat of the Ashley expedition by accident, after tripping en route to my father's warehouse and being trapped in a pile of cargo. The publisher attributed the event to serendipity or perhaps even to an act of divine intervention. He explained that I had ended up on the pirates' boat in order to come back downriver, and that's how I helped get those robbers arrested at the St. Louis waterfront.

It should have made me feel better, but instead I felt like a charlatan.

I prayed a lot that night, asking the Lord to forgive me should the newspaper's inaccurate attribution of my antics to divine intervention be considered by Him as cheeky as it seemed to me.

The publisher's version was little like what I told him. And I regret to say that even my version didn't bear total resemblance to the truth. I said I had climbed aboard the keelboat to give an important message to a friend who was leaving, then accidentally found myself trapped in the cargo hold—which was true. I didn't mention that I really was chasing after a man, just as the gossips said.

Father's publisher friend knew the public far better than I did. When he tidied up my story, he was thinking of Father and the rest of our family, and I have to give them all credit. Father also saw what was coming long before I did, and he tried to put the lid on things. He did his very best, but some things are beyond repair.

The story didn't work. No one was much interested in killers and river pirates and stolen beaver pelts, even though the *Missouri Republic* ran the story front page in several different versions for four or five days. No, folks had their minds and mouths full, talking about the elder daughter of the highfalutin Arthur Davidson.

They were gossiping about how I had fled upriver, chasing after a man, only to come back by keelboat, arriving at the St. Louis waterfront lashed to a mast in the midst of the devil's own revelry, gussied up in men's trousers and shirt and sporting a flame-red harlot's petticoat over the top of it all. It stirred up the city something awful.

Not that I heard the worst of the gossip right away.

No, a full-on, ring-tailed scandal sometimes takes a while to be full born. With me, it took more than a week, during which time I kept to my room with a head cold that nigh unto killed me, though even at that I let on I was sicker than I really was, hoping that Corrin might hear I was on my deathbed and come to me.

He had still not been seen. Father was looking for him at my insistence. He combed the entire city, but to no avail.

After I explained that the pirates had beaten Corrin to beefsteak for trying to defend my honor, Father was indeed ashamed that he'd jumped to the wrong conclusion and horsewhipped him in front of everyone. It was even worse that Corrin's hands had been tied when the whipping took place. Father wanted to make it up to him. But Corrin had shed the lot of us.

Mother tended to me for a few days. She packed my head in hot washcloths, and she boiled water beside my bed so that I could breathe the steam. She lathered me in camphor oil until I smelled to high heaven; she bathed and soothed and comforted me.

Sunday morning I awakened feeling a good bit better. It was early, just past dawn. The curtains had been left open the night before, and I could see that the river was peacefully rolling past, the green trees were in full bloom. The sky held a clear, luminous, blue golden light scudded with spun-sugar clouds. Spun sugar. Toast and honey. I was suddenly hungry enough to eat a river eel.

I slid out of my crisp white sheets, put on my slippers and fleecy robe, then tiptoed past Sally's door down to the kitchen and into the pantry. I had just sliced off a chunk from a fresh-baked loaf of bread I'd found wrapped in a tea towel, pulled out some strawberry preserves, and put on the teakettle, when Sally came in.

Her curly brown locks were mussed, her sky blue eyes were sleepy. She was in her blue night robe, and I knew she had heard me pass her door.

"What are you doing?" she asked.

"I'm hungry. Do you want some bread?"

"No, it's too early. I mean, what are you doing up? Mother said you should stay in bed."

"I feel better. I thought I'd get an early start and go to church this morning."

Her freckled face turned pale. "Don't."

"What on earth does that mean?"

"Don't go to church."

"Why not?"

"*I'm* not going, and you don't want to go either, Emily. I promise you."

"What on earth is wrong?"

"It's those awful gossips."

"Who are you talking about?"

"You don't know because Mother has been protecting you from it," she said, "but the whole town is talking. Saying disgraceful things. And every day it's getting worse."

"Who?"

"You don't want to know."

I felt my jaw go stiff. "You'd best tell me, Sally Lou, or I'll tan your hide."

"You can't. You're not big enough anymore, and I'd just tan yours instead."

When that stubborn streak came up in her there was no getting around it. I had learned that many years ago. I changed tactics.

"Let's don't fight," I said gently. "I just want to know. Who's saying what?"

She measured me, looking out of the same grave eyes as Father, though the colors were different. "Well—I expect you'll know sooner or later. And I guess you might as well hear it from me and get the truth." And then she told me.

That's when I learned about Mrs. Dora McKenzie's saying I'd had a knack for meanness and chicanery for a long time, and how she had warned Barnabus to stay away from me just in time to keep him from disgrace. I also learned about Mrs. James Lee Bradley's saying I was a bit teched in the head, for what other excuse could there be for a young lady to behave so outrageously?

There were other embarrassing items. Folks I had always considered to be my friends were wagging their tongues far and wide, and it seems that Sally's girlfriends weren't letting her miss a thing.

I managed to get hold of my temper and continued making tea. Then I sliced a chunk of bread for Sally in spite of her earlier refusal. She looked so sorry for me, so forlorn, that I wanted to comfort her.

I took out a second teacup and added extra water to the pot. Then I sat down at the wooden kitchen table and looked across at my younger sister. "I'm sorry for what's happening. I know it's hard on you to be involved in this."

"Oh, Em." Tears welled into her eyes. "Why on earth did you do it?"

I thought about it, then truthfully said, "I don't think I can explain."

"Do you even know?"

"I'm not sure."

"Was it because of Mr. McCannon?" Her eyes suddenly sparkled with interest. "Are you in love?"

I surprised myself by coming right out and saying, "Yes. But I'm not sure that had much to do with it."

"What does love feel like?"

"Very strange," I said, thinking.

"Good?"

"Some of the time."

"Bad, then?"

"Most of the time."

"Then why do people fall in love?"

I thought about that for a moment. "Guess the Lord just made us that way, and we can't help it."

"Our teacher says the ancient Greeks believed that love was a form of mental illness. Do you think that's true?"

"Don't be foolish."

95

"Then why did you stow aboard that keelboat? What really happened to you?"

"I went off half-cocked," I said, "thinking more of myself than I had a right to. Pride goeth before a fall, Sally, just like the Bible says. I was prideful. I thought I could hook Mr. McCannon right by the nose and make him jig to my tune if I just had a chance to see him again."

"So you were trying to manipulate him?"

I didn't like the word, but I was bound to tell Sally the truth. I said, "I reckon you might just as well come out and say it, just like that."

The teakettle started singing. I poured two cupfuls, then handed Sally the sliced bread.

She nibbled at it like a little mouse, then said, "I'm not in love with Kenneth."

Kenneth was her beau, a sweet boy of sixteen.

"I wouldn't expect you to be at your age," I said.

"I won't marry him," she said. "Even if he asks me."

"Then I take it he hasn't?" I smiled to myself.

"He wants to finish school first and maybe go on to college. Are you going to marry Mr. McCannon?"

I felt a deep sadness well up in me and swallow my smile. "I don't believe so."

"But why not, if you love him?"

"Because he has gone away," I said, "and I will be really surprised if I ever so much as see him again."

The rumors got worse. When my friend Clarissa came by and told me that people were coming right out and saying I was nothing more than a harlot, I ran to my room and cried the rest of the day. I felt unable to stand the shame and the pain.

Mother tried to comfort me. She said that the scandal wouldn't have been such a big whoop-de-do if I'd belonged to a lesser family. But the well-bred granddaughter of Revolutionary War hero General William Lee Davidson carrying on in such a fashion? Not to mention

96

that Father owned the New West Fur Company, and many people resented his success.

"We are who we are," she said, sitting there and stroking my hair—my face was buried in the pillow to stifle my sobs. "We're expected to keep up appearances. People watch us closely, and a good number of them are envious. They're just waiting for us to stumble and fall."

"And I have stumbled as far as I can go," I said. My face was still buried in the pillow, and I had to lift up a bit to even speak. "I am a fallen woman, Mother. I have been shamed for life."

"Now, hush. It isn't as bad as all that." But she didn't sound so sure.

I turned over a bit and looked up into her sweet, pretty face. She had the same chestnut hair, the same green eyes as mine, and I did love her so.

"Sally told me they're saying I'm teched in the head." I forced myself to smile.

Mother's fine-plucked eyebrows dipped into a frown. "They're saying a lot of things. They'll get over it, and so will you."

But when she left and I tried to sleep, I wondered if I ever would. Even if others forgot. Most of all, I wondered if I would ever get over the aching pain in my heart when I thought about Corrin Brevard McCannon, who had come into my life and was now gone.

Like most dark things, the scandal continued to percolate beneath the surface—the wasp-tongued gossips doing their evil work. Finally, one night the Reverend Mr. Farnsworth and his stiff-backed wife came calling. Mother insisted that I join them all for tea.

It was a grim meeting. Everyone wore dark, severe clothing, as if we were attending a funeral. We even kept mournful expressions pasted to our faces, as if someone in the family had died.

Minnie, our cook and house servant, poured us hot tea and served hot honey biscuits, then carefully shut the door as if she were leaving a sick room.

Father broke the silence, since someone obviously had to. He said, *"Harumph.* Um . . . well . . . thank you for coming, Reverend and Mrs. Farnsworth."

They both primly nodded, then continued to sit straight-backed and silent on the brocade sofa. I noticed for the millionth time how alike they looked—both slim as reeds, with carrot-red hair and dour faces, though the Reverend's hair had more than a speck of gray. I also wondered for the millionth time why ministers had to be so serious about life. Hadn't the Lord Himself found time for picnics and weddings and laughter from time to time?

Father said, "Terrible time we're having with the river this year. They can't get those levees fixed soon enough to suit me. Six planters flooded out downriver and more to come, they say."

But Mrs. Farnsworth was not to be distracted from her immediate purpose. She said, "We have already done our social duty by those poor unfortunates, thank you, Mr. Davidson. Now we are here to help you folks."

Father never forgot his manners. He said, "Thank you for your kindness," but he sounded puzzled, and I could see from the look on his face that they had him perplexed.

"That is, in the matter of the events surrounding Miss Emily," the Reverend added, apparently seeing Father's distress and deciding to help him out.

"The scandal," Mrs. Farnsworth said.

An angry glint locked into Mother's eyes. She said, "We are weathering the so-called scandal very well, thank you. If some folks have nothing to do but wag their tongues and spread lies, that is their problem and not ours. Miss Emily is doing very well."

But I wasn't. I suddenly flushed with shame again at the thought of all the unpleasant talk.

Mrs. Farnsworth turned to me. "What have you to say about that, Emily? *Are* you holding up?"

"Yes'm. I am angry at the tall tales that are being bandied about, but I doubt if they'll bowl me over."

"Um-hm," she said. "I see. And what will you be doing now?"

I thought for a second that she was accusing me of conjuring up some antic to top the last one. But no, she was gazing at me with a stern but kindly look on her face, simply asking a question.

Suddenly I found myself talking to her.

I said, "I expect I shall leave Saint Louis, now that I've seen the truth behind so many Christian facades."

She shook her head. "Oh, pshaw, Emily. It's not just Christians—though I admit that some of the folks at church could be a little more charitable. But everyone loves a good scandal. It heats up their blood and puts some spice in their dreary lives. Pay them no mind, and don't let them hurt you. These gossips are bored, small-minded folk who have nothing in their own lives, so they have to try to feed off the troubles of others."

She surprised me. I hadn't expected to find a kindred spirit in Mrs. Farnsworth.

She said, "My sister is headmistress of a very good girls' college back in Boston. You can learn nursing, teaching, or secretarial. Not that you have to work, of course—" she shot a sideways, apologetic look at Father "—but it might be nice to do something different. I'm sure my recommendation would secure a place for you, should you decide to further your education. And time spent away from this wretchedly uncivilized city might do you a world of good."

I looked at Father. I had been considering teaching. This might be just the thing to do.

He looked interested too. "I'd be happy to explore it," he said, "assuming it's what Emily wants."

I felt my heart sadden. What I wanted was Corrin Brevard McCannon. But he was probably the last thing I would ever obtain.

I forced a smile to my face. "It might be the best for all of us."

"You don't have to leave on account of the rumors," Father said angrily.

"Oh," Mrs. Farnsworth interrupted, "but perhaps she does. I've seen this before, you know, though perhaps the comparison is not exact. You remember the young Harper girl, who got herself with child and her out of wedlock—you remember—last year it was?"

I did remember. The poor thing had been harassed almost to death by her so-called friends.

Mother and Father both nodded their heads.

"She is in Memphis now. Married. Both she and the child are doing quite well. But by the time she left here, she was nigh onto having a nervous breakdown." She peered intently at me. "It could happen to anyone."

"I'm doing fine," I said.

She fixed me with a stern look. "You, Miss Emily, are peaked-looking. There are dark circles under your eyes. This whole wretched family has stopped coming to church. And for what, I ask you? Because of a bunch of wagging tongues."

"It is rather hard to stand up to the storm just now," Mother said.

"Pshaw. When you go into hiding, it just makes things worse."

"Well . . . Emily Anne has been sick . . ."

"And is likely to be again, if she doesn't get a change of scenery."

The Reverend cleared his throat for attention, in the way he always did before preaching. Then he stood, stepped over, and took his hat from the rack. He said to Mrs. Farnsworth, "We've said our piece; now it's up to them. Come on home and make supper."

We went to church that week, Emily looking spruce and trim in a gray linen coatdress, Sally wearing pink, Mother wearing her beige and burgundy go-to-meeting dress. Folks tittered and looked at us some, but it wasn't all that bad.

And the Reverend stood up there and preached a hellfire and brimstone sermon if ever there was one, about falsely accusing your fellow man—or woman, he was careful to point out—and how the Lord Jesus feels about folks who set about destroying one another with wagging tongues. Oh, he said a mouthful that day, all of it intended to exonerate me.

And all it did was set the tongues to wagging again.

The following week I still hadn't seen hide nor hair of Corrin McCannon. Father said there was no word of him among the river folk or trappers. I feared that he was gone for good, headed back West or back to North Carolina.

The gossips were at it with regard to his disappearance too. I was trying to ignore them and get on with my life, but it wasn't at all easy for me. Or for any of the family.

Mrs. Farnsworth brought me some brochures about her sister's school. I spent several evenings in my room looking at them, praying, and wondering what to do.

And then I told Mother I was going to attend. She didn't know whether to be happy for me or sad for herself, but she agreed it would probably be a good thing.

That night the family had just sat down at the dinner table to a meal of chicken and dumplings. I was waiting while Minnie spooned out the food onto our plates; then I was going to tell Father about my decision to go to school.

But before I could open my mouth, he said, "I saw an old friend of yours today, Emily."

Politely, I said, "Who, Father?"

"I think you'll know soon enough. He came by the warehouse to ask permission to come calling on you tonight."

My first thought was that William Baxter was back from medical school. I said, "This is not a good time to have callers. I have something to tell you, Father. I am going—"

"I think you'll want to see this young man."

And something in the expression on his face made me realize who he meant.

"Corrin," I said, my voice a whispery shiver.

Father nodded. "He came to apologize for being a part of your high jinks. I in turn apologized to him because he got beaten to beefsteak because of my inconsiderate daughter. We both ended up having a good laugh."

"But—where has he been?"

"He went south, downriver. He has been finding backers to invest in a shipment of goods to sell at Fort Davy Crockett."

"He's going back to Brown's Hole?" My voice was shaky.

"So it seems. It sounds like he may have a good scheme afoot. I offered to put some of my own money into the venture, but he refused on the grounds that he doesn't want to be beholden to his future father-in-law."

I was struck dumb.

"He'll be here at seven P.M. to speak to the potential bride about other necessary matters," Father said. "You'd best scoop up those dumplings, Emily. You're going to need something that will stick to your ribs if you're going to get through this evening." He laughed.

But I couldn't eat a bite after that. I felt giddy, as if I'd been struck with a sudden bout of the ague. Suddenly I didn't want to see Corrin. I was angry with him for being absent for so long and not letting me know where he went.

At the same time I was counting the minutes, eager and excited to look at his eyes, see the copper brush of his hair, feel his touch. But I was frightened in spite of it, confused and feeling foolish.

But most of all, I was joyous. Corrin was back! He and Father had made up their differences. Once again he was going to ask me to marry him.

At that moment it struck me. And of all the peculiar things that had ever happened, my reaction to his reappearance was bound to be the strangest. Because after all those weeks of worrying about him, all those nights of praying and tossing and turning and hoping, all of a sudden I didn't know if I was going to marry him and go West or refuse and go back East to school.

8

I made my decision fast, once my eyes locked with Corrin's hazel depths and those sparks started flying again. We talked late into the night, holding hands. Corrin proposed marriage once again, I eagerly accepted, and all was forgiven by us both.

One week later, we had a full-on wingding of a wedding, presided over by Reverend Farnsworth. We decided to follow the newfangled notion of holding the ceremony in the church rather than in the parlor of our house. Mother said we'd stand up to those scold-tongued gossips and best them all, and I believe we did that day.

We invited only family, nongossiping friends, and the good church folk who'd been too busy getting on with their lives to waste time wagging their tongues. And the whole church was filled with good-hearted people. I'd forgotten there were so many. And there you have it—a churchful of good folk, as opposed to a handful of scolds. Those tongue-waggers had been ruining my life only because I gave them far more importance than they deserved.

All the same, they weren't finished with me yet. They said the wedding took place only because Father tracked down Corrin with a shotgun and brought him back to make me an honorable woman. After all, hadn't Father been looking high and low for him, and wasn't that a fact?

Sally was my bridesmaid. She wore a pale pink princess dress, with fresh, fragrant lilacs in her soft brown hair. We'd filled the church to the rafters with white and purple lilacs and white daisies and orange blossom strands and other spring flowers.

I wore a snow-white regency gown with white lace and tiny ruffles, whipped up fast by the local seamstress, a Frenchwoman from Paris by way of New Orleans—or so she said—and her work was fine enough that nobody bothered to argue. Wherever she came from, she conjured up a vision of beauty. The dress even had real, white tea roses picked from the garden and sewn on the scalloped hem at the very last minute. The bodice was covered with seed pearls. In my hair I wore a gorgeous wreath of orange blossoms and white roses, with the leaves woven in.

We spent our wedding night aboard the riverboat *Natchez,* named for the Mississippi Indian tribe. We stayed in a lavish, first-class cabin with a brass feather bed and a carpet of velvet pile, fancy gilt-framed oil paintings on the paneled wall, a crystal chandelier overhead, and that big, muddy, romantic river plowing by outside our window one balcony below.

I didn't quite know what to expect on my wedding night. When I had become a woman, mother mastered her delicate frame of mind enough to take me aside and explain that someday I would have children. She drew some scanty diagrams to show me how that would take place. It had seemed an unpleasant way to go about things.

"Just always remember to keep Corrin happy," she said by way of final advice. Then she turned beet red and hurried away.

Now, in spite of my abiding love for Corrin, my stomach was in knots all throughout dinner. At the same time, my heart was fluttering, and each time he looked at me I felt on fire. To complicate matters, a big harvest moon rose high above the distant riverbank. When we walked from our cabin to the dining room, I felt as if I were floating on air. The night was luminous; the moon-glint on the water took my breath away.

We dined on capon and plum dressing, drank from crystal goblets, and Corrin was handsome and charming and attentive as all get out. But for me the romance of the evening was shadowed by the threat of what was to come.

Corrin knew I was nervous. And he knew just what to do about it. He and I sat and talked until almost dawn, planning our future and talking about how many children we would have, and what we would name them all, and how much we loved one another. When we finally went to bed he just held me, as gently as if I were made from blown glass.

Gradually, in a union so natural that I knew the good Lord Himself had given us His blessing, we tenderly discovered each other on that big, wide, muddy river, floating south. I woke up the next morning understanding why God had created us male and female—and feeling happier than I'd ever been.

We weren't exactly on a bridal tour. It seems that Corrin had an uncle in Memphis, a man who had also left the Carolinas for family reasons. Uncle Hiram McCannon had prospered in Tennessee's emerging cotton industry. He and Corrin remained close, and now Hiram was investing in Corrin's trading enterprise. We were on our way to make the final arrangements.

On the afternoon of our second day out, we stood at the stern, just behind the paddle, watching the river flow away behind us, looking back toward home, and talking about his uncle's cotton mill. I was trying to learn something more about his family, as usual; and as usual, he was reluctant to tell me a thing.

I said, "Hiram is your father's brother?"

"Yes, there were three brothers. Hiram is the youngest of the lot."

"You said 'were.'"

"Uncle Lewis was killed in the War of 1812."

"I'm sorry."

"It's all right. I barely knew him."

I'd tried off and on to pursue Corrin's relationship with his family since that night he'd grown so reticent at my questioning. I asked Father about it and learned a bit in return. But Corrin had made clear that his parents would not be attending our wedding, and he'd refused to discuss the reasons. Now that he was my husband, I felt I had the right to know about the family I had married into, and this seemed a good time to find out, so I pressed on.

"Did you notify your family of our marriage?"

"I wrote my mother a letter," he said, shifting his gaze away from me.

"Will I ever meet her?"

"Don't know, Emily. Most likely not."

"Why are they such a mystery? What could have happened to make you leave them and never want to look back?"

He seemed angry for a moment, then said, "I'd just rather not discuss them, that's all."

I ignored that. "Can't you at least tell me what on earth estranged you from them?"

"A serious difference of opinion," he said shortly. "Let's go in—it's starting to rain."

I looked up. The clouds were a good distance away, though it was true they were headed toward us.

I said, "Why do you find it so hard to talk about them? I really need to know, Corrin."

"I'd just rather not."

"But Corrin, they're your *family*. Our children will have their blood. How can you just come West and never see them again?"

He turned, leveled a gaze at me, and then a resigned look came to his face. "I haven't wanted to talk about this, but now I reckon you're right. They're my family. Whatever else, they're a part of me, and you deserve to know."

I stood stock-still, lest I do something to make him change his mind.

"My family came from Scotland in the early 1700s. They settled on the coast, then began to accumulate land. My father inherited it all."

"What happened? Did they lose it?"

"Nothing of the sort. They're still wealthy people," he said, "but wealth is all they have. They're hard. Especially my father."

107

"My father said they were planters."

"They are. My father raises tobacco, cotton, everything that can make him money, and he makes plenty of it. He runs over a hundred slaves on his land. And he runs them hard, just as he runs himself. But running slaves hard has a mite different consequence."

That astonished me as I suddenly realized how wealthy that made him. "So you really are rich!"

"Not me. My father. But his money isn't mine, and that's just as well. It's blood money, and I want no part of it."

"Why blood money?"

"It comes down to black folks and white, Emily. I don't cotton to slavery, and especially when it's enforced with whips."

That surprised me too. In fact, Corrin was just full of surprises today. "Is that why you left home?"

"I left home over a slave girl, Emily. And I'll never go back."

I felt my heart stop beating. I was suddenly afraid of what I'd hear next, but now I had to know.

"What happened?"

He fell silent.

I said, "Were you—interested in her?"

"What do you mean?"

"Well—some masters have children by their slaves. It's disgraceful, I know, but I've heard of it happening."

"That would explain my special feelings for that child," he said.

"Child?"

"I believe she was probably my young half-sister."

"Sister?"

He looked at me and shook his head. "You've certainly been protected from the world, Emily Anne."

That set me off. "I know my share of things and more than, Mr. Corrin McCannon. Is it my fault that you can't tell a story straight?"

108

He laughed. Then he looked sad again.

"It's a long story, and maybe I'd rather not have to face it all again."

"I'm your wife. I have a right to know."

He nodded. "I reckon you do. Mother and Father fought over a black woman, a house slave about my mother's age who'd been with us for a long time. Mother demanded that the woman leave, and then the woman told Mother something that nigh onto drove her insane with rage."

"What?"

"I never knew, but it was easy enough to figure it out after what came next. Reckon the woman told my mother that her daughter was conceived by my father. To please my mother and punish the slave woman, he sold the woman's daughter to a man noted for his cruelty to slaves. Especially to female children."

I pursed my mouth shut. A sudden cold wind off the river brought a sense of desolation and pity that I had never known before.

"I quarreled with my father over the sale. He wouldn't listen, so I took the slave girl to Richmond and helped her link into the underground railway. They sent her north to Ohio to live with a free black family."

"Oh, Corrin. You didn't."

He shot me the strangest look. "Why, of course I did."

"But—that child was your father's property. It was like stealing."

"You think I should have allowed her to be sold to that monster?"

"No, but—surely there was another way."

He gave me another peculiar look. "You've certainly bought the slaveholder's line."

"It's just—what other way could it be?"

"Many ways, Emily. Maybe even the right way. I wonder if you won't see the light, in time."

"What light?"

"God's light," he said. "Freedom."

I tossed my head and ignored his comment about my so-called blindness. There was enough debate about slavery versus abolition, especially after the fight Missouri had been through these past few years. I'd heard my share of opinions, and more than.

Father and Mother seemed to be on the fence when it came to slave issues. Both their families were planters, and they'd always had slaves. My parents seemed to more or less go along with what other folks of their time and age and station were doing and not feel the weight much either way. Though I will say they treated our slave folk a good deal better than most owners did.

As for me, I believed what I'd been taught to believe, and at that moment I only wanted to pursue the part of his past that interested me. I said, "And your father disowned you for stealing the slave girl?"

"Reckon I never gave him the chance. From Richmond, I went West to Council Bluffs, took a boat upriver with Roubideaux, and moved on to the Far West, to the mountains. I've tried to never look back."

"What about your mother?"

"I wrote and let her know where I was going. Didn't want to worry her none."

"But . . . aren't you punishing her for something your father did?"

"Not much difference between them. She's more or less made her own bed, and I reckon she's still lying in it."

"What do you mean?"

"She and the rest of the family chose to look the other way when it came to Father's meanness. Reckon it mattered more that they keep an ample amount of feathers in their nest. Seems I was the only one to take a stand."

"But Corrin—surely you believe slavery is the natural order of things. Slaves are meant to remain in their station. Why, even the Bible speaks of slavery—the rules for keeping slaves are written out in no uncertain terms."

"Have you ever read what it says about slavery?"

"Why, not really, but—"

"The Bible says we're to love one another—do what's best for the other person. To me that means not making some other human being my slave. The Bible does talk about slavery—it tells people who are slaves to obey, and it tells their owners to be good masters. But nowhere does it say slavery's a good thing."

I was dumbstruck. But he wasn't finished.

"The Bible says all believers—black or white, man or woman—are equal before God. Equally accepted, equally forgiven. But you've heard your parents and others use the Bible references to slavery as justification for it, I reckon. And you're like all the rest—you just accept what they say and don't bother to think for yourself."

"That's not fair!"

"You're trained to think just like your parents. They have house slaves. Your father has slaves who work for him in the warehouse, doing the hardest jobs."

"They're not really slaves. They've been with us forever."

"But they *are* slaves. He has the papers to prove it—almost a dozen of them altogether. They work, but they don't get paid. To you, that's just in the natural order of things. But I can't believe it's the way God really wants it to be."

"If we didn't take care of them, who would? They'd be put on the street to starve."

"Maybe and maybe not. They wouldn't starve if folks paid them a fair working wage for what they do."

"Oh, Corrin, I don't know why you're being so dreadful all of a sudden. I expect you're right, and we shouldn't talk about your family. It upsets you."

111

"That's not the only thing that upsets me. But I can't expect you, among so many, to have suddenly stumbled onto the Christian truth."

I tossed my head and said hotly, "And what truth might that be?"

"The truth I was just speaking about. That all men and women were meant to be free people and God loves us all equally. Slavery is an abomination, and one day this nation of ours will rise up in arms to stop this evil."

I shivered at the thought of it. I had seen such hatred on people's faces when the free-state versus slave-state issue was debated, and folks had indeed been killed over the issue. But I understood now why Corrin didn't want to talk about his family. What he had told me was only the tip of it all, I was sure. If it put him in this black, painful mood to discuss it, I was willing to let sleeping dogs lie.

But Corrin had the final word. He said, "How can a nation that values freedom enough to die for it allow slavery in its own bosom?"

"I don't know," I said, trying to leave the subject.

"If only part of the people are free, how long can freedom survive?"

I couldn't answer, so I looked away. Into the muddy churning depths of the river.

Other than that one discordant conversation, our journey was wonderful. We passed a few tiny settlements. We stood on deck and watched the Indians who still roamed the region. In turn, they rode to the river to watch us. We picked up cargo from a handful of wilderness plantations.

But mostly the Mississippi was still unsettled, except for a few cities such as St. Louis and New Orleans. And that's why, when I opened my eyes one morning to see Corrin standing over me, already dressed, telling me excitedly that we'd just made Memphis, I was surprised to look out the window and see a full-blown town breaking out of

112

the morning mist. It was as if it had risen from the green hills while I slept.

Memphis was small by St. Louis standards, but it was growing, and it was a good sight bigger than anything we'd seen yet during the journey.

Hiram McCannon was waiting for us at the docks, and he was a good sight bigger than any man I'd yet met too. He must have stood an easy six feet six inches, and I estimated he weighed close to three hundred pounds, though I never got up the courage to ask. He had the same rust-red hair as Corrin, but it fell away in a wide beard from beneath his beaverskin top hat to become a full broom that included handlebar mustache. He had a florid, apple-cheeked face with bright blue eyes that seemed to look right through you, though in a pleasant and understanding way.

He was driving a custom-built carriage, and his slaves—for the two broad-shouldered black men with him could have been nothing but—loaded our trunks into a wagon. Corrin and I were swept into the carriage on the strength of Hiram's open-armed welcome, and away we rode.

Hiram made polite noises of greeting to me as we rode along and indeed surprised me by knowing something of my father and his business. But it was apparent that he and Corrin were interested in nothing but commerce, for they soon occupied themselves with talk of trade and left me to sit back in the well-padded seat to watch the green countryside roll past.

Hiram had done more than well for himself since leaving North Carolina. Cotton fields stretched off in every direction, and when we drove through a stone gate onto a paved lane, we approached a Grecian Revival house as fine as anything my mother's family owned in Mecklenburg County. Which was all the more amazing, considering the remoteness of the region and the distance the carved pillars and ornate ironwork had traveled in order to pop up in such an unlikely place.

113

I commented on Uncle Hiram's success. He beamed at me and said, "A social experiment that's working, my dear Mrs. McCannon. I've given each and every one of my slaves their freedom, in return for five good years of work. At the end of that time, they're free to do as they wish, and the wages they've earned are theirs to keep as well."

"Wages?"

"Of course. While I hold paper on them, they're not allowed to earn a wage, by law. But as soon as I give them their freedom I can pay their back wages, which is just exactly what I intend to do. In the form of cash or good bottom-land they can sharecrop for me and earn a good living upon, or they can just up and leave, if that's what they want. I've set my first people free this year, and so far every one's decided to stay with me in return for a fair wage."

I was aghast. This kind of talk was getting people shot in certain parts of the world. I said, "Aren't you afraid of what your neighbors will do?"

He chuckled and didn't seem a bit worried. "Not enough neighbors in this part of the world to worry about. Though if people act true to form, that's bound to come too, and far too soon."

Hiram's wife, Addie, was a portly, fussy woman with curly golden locks and a muddled air about her. She anxiously welcomed me, apologizing for the state of the house and the state of her hair, and the hurry she was in, and a thousand other things that didn't matter a wink to me. By the time a house servant escorted Corrin and me to a private suite at the top and back of the house, I felt as if I had just been swept through a small but benevolent hurricane.

Addie and I visited with each other that afternoon to get acquainted. She was an East Tennessee farm girl, married to Hiram some twenty-five years ago, and was one reason he'd decided to settle outside Memphis. I quickly grew to like her.

And then, about 4:00 P.M., we retired to our separate bedrooms again. It seems that Mr. and Mrs. Hiram McCannon had a grand reception planned for us, and it was time to dress up. They were excited and told us over and over again to expect a great surprise.

That surprise arrived just as the rest of the dozen or so dinner guests were getting comfortable, the womenfolk visiting, the men sipping juleps and otherwise settling down for an evening's camaraderie. They'd come from far and wide. It seemed the Hiram McCannons had called out every other planter in the countryside, rich and poor alike.

I was in the parlor, talking to a white-haired woman in a pale blue gown whose name was Fanny Marshall, when a stir of excitement went through the room, and I heard folks twittering, "He's here. They're here. They just drove up."

I gave Addie a questioning look, and she beamed. She put her arm around me, walked me over to where Corrin was talking to some men, and drew him away too. Then she led us out to the front porch.

We saw a lanky, long-legged man bent halfway over to help a dainty, brown-haired woman from the rig. When the woman was safe on the earth, the two of them straightened their clothing, then looked up to where a whole gallery of us watched them.

The man had thick, strong features, with a wild hank of curly brown hair and a beard that started at his sideburns and wrapped around his chin. He doffed his tall hat with a saucy flourish, bowed, and with a wicked grin said, "Howdy, folks. What's for dinner?"

Hiram puffed up to his immense full size, turned halfway toward us, and said, "For those who don't already know him, I'm proud to have the privilege of introducing Tennessee's smartest and toughest Whig Congressman. Meet Mr. Davy Crockett himself!"

That was a surprise indeed. Davy Crockett was already a legend. He had served with General Andrew

115

Jackson in the 1813 campaign against the Creek Indians. He had helped open up the current edge of the American frontier all the way to the Missouri River and a bit beyond. Folks wrote essays about him, good and bad, and spoke of him as if he were part of a ballad or folk tale on the order of Paul Bunyan.

He was always drawn larger than life, and that's why I was somewhat skeptical when I first laid eyes on the real thing. It seemed at first as if Hiram McCannon might be pulling our leg.

But it was Davy Crockett, all right, elected to the Tennessee state legislature only the year before and out in this neck of the woods to do some politicking—and to check into the possibilities of assigning some land to certain interested parties. Hiram was a Whig himself and planned to start early to help Congressman Crockett get reelected.

Corrin and I were seated in positions of honor near the head of the table. Davy and Mrs. Crockett were right beside us. After grace was said and folks began their dinner conversations, I couldn't help but pipe up to Mr. Crockett.

"We are going West, my new husband and I."

"You don't say. Where from?"

"Saint Louis."

"Adventurers, hey? Where you headed to—St. Charles?"

"Farther than that."

"Oh? All the way to Westport and the Blacksnake Hills?"

These were all places up the Missouri River some one hundred and more miles distant from St. Louis, prime jumping-off places for the Far West.

I said, "We are going all the way to the Far West. To help establish a fort."

"Plenty of forts already out there," Mr. Crockett said with a scowl. Then he harumphed, turned away, and answered some fellow's question from down the table. Everyone seemed to want to know what the government was

116

doing about opening up the once-Indian land for planting, whether or not the Indian treaties would be revoked, and everyone had an opinion he wanted to share.

I fell silent and sipped at my turtle soup, which was served from the largest, shiniest silver tureen I ever saw. It became more and more apparent to me that the Hiram McCannon family was prospering. And was well connected too.

Corrin was visiting with the people at the far side of the table, altogether enjoying himself and leaving me to my own devices. I was happy to take a moment to satisfy my appetite and to examine the situation.

After a spell of chatting with some others nearby, Mr. Crockett turned back to me. "Ain't the easiest thing in the world to start a fort, you know."

"Oh, people are already building it. Two mountain trappers who know what they're about. We'll just be going along to live there and do some trading, perhaps some trapping."

"That right? Where you folks aiming for? Might be I could help."

I smiled secretively, then said, "You will surely be surprised. We are heading to a place that bears your name. Fort Davy Crockett."

He tilted his head so that his chin nearly touched his chest and he could peer straight into my eyes. His brows beetled, and his eyes bugged out. "Davy Crockett? Ain't no fort named after me."

"As I said, they're just now building it."

He chuckled. "Cain't be out West. You're bound to be jawin' me, missy."

"No, sir, I'm not."

"Come on now. It must be back around Horseshoe Bend on the Tallapoosa River, where me and Jackson kilt nine hundred Creek Injuns, and me with my arm strapped to my side."

117

I tried to hide the incredulous look I knew was on my face.

"Or mebbe it's in West Tennessee? Back in that area where I kilt me a hundred or so b'ar afore I went to deal with the real beasts of prey in the Congress. Har, har."

"Nossir. It's not in your old stomping grounds. This fort is all the way West. On a river in the Rockies called the Sheets-Kadee."

He scratched his head. "Never heard of it."

"It's in Ute Indian country."

"Ute?"

"Yessir."

"That's a troublesome bunch," he said, scratching his beard thoughtfully. "Hear they're the fiercest of the lot."

"I understand they're more or less civilized so long as they're not provoked."

"You ever seen a scalp?"

I shuddered at the thought and put down my fork, which had been on its way to my mouth with an especially rare piece of roast beef on it.

"Bloody mess, they are," said Crockett. "I wouldn't risk no woman of mine, takin' her into something like that."

"But I do understand most trappers get on well with them. And I have read up on them too. They frequent the easternmost part of the Rockies mostly. Only a few bands travel the high mountains and the western slope, and thus far those bands have given the trappers little trouble." I thought about that, then added, "At least so far as anyone knows."

"So you're headed for the Far Mountains." Crockett squinted, took a new look at me, and said, "Ain't no place for a woman."

"I shall manage fine, thank you."

"Turn you into a squaw afore you're through. They're the only women strong enough to survive in the wilderness."

"Then a squaw I shall become," I said, puffing up with indignation.

He chuckled at having riled me, then turned serious again. "I ain't never been out that way. Not yet. That's what bewilders me. I mean, why'd anybody want to name a fort out there after me?"

Feeling suddenly small, I said, "I don't rightly know, sir. Though I do know that the gentleman who wants to name it is called Philip Thompson. He says he's your fellow Tennessean."

Crockett grinned. "I recall old Thompson. That varmint is the spawn of a snappin' turtle, same as me. We took a flatboat upriver together once, but whereas I came back, he jest kept on goin'."

I said, "But another of the fort's founders—a Frenchman name of Prewitt St. Claire—thinks they ought to call it Fort de Misère."

"Fort Misery?"

"Yessir."

He scowled something fierce, and I thought he was going to lambast me. But just as quickly his face turned sunny, and he said, "Fort Davy Crockett, hmm?"

"Yessir."

"Wal. It beats namin' something after the miseries, now don't it? Reckon Davy Crockett is a right fine name at that. Come to think of it, I'm fond of using it myself."

"Maybe they want to honor you, sir."

"Yas. Wal. Might be honored at that. You just make sure them folks what are so all-fired anxious to use my name do me proud and don't pin it on some scurvy cottonwood lean-to."

"You will be proud," I said, with a certainty born of absolute ignorance.

After the party, Corrin was sullen. I sat at the dressing table—a fine oak affair with all sorts of fancy drawers and brass handles and an oval mirror as big as me. I brushed out my hair, counting the strokes, then glanced over my

119

shoulder and caught him glaring at me as he unbuttoned his shirt and hung it up.

I turned then and finally asked him what was wrong.

"I can't believe you, making calf's eyes at that charlatan," he snapped.

"Charlatan?"

"Crockett. The man's a phony. A humbug. Why, if it wasn't that the Whig party needs his vote in Congress, he'd still be out in the wilderness trying to learn to read."

"I thought he was charming—in a sort of rough-spun way," I said. Corrin was jealous of the attention I'd paid to Congressman Crockett! I was delighted!

"He's a man of poor character, from all I've heard. Treats his wife abominably."

"I can't speak for that, but he was a perfect gentleman with me."

Corrin turned livid. "He's going to lose this next election, mark my words. The man's too controversial a figure, and he plays havoc with the truth."

"Then maybe he'll come West," I said, "and live at the fort that's named for him." I tossed my long mane of hair and brushed some more.

"Over my dead body," Corrin said, grinding his teeth.

He was getting seriously riled, so I quit provoking him for the moment, finished my toilette, then went and sat on the edge of the bed, where he was already burrowed under the covers.

He looked miserable, but I just couldn't give it up. It was fun to get the better of him for once. After I'd teased and cajoled him for almost an hour, he finally admitted he was jealous. That cleared the clouds. I laughed and told him I'd been doing it on purpose, and we got on fine again.

And he was right. Davy Crockett did lose the next election, by a landslide, and not long after that he abandoned his wife. But to tell the truth, I'm still proud of the night I met Davy Crockett himself, even if he wasn't what

I'd expected him to be. I was going to spend the rest of my born days with Corrin Brevard McCannon, and I loved him beyond life itself. But meeting Davy Crockett was a thing a woman might only get to do once in a lifetime. I suspected it was something I'd live to tell my grandchildren about.

9

Four days later we were back in St. Louis at my parents' house. Mother and I were busily preparing for our departure, while Corrin and Father worked at the warehouse, packing trade goods and counting supplies and preparing the necessities for the trip West.

Father put money into Corrin's enterprise after all.

He said, "Folks will need supplies, no matter what and no matter where. Trading is a smarter proposition than trapping, and one that bodes for a better future. I wouldn't mind hedging my own bets against the possible demise of the fur trade."

And so Father convinced Corrin to take a substantial investment from him. And the moment he accepted, Father immediately took over the details of Corrin's "expedition"—as they were now calling it—and nigh unto drove Corrin and me both crazy.

Suddenly we were the McCannon-Davidson Expedition, headed West to trade with the trappers and Indians and to do some trapping ourselves, if it came to that.

A full-blown expedition requires expeditioners, and so we were soon in charge of twelve well-armed teamsters to handle the thirty pack mules, and a cook to tend to our stomachs during the long trek West. Father and Corrin both explained that the big Conestoga wagons that had brought settlers to Ohio and Missouri were too cumbersome to make the journey to the Far West. There were no roads where we were going. I was troubled that night as I finally began to realize just how remote our destination was.

The day before we were to depart, Mother and I went down to the warehouse to watch the hustle and bustle as the goods were loaded onto the riverboat.

We had booked passage on the paddle-wheeler *Independence*, which would carry us upriver to the Missouri, then up that rougher water all the way to Blacksnake Hills, the jumping-off point for the Far West. There we would take to the land, traveling by mule train over prairies and foothills until we at last came to a pass in the Rocky Mountains that would usher us out onto the westernmost slopes. There we would set up shop with Thompson and St. Claire at their fort in Brown's Hole.

Corrin and I had sat up nights, too excited to sleep, looking at the rough-hewn maps others had drawn of the region. He drew me a line to indicate our path and told me colorful and fearsome tales of what to expect, though I felt he was embellishing a great deal in order to entertain and interest me.

And when he once again mentioned giant lizards embedded in rock, I hit him with a pillow. "Land sakes, Corrin. You sure do think I'm naive."

He shot me a peculiar look, then said, "You'll see."

"You just never get tired of teasing me, do you, ever since I asked that simple-minded question about the Flatheads?"

"You'll see," he repeated and burrowed his head into the pillow. Within minutes he was asleep.

I'd pored with Corrin over the inventory lists and the prices we would receive for each item. I was astonished by all the goods we were taking with us. He carefully showed me the profits we hoped to make and the returns of those profits to our investors, his Uncle Hiram and my father.

We planned to make a tidy profit that first year. On top of that, Corrin would still be able to do a certain amount of trapping to further enhance our income. And as he'd told me some time back, a good season could bring a smart trapper $100,000 or more—so long as he didn't squander it or let the big companies rob him.

In short, if all went well, we stood to get rich. I was thinking we could spend a few years out there trading—hard years, to be sure, but adventurous ones. And then we would come back to St. Louis and build a huge house beside Mother and Father's, right there on the river. The gossiping tongues would give way to admiration for my courage, Corrin would have the wanderer's itch out of his bones, and we'd be set for life.

I watched the workmen load the goods into the stately riverboat, which sat high above the waterline and well above the wharf. It was white, with gingerbread trim, though not so elegant as the *Natchez*. This was a working riverboat, designed to haul trade goods and people upriver, furs and more people back down.

We were taking flour, blankets, needles and thread, and piles and piles of muskrat and beaver traps. Bridles and spurs, two saddles for each pack mule. Case upon case of rifles, mostly to trade with the trappers, though Corrin said the Indians had long since gotten their hands on firearms and it was nothing new to have to face an Indian who was more than capable with his own gun.

"I'd trade guns with an Indian, depending upon whether he was likely to use that gun on a white man or a buffalo," he said. "There's good Indians and bad."

Father said, "Just don't do any trading with the Pawnee or Kiowas or Arapaho. Not if you're planning to make friends with the Ute."

"No fear. I've never even heard of those tribes coming as far west as we'll be—leastwise, not to trade. And mark my word, we'll be avoiding them as much as possible along the way."

The Hudson Bay Company and the British controlled the Northeast, the Canadian border, and well down into the U.S. territories, and they thought they owned all the fur in that region. When they were challenged, they had a way of fighting dirty—which I expect is where Astor learned so many dirty tricks, since he was the first to fight them one-on-one.

Anyway, they had long since competed by liquoring up the Indians, and many trappers and traders had followed suit. Though Corrin was bound to get ornery once in a while, and had taken a snootful himself on that keelboat ride with Mike Fink, for the most part he despised alcohol, and especially when it was used to deliberately corrupt others. So he had decided not to do business that way. There was no whiskey in our stockpiles.

Rather, we took along barrels of glass beads in all the colors loved by the Indians; fine-looking mirrors, finger rings, bells, wristbands, earbobs, axes, powder horns, knives; copper, brass, and tin kettles; bolts of wool and cotton cloth in all the colors of the rainbow; tools for hewing logs, tools for building, tools for making adobe bricks; lead, flints, gunpowder, more rifles, and silverworks; belt buckles and moccasin patterns gussied up by folks back East who were already trying to horn in on the Indian ways.

A veritable mountain of goods was loaded into the hold, all of it carefully protected by tarpaulins and packed in wood or sealed in bags inside waterproof oilskin.

That night at the dinner table a strange feeling was in the air. Father seemed to alternate between sadness and envy. Mother's eyes teared up every time she looked at me. Sally was angry with all of us. She was angry with me for getting married and leaving, angry with Mother and Father for not letting her go along, and angry with Corrin for starting it all.

I spent an anxious night and awakened once to find Corrin at the window, wearing his wool night robe, staring out at the stars that twinkled in the ink-black sky.

I went to stand beside him, and he put an arm around me. He smelled of soap.

"I don't know, Emily. Do you really think this is the good Lord's plan for us?"

"I hope so. It's a little late to back out now."

"But not too late." He turned to gaze down into my eyes. He was really worried. "What do you think? Do you want to go, or am I just pressuring you into this?"

"I want to go, Corrin. I really do." I felt almost breathless as I said it, so eager was I to be under way.

"It's going to be hard on you. Harder than for me."

"Because I'm a woman?"

"Yes. Exactly that. Tell you the truth, I'm having second thoughts about taking you along. Now that we're almost ready to take the final step, I feel selfish and short-sighted."

"I don't want to live without you."

"I reckon if push came to shove, I could stay here."

"No! It would break your spirit. I'm sorry I ever tried to persuade you otherwise."

He nodded, obviously relieved. "Or I could go alone this first trip, get things settled out there so I'd be more certain of what I'm taking you into. I've tried to learn about what's happening in Brown's Hole, but most of the traders these days are coming from the upper Missouri, the Yellowstone, even the Teton Basin. Astor's American Fur is getting strong up there, and Ashley's folks won't be far behind them. Not much word from the Brown's Hole region. In fact, none at all."

"What could be so different?"

"I don't know. Plenty of things. Indian uprisings, bad weather. A lot can happen in two years."

"If there's something wrong—like an Indian uprising—we'll know before we get there. Won't we?"

"Maybe, maybe not. Depends on if there are survivors."

"But you said the Ute and Snake Indians leave white folk alone!"

"I said some of the bands do. Leastwise, they did back when I was there. But I've heard recent rumors of some lowland bands of Ute attacking a fur party or two down south and east of where we're headed."

126

"But Corrin! I thought we'd be safe...well...at least somewhat safe."

"I don't reckon I ever promised you that. There's risk in everything."

"But I thought the Ute were somewhat civilized!"

"Some Ute are, and it depends on how you look at it. One thing about the Far West, Emily—things have a way of changing on you, right beneath your nose. And being gone for two years...well...I'd say some of it depends on what sort of white folks they've encountered during that time and whether or not they're at war with any of their enemies and decide to add us in among ém."

I set my jawline firmly and refused to be discouraged. "I'll just pray that the Lord will travel with us. We'll be in good hands."

"I mean it. Things will be harder than you expect. You just don't know. Living here in your parents' house these past few days, I can see how easy you've had it. You'll—"

I felt a flash of anger and pulled away from him. "I'll just do what I have to, Corrin. Don't tell me I won't measure up."

He looked down at me, his eyes sad and serious. "No, that's not what I meant at all. It's just that—"

"Hush." I moved back inside the comfort of his arm.

"Can you even fire a rifle?" He laid his arm around my shoulder, but his body felt stiff as a board.

"I'll just have to learn, won't I?" I cozied up to him some more.

"And what about cooking? I hadn't realized that you've probably never cooked a meal in your life."

"I have, on occasion. Minnie taught me how to bake cakes, and cook a whole turkey, and many other things."

"We won't have a fine wood stove and plenty of kindling in the mountains, Emily. We'll be lucky to have a fireplace, and most likely you'll cook in a pit beneath a smokehole for a while."

"Then I'll just have to learn how to cook by campfire or however I must. I can do it. You'll see. We'll be just fine."

I felt him begin to thaw a little.

He said, "If things get too hard, we're going to give it up and come back."

"Not on my account we won't."

"You've no idea what you're getting into. You were right in the beginning—no decent man would take his wife into the wilderness. I let my loneliness and my love for you get in the way of my good sense, Emily. We had best reconsider—"

"Very well. If things get too hard, we'll just come back, and that's the end of it. Now come back to bed."

Corrin lay down beside me, but he was anxious and restless until dawn streaked through the windowpane. During that long night some of his anxiety wore off on me.

Or maybe trouble had been brewing beneath my skin all week, and he'd sensed it. Because next morning, just as we were about to board the riverboat, I changed my mind and couldn't take another step. The crowd was pressing me, there was so much hustle and bustle about, and abruptly I felt as if some palpable weight had filled the air to hold me back, a foreboding that literally took my courage and breath away in one fell swoop.

I was suddenly terrified at the enormity of what I was about to do. Frozen solid.

"I may never see you again," I said, turning to Mother and Father, feeling like a young child again.

They moved around to stand in front of me with matching looks of helplessness upon their faces. There was a tremor in my voice as I repeated myself. "I may die. I may never come back to Saint Louis."

"Corrin will take care of you," Father said gruffly. He hugged me, then held me at arm's length and looked down into my eyes. "I've come to have great confidence in that young man. If anything goes wrong, he'll get you home. If not—we'll see you next year when you both come home for new supplies."

"I'm afraid," I said, holding back the tears.

"Of what?" Sally said in her most saucy voice. "There's nothing to be afraid of out there but barbarian Indians and grizzly bears, rattlesnakes and killers and robbers and such."

"Hush up, Sally Lou," Mother said sharply.

"Well, if it's all right for her to go, why can't I? She's going to see all sorts of things—mountains, savages. Land sakes, Mother. Can't I just ride along to Saint Charles and take the next boat back?"

"This is Emily's bridal tour—at least the nearest thing to one that she's likely to have. I wouldn't allow you to go along if she were going only to Saint Charles to stay."

"I had expected as much," said Sally. "You have always loved Emily best."

The exaggerated pout on Sally's pretty face made me laugh. I said, "Sally Lou, as soon as I am set up out there, I am going to arrange for you to visit. We'll find you a trapper husband—some gnarly, savage old thing with hair sprouting everywhere—and you can turn squaw and stay out West as long as you like."

Sally said, "You mean you'll find me someone primitive, like Corrin?"

Corrin pasted a pretend scowl on his face.

Sally laughed too, my parents laughed—relieved—and suddenly my attack of melancholy was replaced by the realization that I had a fine, rollicking adventure in front of me if only I'd brace up to the challenge and hold my chin high.

All the same, it wasn't easy to tell my family goodbye, but it helped some that the departure of the riverboat was such a grand, busy event. It was no light undertaking to go off into the wilderness in 1822. Many went and were never heard from again, and even those who would come back could expect to be absent for one or more years. I was again pondering these things as Corrin and I began to ascend the gangway.

Suddenly a man in black worsted, with a bright blue stickpin in his silk knotted tie, began to cause a commotion on the dock. He was impossible to miss. His sprout of neck-length hair and wide beard were both so white as to resemble cotton.

It took me only a moment to realize that he had been tippling and was having trouble threading himself onto the gangplank. Folks on both sides were trying to help him. And as the realization spread that he was making a fool of himself, more people turned that way and began laughing, enjoying the spectacle of such an august-seeming gentleman almost falling down drunk. And then he appeared to deliberately weave to exaggerate his condition even further, happy to be the center of so much attention and happy to entertain.

Fortunately the crew members were not amused. Two strapping young lads marched past us and down the gangway to lift the man by his belt and heave him aboard, brushing past us en route.

The peculiar man leveled a suddenly lucid gaze at me as he accidentally grazed my shoulder. There was a diamond-bright hardness in his blue eyes as he slurred a greeting. "Beg pardon, ma'am. Ebenezer Crow at your service, and—"

But by then they'd rushed him past and onto the deck, where they summarily dumped him beside a pile of carpetbags. He rolled over and sat up, a surprised look on his face. Corrin and I made it a point to give him wide berth as we came aboard.

A number of others were equally unable to board of their own volition, for the latecomers included many a rapscallion. Finally, a leathery-faced man of coal-dark countenance slipped on at the last minute, showing his ticket of passage to a startled porter, then went to the larboard side behind a great bank of machinery. Corrin promptly excused himself and joined him.

He was gone for only a moment, and when he came back, I said, "Who, pray tell, is that black man?"

"Fellow's name is Hank, and he'll be riding in slave steerage with the other slaves."

I was shocked. "You bought a slave?"

He looked offended. "Hardly. Hank is with our party, but they wouldn't let him ride with the white folk. I considered making a to-do about it, but I'd likely just get us all thrown off. Then we'd have to wait for the next boat—which would most likely have equally uncivilized rules with regard to white folk and dark." Now he looked as if he wanted to strangle someone, though fortunately not me. He was even flexing his hands.

I said, "Who is Hank?"

"He's hired on as a guide. Other than me, he's the only one of us who has ever been through the South Fork and on into the western Rockies."

"You mean black folk travel out there too?" In Missouri even the free slaves were deferential, walked on the other side of the street, and stayed in their place. It never so much as dawned on me that there would be black men working in the Far West as trappers and traders and such.

"Some. Not many. But then, there aren't many folk of any color, except Indians."

"Why did you bring him?"

"Because he's a genius when it comes to pathfinding."

A sudden gust of fear struck me. "Then you're afraid we'll get lost?"

"No, but I plan to make good and sure we don't." He searched my eyes for a long time and seemed about to say something. Then he decided against it—I actually saw him shake his head and tell himself no. Instead he said, "Hank has been West more recently than me. In fact he just got back to Saint Louis."

131

"What did you start to say?"

"Nothing."

"You did, Corrin. What did you start to tell me?"

"Just never mind. It's nothing you want to know."

"Something about Hank, isn't it?"

"Never mind."

"Tell me."

"I can't."

"Corrin, we're supposed to be one flesh before God. I am supposed to share in your life, aren't I?"

He grinned that lopsided grin and said, "That might not include my every waking thought."

"Come on, Corrin. It was something deep—I could see it. And if it involves me or you, I have the right to know."

"It would just upset you."

"Then it's bad, isn't it?"

"Not necessarily. Actually, it's downright good, if it works out right."

"Tell me."

"Can't. But I'll tell you what. Get out of my hair for a while, and I promise to reveal everything once we reach our landing point."

"That's too long! I'll go crazy!"

"And I reckon you'll drive me plumb crazy too, but it's something I'll have to live with. I'd be taking a risk for both of us if I tell you now, and I just won't do it."

"I'll guess then. It does have something to do with Hank, doesn't it?"

Corrin's lips drew up as if they'd been stitched shut. Anger flashed through his eyes. "Leave it alone, Emily. Don't speak of it—and certainly not to anybody else. I'll tell you as soon as it's time for you to know."

I knew I wasn't going to win the argument, so I decided to take it out on Hank.

"I don't see why we have to take him along. Does he know anything about Brown's Hole?"

132

"Nothing. But he knows the mountains. He's been up the Yellowstone, trapping there in some of the hardest places. He's worth his weight in gold, Emily. Mark my words, you'll find that to be true if anything ever was."

It was also true that I was only beginning to know my husband. When we got upriver, I learned that Hank was a runaway slave who had indeed been to the Far West before, returning with a fortune in beaver pelts and a price still on his head. His master, a rabid slaveholder, took Hank's disappearance personally, learned he had been in St. Louis, and put a $500 reward on him.

But Corrin didn't tell me any of this until we were well along in our journey and it was far too late to change anything. Then he finally explained that he had come across a group of men who had robbed Hank of his earnings and were ready to hog-tie the slave and send him back to Virginia in order to collect the reward. Corrin freed him, spirited him away, hid him, and brought him aboard as his own slave, passage paid, at the very last minute—a risk that could have gotten my brand-new husband hanged!

At least he didn't want to bring me in on it, though I reckon maybe he just didn't trust me not to wag my tongue and give the whole plot away.

Corrin was impetuous and determined and bound and beholden to single-handedly save the whole human race from itself. On top of that he had an ornery streak that ricocheted him off the straight and narrow and straight into trouble time and time again.

But it would be a while yet before I would see much of that side of him. At the moment, boarding the steamer and taking care of the details of travel, he seemed like the most dependable, honorable, safe man in the world, even if he did have a secret about a black man who was traveling as a slave.

I needn't point out that those who traveled upriver were not always the most moral and decent members of St.

Louis society. As I watched the motley mixture of people who came aboard, it crossed my mind that there might be killers and thieves among us, escaping from an evil past. Trouble even before we reached the wilderness. I shivered at the thought and leaned in close to Corrin.

He sensed my renewed misgivings and held me tight.

The riverboat's chimneys were smoking; the crowd was excited. As the paddle wheeler pulled away from the wharf, backed into the current, and swung slowly around to head north, Mother, Father, and Sally stood there waving. I saw Mother put a handkerchief to her eyes.

I pulled away from Corrin and watched with tears streaming down my face, my right hand gripping the railing, white-knuckled, while he feebly held my left hand and looked helpless. I said, "What if I never see my family again? What if my foreboding is right?"

Corrin stroked my hair and pulled me close again. "You will. I give you my word. You'll weather this fine, and we'll both come back again and—"

His words were lost in a sudden volley of musketry, followed by an uproar on the docks and a matching volley from a group of revelers there, celebrating our departure. The drunkards aboard joined in the hooting and shouting, another volley of musketry went up from the top deck of the riverboat, another volley from shore followed, and the din of the crowd was enough to break your eardrums. We stood watching as the antics continued on both deck and on land.

Soon we were well under way, and St. Louis shrank into the distance behind us. The uproar continued until we were well upstream, though dwindling as our distance from the city increased. Then the passengers turned from celebrating to practical matters, and the deck itself now became a labyrinth of confusion as the latecomers tried to sort out their luggage and the crew members tried to discern what needed to be stowed and what belonged to whom.

Corrin and I were fortunate to have booked passage in time to receive well-appointed accommodations. But many late arrivals had yet to be assigned sleeping quarters. Some were arguing with the crew, and there was chaos all around.

As soon as St. Louis disappeared from view, Corrin and I found our cabin—not so fancy as the one we'd shared going downstream, but comfortable, considering that this was a working riverboat instead of an elegant, floating palace. We had been given blankets and clean bedding, since we were expected to make up our own cabin.

By nightfall, the boat was toiling steadily upriver, and we were settled in and ready to partake of the simple meal of cornbread, beans, and fatback that was offered by the steamer's kitchen.

Our long journey had begun.

10

It was only mid-May when we left St. Louis. And it was astonishing, the things that had happened to me since that day I'd gone to Effie Keeling's to buy a hat. I stood alone on deck the second day out and thought about it all.

From the day I helped deliver frocks to the Bridger farm till the day Corrin and I went upriver on that paddle wheeler was less than two months. Under normal circumstances, the speed of my betrothal and marriage would have been a disgrace. But since I was already disgraced, folks had seemed to agree that a hasty marriage was the best possible solution. And I thought I knew Corrin.

St. Louis had been warming up, but the high mountains were still deep in snow. Water from the spring thaw was feeding the tributaries that flowed into the Missouri and Mississippi, turning them choppy and turbulent. The current was strong, but the *Independence* was a sturdy paddle wheeler. It cut through the rough flow like scissors through brown watered silk. The boat could make some 44 miles per day, going upstream, a newfangled miracle if ever there was one. It could make an unbelievable 123 miles per day coming downstream, assuming it caught the fullness of the spring runoff on its way back.

But should the spring waters dissipate before the riverboat's return downstream, it might well be trapped upriver until the following year's thaw. In order to avoid this, each day the crew checked to see if the water was dropping. And one never knew how much snow might melt until it suddenly arrived in the form of heightened water or flood. So a boat might find itself either stranded on a sandbar or rushed along out of control on an overnight torrent that could flush it straight past any sign of civilization and out into the sea.

Paddle wheelers, like keelboats, were designed to sit high for minimum draw. The Mississippi and the rivers that fed her all had a tendency to run shallow here and there with sandbars and tree snags and other unpredictable hazards—which was why high water was so necessary to the journey and why early spring was a prime time to travel upriver.

That second morning we put into shore twice to pick up cordwood. The wood powered the steam engine, which powered the paddle wheel, which in turn powered the boat. Fortunately there was usually ample deadwood and drift-wood along the river, except for those places where the banks had flooded wide and everything was covered over or soaked through.

I had heard of the crude boilers catching fire and exploding, blowing up the whole boat. So I watched with some trepidation as the first batch of cordwood was loaded and stowed in the wood room. I worried some more while the boiler was restoked. But the boilermen seemed compe-tent, and I soon decided to give up that particular fear.

Whereas the *Natchez* had polished oak staircases, ours were simple wood. There were no carpets. The mattress in our cabin was well worn—though devoid of "livestock," as Corrin put it. It had been cleaned before we used it.

The finely furnished salons of the *Natchez* gave way here to roughly finished rooms where plank tables were set up to feed the passengers all at once and from the same sim-ple fare. And yet we had paid twice as much for passage on the *Independence* as on the *Natchez*.

The destination was the thing. Folks aplenty traveled the lower river. But only the hardiest took the upper-river tour. And the tour up the wilder Missouri, beyond any pre-tense of civilization, was left to only the most adventurous—or greediest—souls.

By the time we followed the wide loops of the Mississippi and fought the current, the journey from St. Louis to the mouth of the Missouri, then on to the Blacksnake Hills, would take ten to twelve days. We reached

137

St. Charles at 4:00 A.M. of the morning we left, passed her by as it was turning daylight, and from then on felt as if we were already in the wilderness; heavy, deep forests crept right down to the riverbanks.

When the weather was clear, the moon was out, and there was ample cordwood aboard, the boat ran all night. And that worried me for a while. I was afraid the pilot might hit a snag. I had lived on that wily old river long enough to hear an abundant number of horror stories about its wicked and deceptive ways. But our pilot seemed to know his job; we made clear passage, and by the fourth day I was beginning to feel at home.

Reckon that was always one of my strong points—I was adaptable.

On the fifth day out, Corrin and I sat down to a dinner of roast venison and potatoes—some of the crew had gone hunting as an aside to one of their trips ashore for cordwood, and the passengers reaped a part of the bounty that night. I was wearing my gray silk shirtwaist with a pink ribbon and cameo at the throat, and a gray homespun skirt. I was still way overdressed for the occasion.

There were only a few other families on board, the Franklins among them. They came into the dining hall as we started our meal. The husband was a dour, sacklike little man who never seemed to let a smile crack his face. The wife was a small, mousy critter wearing a dress that might have been cut from a flour sack, and the two flaxen-haired teenaged daughters were straight-backed and large for their age. They would have been handsome girls except for their plain faces. The mother's clothing was shabby, but the girls wore fine new dresses, though practical and cut from the simplest calico.

I had spoken with the wife a time or two, and now I nodded a greeting as they went past and found their own table. She barely drew up the courage to nod back.

I was getting to know most of the passengers by sight, though I had no intention of becoming a social butterfly. Not with that crowd. Still, a few of them gave me pause and made me wonder about their origins.

I was interested in two copper-faced Indians, one tall, one short. They looked just alike except for that, and I took them for mismatched brothers. They both wore black beaverskin top hats with eagle feathers stuck in the brims, buckskin-fringed vests, homespun shirts, and twill pants with buffalohide belts. I learned that they plied the river—up, then down again—running a card game. It was no secret that the Indians, for the most part, liked to gamble.

These two seemed furtive rascals, and I kept an especially close eye on Corrin when they were around, lest they seduce him into a card game and fleece him of our operating capital or simply pick his pockets.

And then I had seen the gentleman with the black worsted suit from time to time. The one with the bright blue stickpin in his silk knotted tie and the bright blue eyes, who had to be carried aboard. He was impossible to miss. His white-cotton neck-length hair and his wide white beard made him stand out in any crowd. He had sobered up and was acting the perfect gentleman these days, so I chalked his earlier antics up to excitement at the thought of boarding the riverboat and a bit too much celebration.

Now that gentleman entered the dining hall, lifted a wooden plate off the stack of clean ones, picked up a tin fork and knife, then passed the cook table slowly as the servers filled his plate to brimming. Then he stood looking around the room—and sashayed our way.

He stepped up to Corrin, stood at attention, and said, "How do you do? I am Professor Ebenezer Crow. I have been told you are Mr. Corrin Brevard McCannon, of the McCannon-Davidson Expedition, and I wonder if I may have a word with you?"

"Have a seat," Corrin said and gestured to a spot across from me and catercorner to him. He then indicated me. "My wife, Emily Anne."

The man slid onto the plank bench. "How do you do, Mrs. McCannon? And are you enjoying your trip?"

"It has been most interesting."

"If I may be so bold, you are a very courageous young woman to undertake such an expedition. Albeit in the company of your fine-looking and equally courageous husband."

"Thank you," I said simply, not knowing what else to say. That diamond-hard glitter was in his bright blue eyes again, though his speech was so polite and fine that the best quality butter wouldn't melt in his mouth.

Corrin just sat there silent, a look of distaste on his face.

I said, "So you are a professor?"

"Yes, indeedy."

"And what do you teach, sir?"

He puffed up. "I have given up teaching for the moment. I am on an expedition of my own. Under the auspices of the United States Government, I am studying Indian lore and habits. A sort of modern-day Lewis and Clark, *harumph.*" He actually took a bow, though he remained seated.

"That's a pretty tall order," Corrin said, trying to fight back a laugh.

The professor ignored him and puffed up even more. "However—*ahem*—in my normal guise I am a professor of unusual philosophies, knowledgeable in anthropology and biology and Indian linguistics. I am also adept at the practice of phrenology and certain of the healing arts. I plan to do a comprehensive study of Indian herbs and healing lore as a part of my contribution to the knowledge of mankind."

I tilted my head, interested in spite of his pompous air. I said, "You're traveling all the way upriver?"

"Partway. I am about to begin a scientific assay of certain of the most savage Indian tribes."

"And which ones might that be?" Corrin asked politely. He took a bite of his venison and chewed it with relish. It was good, tender meat.

"Arapahoes, Sioux, Cheyenne, Snakes, Ute, Kiowa, whatever comes my way."

"So you'll be departing at Blacksnake Hills and traveling west on land?"

"Indeed, I shall be."

"Alone?" Corrin frowned, puzzled.

"Ah, no, indeed. I shall meet up with my party there. They came upriver several weeks ago to prepare the pack train that will take us into remote and hitherto unexplored regions."

"Well, I wish you luck," Corrin said.

"I shall need more than luck. I shall need all my formidable skills, as well as the considerable Indian lore I have already accumulated during my long and esteemed journey through the halls of wisdom."

"What tribes have you already studied?" I asked, more curious in spite of myself.

"I have done a comprehensive study of the Natchez, for one."

"I have heard a bit about them," I said. "Weren't they a tribe that lived several hundred years ago in the lower Mississippi Valley?"

"Ah, you are a well-educated young lady. I am impressed, yes, indeed. But I remind you that I am the reigning expert on the subject. I question others' conclusions, and my forthcoming dissertation is far from complete. I had thought of publishing on just the Natchez Indians, to set the record straight, but there is so much, so very much, to tell the world about all our red-skinned brothers and sisters."

"Tell me everything," I said, suddenly excited at the prospect of understanding the world of Indians. After all, I was about to enter a part of it. And though I had seen them come and go in St. Louis, all in all I knew little about them.

141

Corrin rolled his eyes to tell me I was being foolish to listen to the man.

But the professor was pleased as molasses by my curiosity. "Ah, yes, indeed," he said. "I shall be proud to oblige. You see, the Natchez were the most peculiar tribe of folks. They built huge mud pyramids to rival those of the ancient Egyptians, all up and down the Mississippi River Valley—"

"Strange no one has ever seen one," Corrin muttered.

The professor craned his neck and peered at him. "Beg pardon?"

"Nothing," I said, giving Corrin an irritated, sideways look. "My husband is given to muttering while dining on venison." I turned my best smile to the professor. "Pray go on."

"Well—some of this is hard for a layman to understand—or laywoman, if you'll pardon me, my dear—"

Corrin shot him a mean look, and the professor immediately said, "If you'll forgive my forwardness for calling you 'my dear.' Indeed, it's just that I had a daughter once—you remind me a good deal of her."

"Really?"

"Ah, yes, but she was taken by the Cherokee, a terrible fate. Died down in Alabama a few years back. Scalped of her long blonde tresses."

"How sad."

"Yes, pitiful," Corrin piped up.

The professor said to him, "Eh?" He craned his neck again, as if having a hard time hearing.

Corrin looked at me, rolled his eyes again, then said, "Never mind."

"Tell me about the other Indians," I said.

"I have studied the ancient Hopewells. Earth dwellers who lived in vast labyrinths beneath the ground, with their own lakes and rivers and everything they needed. Even blind deer and beaver—for the animals lived in blackness, and the game had no need for sight, I'm told, though their hearing was especially keen."

"I see," I said. I shot Corrin a disbelieving look.

He smiled with satisfaction that I'd finally realized the man was a humbug, then took another bite of steak.

That "I see" was apparently all the professor needed to fly off into another monologue. He said, "And then there were the Floridian tribes. I studied the Apalachee and Timucua and Calusa for many years. A fascinating species of human being. They thought the sun was a woman and worshiped her—indeed, worshiped a woman, if you can imagine. And they tattooed themselves all over, often in a sort of Scottish tartan plaid that rivaled the tartans of the greatest Highland chieftains. In fact, one of my premises is that these strange natives might in fact be somehow related to the Scots—"

He stopped short, suddenly frowning at Corrin, and as I looked at Corrin too, I realized why.

Corrin had the most incredulous expression on his face, and his cheeks and mouth were puffed up as if they were about to explode. I could see that he was doing everything he could to suppress a laugh that might well expel his dinner like a cannonball.

He bobbed twice, managed to swallow, his napkin to his mouth now, and then he indeed guffawed. He laughed till tears streamed down his face, and when he had settled down some, he said, "Where on earth did you hear all that balderdash?"

The professor went stiff as a board. He puffed up like an adder. "It is an intellectual fact, sir. I have studied them myself and came to those very conclusions. I will have you know that all the reigning experts agree completely with my deductions."

He looked as if he were about to stand and throw down the glove that would challenge Corrin to a duel.

My husband apparently decided to douse the flames of anger. "All right, excuse me. It's just that the idea of a

143

Natchez Indian tattooed in the clan of my forefathers is a bit much for me to contemplate." He forced his face straight, though I could see it took effort.

The professor, however, didn't seem to notice. He turned back to me. "Ah, the wonders I have beheld. The remarkable habits of the Kansan Indians, whose domain we shall soon sail right past. The savage antics of the Wichita tribes—"

"Tell me," Corrin said, "is it true that the Flatheads have heads which are only a few inches thick and are otherwise flat as pancakes?"

I kicked him under the table, but my legs were too short to get up enough steam for him to feel it much.

He barely glanced at me, his eyes twinkling, before he turned back to the professor, a serious look on his face.

"Well, now," the professor said, stroking his beard and seeming to think hard. "I have indeed heard certain peculiar things about that group of savages."

Corrin was loaded for bear now. He said, "I have been told that their heads form a straight line from the nose to the top of the forehead. They are made that way by their mothers, who bind them in compressing machines right after birth that make their eyes pop forward while their heads are flattened like pancakes. I have been told that they believe this is a sign of great beauty or handsomeness."

I suppressed a volley of outrage. Corrin was making fun of me and the professor to boot.

But the professor was looking at him with a peculiar light in his eyes, as if wondering if he had found a kindred spirit.

Corrin helped him decide. With the straightest possible face, he said, "I understand that west of the Rocky Mountains the flattest possible head is the savage idea of beauty. I have it on the best possible authority."

"Well—that is most interesting. I shall make it a point to look into that, yes, indeed." The professor was still giving Corrin a peculiar look.

Not to be outdone, I said, "And I understand that where we're going there are giant lizards trapped in the stone cliff walls, and giant elephants with tusks as big as a house buried under the ground—"

Corrin looked at me and laughed out loud.

The professor looked shocked. Slowly, seriously, he said, "I, too, have heard about the giant elephants. Mastodons, they are called in the scientific literature. Great scot, you don't mean to tell me—but where are you children going, anyway?"

"Place called Fort Davy Crockett," Corrin said.

"Where is that, exactly?" The professor's eyes were wide with wonder.

"Place name of Brown's Hole, due west of the Rockies."

"And you say the giant lizards and elephants have been seen there?"

"I have it on the best authority," I said, giving Corrin a mischievous look.

"Live," Corrin added with a twinkle in his eyes.

"Ah, but—"

"He's not serious about that," I said.

The professor said, "But—in the western Rockies, you say? That's a lot of territory. You—you wouldn't be so kind as to draw me a map, would you?"

Corrin shrugged his shoulders. "Don't see as how it would hurt anything."

The professor pulled a tattered envelope from his vest pocket, handed it to Corrin with a stub of pencil, and said, "Please, sir. I would be forever beholden to you."

Corrin looked uncomfortable at the man's sudden deference but drew him a rough map of the western Rockies and Brown's Hole nonetheless and politely handed it back. He said, "Do you have some reason for your curiosity?"

"My word, yes. The giant lizards and mastodons. Why, if a man could find such things and bring them back to civilization for display—don't you see? There's a fortune

145

to be made." A suspicious look took hold of his face, as if he suddenly suspected competition. "What are you folks going to do out there, anyway?"

Corrin shrugged. "We mean to do some trading."

The man's face turned artificially sunny. "Ah, but if only I could go along. I would give anything to see those lizards. I would consider changing all my plans—"

"But we aren't going to be hunting any lizards, whether they're giants or small enough to climb into your shoe. Fact is, we'll be even less likely to chase after them if they're giants. And we aren't doing any trading till we get there," Corrin said slowly, as if beginning to see a plot brewing. "Here or there, I don't plan to listen to any hare-brained schemes or be horse-traded out of so much as a thin copper coin."

Astonished by his rude behavior, I said, "Corrin!"

The professor looked suddenly guilty. He abruptly looked over Corrin's shoulder, picked up his half-full plate of grub, and said, "Ah. If you'll excuse me. I see the person I was to meet for dinner. Thank you so very much for your charming company."

But when I looked through the crowd to see who he'd met, he was no place to be seen.

11

The mouth of the Missouri was only some twenty-two miles above St. Louis. We traveled up this rougher, narrower river for the better part of a week, northward and westward toward the far mountains. Day after day the boat churned through the deep, choppy, spring-roughened water until the days became tedious and I became restless and irritable with little to do but watch the sameness of the riverbank roll past.

We stopped at an occasional remote post to pick up supplies or a passenger. But for the most part our stops were either nighttime layovers, when the weather dictated, or frequent pauses to replenish the cordwood.

Corrin and I began to know one another better during that long river journey. We began to learn each other's idiosyncrasies and annoying habits and flaws all at once, for we were cooped up tight in our small cabin and had few excuses to avoid one another.

Finally we had a spat over some small thing—I believe we fought over the palatability of the bean soup at dinner the night before. I complained, Corrin said he doubted if I could cook anything much better, and I flew off the handle.

He marched out and went for a long parade around the deck, then came back two hours later and apologized, but we sat down and talked and decided we both needed a bit more room. We were two headstrong people—independent, used to doing things our own way and with little interference from outside. It was going to take some doing to settle down and become fully comfortable. Perhaps we never would, and perhaps that was best. If there was anything I did *not* want in a marriage, it was boredom.

On the eighth day out, the weather turned on us. The paddles labored; the feel of the boat changed. Corrin and I sensed the change inside our cabin when we awakened at daybreak. We went for a short walk to see what the trouble was and found the crew half frozen, working beneath the lash of a cold, heavy rain. The sky was leaden; rain curtains all but hid the shoreline. And the wind had risen with awesome force.

The miserable weather made people listless and mean-spirited, and they elbowed one another around the deck and complained no end. But that was only the beginning. The rain pelted down till the decks were slippery and the captain suggested we all return to our quarters. Those few penurious refugees who had been berthed outside were sent packing to the dining hall to weather the storm therein.

The icy river water pounded at the boat. The wind grew wilder, and when there was a gap in the curtains of rain and I could see the bank, the ancient trees seemed grim and almost alive, like a tangled green-black horror with gnashing teeth, whipping animal-like back and forth.

I was sitting on our berth shivering, wrapped tight in a blanket, shooting dark looks at poor Corrin and wishing I'd had the good sense to stay home, when a sudden shudder rocked the boat. It struck again and pitched me off the bed as if an invisible giant's hand had yanked me up and thrown me.

I was on the floor, looking up, trying to figure out what had happened, when Corrin loomed over me. "Emily, are you all right?" He bent over, looking at me intently, as if afraid to touch me.

"Get me up from here, Corrin McCannon. I'm—" I shook my head as a dizzy spell struck. I shook it again, trying to clear it enough to realize what had happened. I tried to stand.

Corrin reached out to help me, but I shook off his hand, angry for some reason, then fell back to the floor, which tilted right out from under me so that it stood at an angle.

We heard shouts then—the crew and the pilot yelling orders and curses, all in a frenzy. Thinking we were about to sink, I leaped up, and we managed to grope our way outside—to see that we were stuck tight in a chute of the river channel, listing, prow facing one bank, stern facing the other, and the river water pounding at the upriver side in its full fury.

"Sandbar!" someone shouted. "We've hit a sandbar—turned us crosswise, and we're stuck fast! Full steam ahead!"

"Cain't do it," another voice shouted back. "That blamed lurch doused the larboard furnace! Got us a hank of a tribulation here to get that rascal going again!"

"Halloo!" another voice shouted. "Is that a man overboard?"

"Logjam!" shouted yet another man. "Halloo—halloo, there—nah, ain't nothing but a logjam over there in the fog."

There was such chaos that I could scarcely keep track of it all, and on top of that my head was still spinning from my fall.

Water rushed down the deck like a waterfall, pounding on the upward side while the downward side was at a slight tilt. We were stuck fast all right, and the rain grew harder. It was all but impossible to stand, and people were scattered here and there, holding onto posts and railing, trying to make their way forward to see what was going on. Certain of the supplies had also slid to one side, making the job of righting the paddle wheeler far more difficult.

"Stop," Corrin said to me, as I started forward.

I was happy to do just that, since I was about ready to fall forward due to the list of the boat.

"Time to pray," he said, holding me tight in one of his strong, thick arms.

He braced himself, braced me against him, then held onto my hand, and pray he did, without embarrassment. He just stood there and spoke up into the rain, pouring full into his face. He asked the Lord for my safety and for all the passengers' and crew's safety, and then he asked a blessing for our expedition and prayed that everything would work out just right.

I wasn't exactly accustomed to that sort of prayer, though I did believe that prayer worked. But perhaps, I thought, it worked better when spoken inside a church by a minister—that is, by someone who served God regularly rather than only in a pinch.

I was skeptical. But at the same time, I was grateful that I'd had the good sense to marry a man who would put God first, especially while in the valley of death.

And the valley of death seemed to be exactly where we had landed. Evening was descending, it kept growing colder, the rain poured down, and everyone was drenched. Certain folks started sobbing, and the crew seemed just as discombobulated as the rest of us.

I reckon the Lord had the help of many a pair of strong, determined human hands that evening. For something happened just as the night was descending full upon us. I felt yet another lurch, and someone shouted, "We've worked her partway free! All passengers to the starboard deck! Hang on tight—come on now—hurry it—we've got just a short time to get this lizzie turned around and headed upstream."

I felt the engines catch, heard them choke and complain, then take hold. The paddle wheel began to turn. The boat suddenly broke all the way loose with a ferocious wrenching that ground her timbers and shook the decks. I hung onto Corrin and onto the railing at the same time, feeling her shudder and quake, then suddenly tilt upright with a crash that set her decks level again.

Corrin jumped up and down. "Whoo-hee!" He laughed and spun me around, not taking into account that I was already dizzy or that the deck was so slick we were close to ice skating. His face was full of sunshine that glowed in the dusk. He gave me a swat. "You go on below deck, get dried out and cleaned up."

I moved to the hatchway that led inside, then turned to watch him. He was so happy, whistling, helping the deck-hands set things straight, and working as hard as he could. How I loved that headstrong, rust-haired man!

We traveled farther up the boiling, churning, muddy Missouri than many folk did. At the mouth of the Kansas River, the Missouri made an abrupt turn, and we put in to shore to discharge the travelers who were bound for the Spanish South on the route called the Santa Fe Trail. Some folks also took that route when headed north, then peeled off when they reached the foothills of the Rockies and the Arkansas River. But Corrin had decided to keep to the pad-dle wheeler and the Missouri as long as possible in order to make the journey somewhat easier for us all.

I grew excited when we berthed at the great bend at Westport Landing to drop off those passengers and supplies headed to Santa Fe. This was the last port before we would reach our own debarking place.

Westport Landing was disappointing though. I had heard the name so often, spoken with such reverence, that I expected a great deal more than I got. The small settlement was made up of tents and muddy horse pens, without so much as a wooden building to be seen. The storm had come through here too, and most of the folks looked tired from fighting the weather.

We stayed aboard. The boat put back out into the middle of the river almost immediately, then wheeled on north to the mouth of the Platte. Several primitive trading posts (some no more than cabins) and forts (some no more than a single rampart atop an equally primitive cabin) had been set up by various fur companies and traders in the region. According to Corrin, forts and trading posts waxed

151

and waned. At the moment one decent-sized fort and two unimportant trading posts existed near the mouth of the Platte. There we would leave the river and journey inland.

We were rounding a tree-clad bend two days later, I was sitting on a chair on deck and swatting mosquitoes, thinking about everything I'd left behind and letting myself get into a blue mood, when a volley of musket fire thundered through the pristine air, followed by the boom of cannon.

I leaped to my feet along with everyone else. Even the deckhands all stopped short, threw their hats in the air, and shouted. I had seldom seen such a frenzy of activity.

"What is it?" I asked Corrin, who came to stand beside me.

"We've reached the fort. See it?" He pointed toward the bank, and now I could see the smallest outline of a wood rampart partly hidden by the trees.

"The arrival of a boat is one of the great events of the year to those poor lonesome trappers and traders. Think of it, Emily. We're bringing mail and goods to eat—items these folks can't do without but don't see near enough of."

"Spoken like a true trader," I said with a smile. But my own spirits soared at the excitement around me. The river was something I knew, even if I had never been this far upstream before. But reaching the fort that was our doorway to the Far West. Ah, this was grand adventure indeed.

Before long I could see a small handful of log buildings. As we proceeded toward shore, renewed volleys of cannon and musket fire greeted us, ringing in my ears till I wondered if the shooters wouldn't expend an entire riverboat's supply of ammunition just in celebration. But no, because now folks aboard the paddle wheeler were firing too, vigorously responding to the fort's welcome. There seemed to be plenty of gunpowder to go around.

The pier was raw, rough wood, lashed and bolted together, but the boat paddled grandly up alongside as if she were docking at the fanciest city in the world. All the passengers stood proudly at the railings, letting the primitives get a good gander at us before we, too, turned savage and thorny due to our own time in the wilderness.

It seemed that most everybody at the fort and trading posts had turned out, from a handful of soldiers to storekeepers to charlatans to trappers to Indians. We had no more than touched the dock when a bevy of rascal traders leaped aboard, opened the holds, and began unloading the goods, mostly ignoring the people altogether.

I felt a bit insulted, having expected to be celebrated as an adventuress for my journey north and west. But in no time it was explained that both the pilot and the fort dwellers were in a hurry to unload and be rid of us, for they were fighting the spring rise. No one wanted to be stranded by low water and have to sit at such a fort for a full year.

More important, many of the folks who were waiting were trappers fresh back from the Far West, the Far North, and other places where there were beaver, otter, and fox aplenty. They had brought in their furs and were anxious to unload our cargo in order to put theirs aboard. The sooner they could get their furs loaded and get downriver to sell them, the sooner they could get to the real celebration of squandering their earnings.

One thing I was to quickly learn about trappers: if they made a penny on a plew, it was all likely to be gone almost as soon as it hit their pockets. It was a rare man who could go into the mountains, work hard trapping all year, then hold onto the money when he finally got paid.

Three hard-faced bourgeois, overseers of the company trapping expeditions, seemed to have the most pelts—in fact, stack upon stack of them.

Corrin felt them out, then came and told me what they'd said. They were representing John Jacob Astor's American Fur Company.

In 1822 we weren't many years past the American Revolution. The nation was still aborning—the Northwest Territory was the edge of civilization, and the Far West extended from there all the way to the Pacific Ocean. Certain trappers—John Jacob Astor among them—had explored up the Columbia River, after Lewis and Clark initially mapped that area. Astor set up a few posts there to trade with Russia and China. But in between, in the land of the Far Mountains, the region was largely uncharted territory. It truly was the last frontier.

Spanish explorers had been into parts of the region, mostly looking for gold. An occasional Spanish settlement had been left behind—Santa Fe, for instance. And a few of the hardiest trappers had been bringing in beaver plew from the Far West for half a century or more, at their own peril.

Part of that peril was still the British. They controlled Canada and much of the Northwestern forests and forayed widely into land claimed by the United States. They hadn't quite given up the idea that America was still made up of their colonies.

The Hudson Bay Company, the British trapping conglomerate, was happy to use the Northwestern Indians against the Americans every chance they got. It was nothing for a trapping party to be found half-skinned and long dead, with British musket balls right alongside Indian sign and arrowheads. More than once, American trading posts and forts were burned to the ground by Indians who'd been bought off by the British in various ways—often with pure rotgut whiskey.

To counter the British franchise and their skullduggery, certain American fur companies took up their underhanded methods. Profit was the thing, and the company that couldn't turn a profit didn't last long.

Father's New West Fur Company managed to stay out of the fray, since he didn't send out trapping parties of his own. He operated mostly as a middleman. He bought furs from independent trappers and sold them to the big fur merchants, who shipped them down to New Orleans, from where they were mostly shipped on to Europe.

But one man held most of this European trade—the German-born John Jacob Astor. His methods of doing business were about on a par with those of the British, for he'd learned from them. He'd been in the fur trade since the late 1780s, and he knew every illicit trick in the book. Astor's American Fur Company was a thorn in everyone's side.

I glanced now at the three hard-faced bourgeois and their stacks of pelts. The bourgeois managed company business with regard to expeditions and forests and streams, whereas the company's high-muckety-mucks sat in their offices in St. Louis and New York and cracked the whip.

But in the forests and at the company trading posts, the bourgeois did the whip cracking, sometimes literally. They had absolute authority, right down to being able to shoot a man, for they were supreme law in the wilderness. Some folk claimed that the bourgeois were men of great dependability and integrity. But if you ask me, any man who would do business in such a way is suspect already. And if I hadn't already known that from listening to Father's conversations, I'd have seen it in those men's faces. They were hard and lean, like ferrets on the hunt.

It turned out that even Ashley wasn't all Corrin had thought him to be. Though he was a decent enough man, he was bound to take care of what was his, and sometimes that meant cutting corners. Corrin and I both had a lot to learn about human nature.

Anyway, the big companies hired their trappers in batches, just as Ashley had hired Corrin during our ill-fated expedition upriver the first time. They were put on salary and sometimes given bonuses if they trapped enough. Trouble was, while the trappers were out in the wilderness trapping for the company, the company was busy tallying up every bean those trappers ate, every side of venison the hunters brought to them. They then multiplied everything a few times, to account for the expansion of the owners' bellies, and billed it against the trappers' harvest of plews. By the time the trappers and the company compared notes, the company came out ahead nearly every time.

Only a few of the most respectable companies allowed their trappers to get ahead. And so, when I looked into the faces of those three hard-faced bourgeois, I could see by the leathery set of their jaws and the hard glint in their eyes that I was looking at men who would more or less do anything to obtain a beaver plew.

"I'm glad I pulled out of the Ashley Expedition," Corrin said after a brief conversation with them.

I tried not to look smug. "And why is that?"

"The way the companies do their trapping. Those men came right out and laughed at the way they'd hornswoggled their trappers this year. Claimed they were making ten eagles for every copper they paid them. Seemed to think I was on their side since I'm running an expedition, and they let their tongues wag at will."

"That's American Fur for you. Astor is far worse than Ashley, any day of the week."

"Yes, and if I had my druthers, I'd rather be up against Ashley anytime rather than Astor. What worries me is that these folks are planning to move farther west when they get back from St. Louis. They seemed to think I was planning to do nothing but trade, and they talked a good deal more than they would have had they known I intend to trap."

"Corrin. You hornswoggled *them*. Good for you!"

"True, I let them believe what they wanted to. I wanted to get a better feeling for what we're going up against. And though they were a bit more closemouthed about their forthcoming plans than about their recent thefts, they let enough slip to worry me."

I was suddenly made anxious by the troubled look on his face. I said, "Corrin—are they coming to McCannon's Country?"

He smiled. "Not quite. But they are planning to help set up a big rendezvous farther north on the Sheets-Kadee.

May have already set up a post there—these fellers weren't sure."

"Oh, Corrin. Are they going to be trouble?"

"They're most likely always trouble. They bring in their trappers and comb the country of all beaver and most other wildlife for miles around, then move on and do the same, over and over. It's a bad way to do business. One day there won't be any beaver left."

I found that nigh unto impossible to believe. Why, there were thousands upon thousands of miles of wilderness in front of us. But at the same time I remembered Father's concern that the beaver trade would one day die out.

I said, "Where on the Sheets-Kadee? How far from the fort?"

"A few hundred miles north and west. Far enough. But close enough too, if you get my meaning. Close enough to be potential trouble. They've even given the river another name. Call it the Green River. A white man's name for country being claimed by white men."

"Well, you can't fault them on that account. We're white too—and moving into Indian domain."

"Yes, but we don't plan to pillage it and leave it a wasteland when we leave," Corrin said. "And we aren't likely to shoot our way in or leave a bunch of liquored-up Indians in our wake."

That was my first realization of the friction in the wilderness side of the fur trade. Father had talked about it, but it had never been real to me. I had never seen it as interfering with my own life in any important way until that moment.

Now, looking at those three hard-faced bourgeois, I began to realize that this expedition would indeed lead us into trouble.

But certainly no more trouble than we could handle. I was equally sure of that.

The evening we reached the fort, the riverboat held a banquet to celebrate. The next night, the folks from the fort returned the compliment. The bourgeois, the card-shark Indians, the Franklins, and the cotton-haired, diamond-eyed professor joined the festivities with the rest of us.

By the time our goods were all set aside under oil-cloth and tarpaulins inside the fort, our mules taken out of the livestock pens, and the riverboat cargo deck packed tight with furs, we had eaten as much as we could hold. We were left more or less stupefied by food and revelry as the boat readied to leave the dock early the next morning.

A new batch of folks now lined the decks—rough fellows this time, ones who had already been to the wilderness and were coming back with the wear and tear to show for it, including those bourgeois.

The mysterious Hank was helping us count supplies, and we were talking to our mule skinners and making plans on how to proceed on west.

As the boat pulled away, I looked up to see the man with the cottony hair, Professor Ebenezer Crow, bearing down on us.

Corrin frowned when he saw him and gave me a sideways glance of impatience.

But the professor either didn't see Corrin's expression or didn't care, because he burst right into the middle of our accounting and, with wild gesticulations, said, "The most awful thing has happened! Ah, alas. I can't tell you how tragic this is."

"What now?" Corrin asked dryly.

"The people who were to meet me. My expedition. They have been waylaid by Indians, butchered to a man. Ah, alas—I don't know what to do. I—"

"Which Indians got them? The Natchez or the grubby ones that live in the ground?"

The professor puffed up with a hurt look on his face and scowled at Corrin.

"I reckon you want to borrow money to get back downriver," Corrin said.

The professor's head melted out of its stiffness, as if he was overwhelmed. "Ah, kind sir. What a generous offer. I could still just barely row out and catch the boat. But I could not presume to take your money—"

"Just as well, because you aren't going to get any of it," Corrin said with a scowl so deep it knit his rust-red brows together.

"Ah, but, sir, I have resources to repay you. The University of Boston itself is the benefactor of my expedition."

"Thought you said it was the United States Government."

The professor barely blinked. "They both have a hand in the expedition. It is a very important undertaking. If you could see it in your heart to befriend me—"

Corrin's frown deepened.

The professor said, "My stipend would easily reimburse you—"

Corrin's face went dark.

I stepped back out of the way.

"Unless—" hope sprang into the man's pleading face "—perhaps you could see a way I might go West with you? Admittedly, I am white of hair, but I can work as hard as the next man, and I have wisdom we might draw upon in hard times. I would do anything, pay any price, to see the land of the giant lizards and mastodons."

"Looks to me like you can't pay anything," Corrin said. "Reckon that's why you're trying to talk your way into my party and free eats."

"Sir, I would not presume so much. I understand it would require a great act of charity for you to take me along on such a journey, alas. And perhaps it is too much to ask of you. But barring that, if you could only see clear to finance my trip back downriver so I could reinforce my resources, I would gladly give you a marker on the university's account.

It's as good as gold, sir. You have my word on that. And I shall be coming to Brown's Hole shortly. At worst, I could repay you then."

Corrin's knuckles bunched up. "You think I'm fool enough to believe you'd travel more than a thousand miles to repay a debt? Reckon you'd best take a running hike, Professor So-and-So. You're a flimflam man if ever I did see one, and you're not going to flam me nor mine out of one thin copper coin."

"But, sir. You are the only person I know. I am left in this heaven-forsaken wilderness fort alone—"

At that moment, one of the two Indian brothers—the squat little blunt-faced fellow dressed in fancy city clothing—loomed into view, spotted the professor, and shouted, "Hey, there, Ebeneez! You get the ante yet? Boys sent me out to tell you the pot's melting—you don't get back right soon you're out of the game!"

Corrin's face became a thunderburst. He leaned forward as if to hit the professor, and the man's face turned white as his hair. He spun on his heel and took off at a dead run.

12

That was our last night before going inland. We slept in the fort in a small chinked room on a mattress half filled with hay that poked through the thin covering. Itching kept me awake half the night. And if it wasn't the mattress bothering me, it was the horsehair blankets that came with the rough-hewn bed. The trappers and others going downstream were giving themselves one last hooraw, and the distant shouts and music kept me awake too.

On top of that, I was so lit up with excitement that it was all I could do to think about sleep, even though I was exhausted to the bone. Every muscle ached from carrying and repacking my clothing and other things throughout the day.

Finally Corrin got up and opened my travel packet, took out my red and white quilt—the one I'd brought from home—and gave it to me. I wrapped it tight around me, breathed in the lavender water that was still on it, and lay there homesick for a while, thinking about Mother and Father and Sally and wondering if they also missed me. I finally fell asleep.

I awakened at the crack of dawn with sunlight trying to pour through the oilskin window but only leaking in a bit.

Corrin was nuzzling my neck. "Wake up, Emily. This is the day we go West!" He fairly beamed at the prospect, his hazel eyes filled with a contagious kind of excitement.

Not that I needed his excitement to kindle my own. I popped out of bed instantly, as if a bolt of lightning had shot through me. This was indeed the day we started for the Far West, and I had never been more eager to be under way.

The fort was alive for me that morning, the air crisp with spring. I heard the sounds of blacksmith anvils, snorting horses, folks calling to one another—all the hustle and bustle of frontier activity one might expect in a fort, big or small, on the day an expedition would leave. We ate a hearty breakfast of flapjacks and bacon, hot coffee and fresh eggs. And then we did the final bit of packing.

Just before our caravan pulled out, Corrin handed me a rolled-up bundle of buckskin with fringes hanging down. "I reckon you're going to need these before we're through," he said.

I unfolded the packet to find a pair of thigh-high buckskin moccasins, the kind with thick buffalohide soles.

"Thank you," I said, puzzled. "But I have my walking shoes and several extra pair." I smiled and flirted with him. "Are you trying to turn me into a squaw?"

"You could do worse than learn some Indian ways," he said. And then, busy, he abruptly walked away.

His indifference angered me, and I stuffed the moccasins at the bottom of our wagon, beneath the pallets and bags of flour and such that would make up our bedroll on those nights when it rained or was too cold to sleep in a tent.

The hard part of our journey began that day. Had we known just how hard, I reckon we would have turned back right then. But we were young, foolish, and thought ourselves invincible. Death was something that happened to old folk or fools, not to sensible, hardworking young people who had the good sense to tend to their own business and keep their eye on the hills, as the Good Book said.

We had grown into a full-on party of travelers. Twelve mule skinners made up our caravan, and they were for the most part able-bodied young men searching for adventure, eager to please, and in a high state of excitement at the prospect of going West to help start a fort.

And then there were the thirty pack mules and all the rainproofed goods they would carry. Two dray wagons would haul the supplies as far as the terrain would allow, to keep the mules fresh, and two equally able teams of work horses would pull them.

And then there were the mule skinners' riding mounts, all fine examples of horseflesh handpicked by Father and Corrin from the best in the St. Louis marketplace and fleet enough to outrun Indians, if it came to that.

I'd helped unload my bay mare, Little Bit, a healthy three-year-old that I had raised from a colt. We all agreed she was sturdy enough to make the trip, though she was a little unsteady after being so long in the livestock hold. We combed and groomed and fed Corrin's larger new mount, Packy, too, and there were various other animals and odds and ends to attend to.

We planned to follow the land route to the mountains, a slightly blazed trail alongside the Platte. When we reached the South Fork of the Platte, some one hundred twenty miles upstream, we would ford it, head south, and follow it as long as we could. Then we would forge our way inland through a little-used mountain pass Corrin knew about in order to cross the steepest part of the Rockies we would encounter.

One night he held me close and talked of endless fields of bluebells and wild larkspur, of crystal-clear streams, of regal pines. It would be a lonely, difficult journey, he said, but one so beautiful I would remember it all my life. The thought of that place alone kept me going many a long mile.

At the same time he showed me his map and laughed as he pointed at the mountain pass. "Beware, Mrs. Emily McCannon. Beyond here, there be dragons."

Behind a toss of my head I hid the little shiver I felt at the prospect of such an adventure. "And I suppose they live right beside the elephants and giant lizards that are embedded in the earth?"

Corrin laughed, but later that night I saw him studying the map again, looking particularly at that place where we would cross the mountains. And he was frowning, worried as all get out.

We weren't the only ones going West that day. The Franklin family from Fort Charles had ridden partway upriver with us. I spoke to the wife once or twice, mostly because she stayed to herself and seemed so timid she nearly jumped out of her skin when I even looked at her. Her name was Shirley, and she hardly dared look you in the eye. I pitied her and wanted to draw her out—maybe even see if she could smile.

The two handsome teenaged daughters, who boasted wild, long manes of hair the color of ripe wheat, sassed her no end. They were well taught by their withered-up little skunk of a father, who amply provided the lessons the daughters needed to learn such ill behavior toward their mother and his wife. Jeb Franklin did nothing but lambaste that poor woman every time he opened his mouth.

As we were pulling out to go West, the Franklins and their two small wagons just naturally attached themselves to our larger party. After that, there they were—tagging along to make up the end of our parade.

After about an hour, I was riding in one of the wagons, resting my weary bones, giving Little Bit a rest, and asking Hank all sorts of questions that he seemed reluctant to answer. He was wiry-haired, chocolate-skinned, and he'd been well trained to hold his tongue. But the Far West appeared to have changed him some, so that at times he seemed almost like a free man. Now and again, when you least expected it, he'd come right out and speak his mind as if he'd never been a slave at all.

Hank was along to act as guide insofar as he knew the terrain. But for the most part we were to rely on Corrin, for he was the only one among us who had been anywhere near Brown's Hole itself.

Corrin rode up beside me, tipped his hat to Hank, then reined in and professed his irritation to me. "You'd think Jeb Franklin would have the decency to ask me if I cared to have him along."

I was tired already and grouchy. "I don't know him— I barely know his wife. I can't tell you what I think he'd do."

"Might be handy to have him along," Hank said slowly. He was like that, slow and easy and kind of heart but clear thinking. He had a thicket of short, wiry gray hairs on his chin that passed for a beard; he wore an old mule skinner's hat and homespun clothing.

Corrin's frown deepened. "Maybe. But I don't like him taking advantage."

"Might not be taking advantage at all," Hank said evenly, looking into the far distance to where a little squall of rain was causing a portion of the fields to turn gray. "Maybe wouldn't hurt to check it out before y'all go off half-cocked."

Corrin didn't take offense, though from the frown on his face it seemed that he was still concerned. He said, "I'm going to ride back and have a word with him. I reckon he's welcome to whatever protection we can provide, but he'd best be warned that he'll be expected to abide by our rules."

I watched over my shoulder as he rode back and stopped beside the man, who was mounted on a fine-looking sorrel. They spoke, the man more or less hung his head and looked humbled, then nodded a few times as if he were yessiring Corrin. After a time, Corrin rode up past us, on his way forward to check the mule train. He gave us a broad, beaming smile and tipped his hat. The talk had apparently gone well.

When we rested for the noon meal, the Franklin family joined us for a pot of grits and potatoes with collard greens and other more-or-less fresh vegetables we'd brought along from the fort. We visited while we rested, though they stayed mostly to themselves. Seems they were on their way to Fort John on the upper fork of the Platte.

This meant we'd be parting when we reached the forks of the Platte, but that was a good ways distant. Traveling all that way with strangers might turn out to be stressful, I thought, if they proved to be incorrigible in any way. But where the Platte split into north and south, Mr. Franklin said, he would be met by a delegation from the fort, which would escort him on upriver. He was to be employed as a clerk to oversee the fort's provisions. He would work under his brother, who was bourgeois—fort overseer—which was why he expected a special welcome.

Corrin and I discussed the matter late into the night and finally decided it might be practical to travel with as many able-bodied people as possible.

He convinced me when he said, "I wasn't going to mention it so as not to worry you. But I reckon you ought to know. Back at the fort I learned that the Blackfeet are on the warpath again."

I shivered. From time to time the Blackfeet engaged in imaginative methods of torture against nigh unto anyone, white or Indian, who came into their territory.

"Oh, Corrin. Should we go back?"

"No, it shouldn't affect us, but I did want you to know in case you hear of it from someone else. Better you know the facts rather than listen to some embroidered and no doubt far bloodier version of events."

"Will we encounter any of them?"

"Reckon not."

He went on to explain that the normal Blackfoot territory was well north of where we'd be traveling, but still it appeared that the idea of meeting with any Indians at all gave him second thoughts, just in case they might be in a mood to imitate the Blackfeet.

"When will we see Indians?"

"Never, unless they want us to."

"I mean, when will we enter true Indian country?"

He told me that we would soon be entering the land of the Sioux and Pawnee. These were seminomadic plains Indians. They were buffalo hunters who also built hide villages and planted crops. Corrin had been through this region twice before. He'd even traded at the big Pawnee village known as Loup Fork, not far north of the Platte.

166

"They're fascinating folk," he told me. "Their lodges are huge, circular structures made from hide, and they raise the best corn, pumpkins, and squash you'll ever see, though we won't be so fortunate as to draw from their stores this time through, since their planting season has just begun."

"But are they civilized?"

"Depends on what you mean. The Spanish had a hand in turning them against our trappers years back. Some folks say you can still find a Spanish flag in a Pawnee village from time to time."

"Corrin. You know what I mean. Will they try to attack our party?"

"Can't say. No trading posts have been built in their territory. That tells me something. And I've heard from some of the trappers who traded at Fort Santa Fe that the Pawnee are likely to attack any hunting party, unprovoked. Some folks dread them as much as any trapper ever dreaded a Blackfoot or Crow."

"Then we're in trouble," I said despondently.

"Not necessarily. I got on right well with them, last trip through. And I've heard good reports as well as the bad. Because of the Spaniards, they're used to white folk, more or less. That's an advantage. Old Zebulon Pike met with three of their bands back in 1806, and he came through with all of his skin and every hair on his head."

He went on to tell me that the famous explorer Major Long had powwowed with the Pawnee during his 1819 expedition, and indeed we would be following some of Long's route into the Rockies. The Pawnee along our chosen route had allowed Long through and would most likely do the same for us.

"Unless there's something goin' on we don't know about," Corrin explained. "That's the way it is out here. When you're figuring on trouble, you always have to factor in the unexpected."

I shivered again and burrowed deep against his warm, flannel-clad side. "Then we'd best have along as

167

many folks as possible," I said. "Aren't there others going besides the Franklins?"

"Not our way."

By the time we had done all that talking, we were both convinced that the Lord had put us and the Franklins together for mutual protection. It was true that the more folks there were who traveled in a party, the less likely they were to be attacked.

Corrin was almost asleep when I said, "But why would the Franklins come upriver by themselves in the first place?" I had been studying the idea.

He gave me a sleepy grin. "Reckon they aimed to hitch up with somebody, and we happened to come along at the right time. Just as well. We can use the help. Now get some rest—we have a big day ahead."

After that, the Franklins just became a part of our caravan. They settled into the motion of things as naturally as if they'd been part of it from the beginning, and I came to enjoy having Shirley along—except for those times when her two surly daughters sassed her, and then I spoke to them in no uncertain terms. I informed them that if I'd ever spoken to my mother in such a fashion, I'd have had my britches tanned till they caught fire.

The oldest girl, Sharon, was the saucier of the two. She was fifteen, skinny as a sapling, and the meanest-spirited thing I ever did see. When she spoke rudely to her mother and I threatened to tan her hide, she tossed her pigtails, pinched up her face at me, and said, "You just dare touch me, and I'll have Pa take care of you."

"Yes, and I expect I could handle him too," I said, getting angry. "And what I leave over, Corrin can whip with a switch."

The girl was surprised at first, as if no one had yet dared to put her in her place. Then she huffed up like a sage hen and started to speak to me in an even worse manner than she used on her mother.

I was fit to be tied.

Shirley doused the forthcoming fight by gently touching my hand and looking shamefaced.

Though it nearly made me explode, I bit my tongue and held my temper, and her ill-mannered daughter laughed at me and ran back to their wagon, leaving Shirley to ride along on the wagon seat beside me with tears welling up in her eyes.

I wanted to follow after that ill-mannered child and tan her within an inch of her life.

I was keeping to a rutted road that was as much dried-out creek bed as thoroughfare, holding the reins tight and giving the regular driver and my hot, blistered feet both a breathing spell.

That poor befuddled woman just sat beside me, silent for a time, then she said, "La, Emily. I just don't know. Those girls are completely out of hand, but I just can't expect them to know any better. They've never heard anything but the way Jeb treats me."

"Pshaw," I said. "I'll teach them a lesson or two before it's done."

She actually smiled at that, a rare thing for her worry-withered, thin-lipped, sunless face. "You amaze me, Emily. You are such a little slip of a thing but feisty as all get out. I wish I could be more like you."

"Just don't let them speak so disrespectfully to you," I said. "I can't bear to hear it."

But even as I said that, I knew it wouldn't be all that easy to change their ways. That got me to thinking about having children and about all the grief I'd caused Mother and Father, not to mention what Sally had handed them in addition. I vowed in that moment not to ever have children. I would take care of Corrin and myself, and that would be more than enough.

We were on a far different sort of journey from the one that had brought us upriver. The first day on the trail, I learned the meaning of hard work. The wind blew incessantly, turning my skin gritty. On top of that, it was hot when the clouds sailed past and exposed the full heat of the sun, and I worked up a sweat to add to the dust.

I rode Little Bit most of the time, but I didn't want to wear her out before we'd so much as seen a mountain, so I tried to walk some. I had always enjoyed walking, and the horses and mules kept to an easy pace, since the skinners didn't want to exhaust them either. It was no trouble keeping up with the caravan in spite of my short legs.

Halfway through the morning I got in the back of the wagon and pulled my walking shoes off my overheated feet. My black stockings were ripped to shreds by the many brambles. As I tore off what was left of them, I almost cried from relief.

I sorely missed the steamboat, which had seemed primitive and uncomfortable to me before I saw the cut of the land-bound segment of our journey. The glorious blue mountains I had come to see were nowhere to be found. The land spread out monotonously around us, though it was already touched by streaks of blue and yellow spring flowers amid the newly greening grass.

By midday, when the sun was hot and beating down, I longed for the steamer's cabin, where we more or less had privacy, for the dining room where our meals were already prepared and all we had to do was sit down to them, even if they didn't match the caliber of cooking found in my parents' home.

But others had it a whole lot worse, I knew. The trail was barely blazed, and each spring any new travelers had to blaze it afresh. On top of that, they had to wait to begin their journey till the prairie grass was growing in order to feed their stock along the way, as well as having to wait for river breakup.

The Platte grew broader as we traveled upriver. Where it poured into the Missouri, it had been turbulent, thick with tree limbs, and churning with melt-off. Now it was filled to its banks and above with the muddy rage of spring floods.

When we first reached a bump high enough for me to see across the river, I gaped in amazement. It was close to a mile wide—as wide as the Mississippi! And muddy? If I were ever to miss the mud part of the Mississippi, all I had to do was plight my troth to the Platte.

But it was a deceptive river. Only a few buffalohide canoes dared navigate it, and those only in springtime and going downstream. The river had formed atop shifting sands that kept it from cutting a deep channel; it tended to run shallow almost everywhere. Sandbars peered above the surface, and quicksand bogs lay just beneath the surface in the most unlikely places—or so Corrin said, when he caught me kicking off my shoes and stepping into the muddy stream to soothe my feet. At places the Platte took off in all sorts of channels, so that it looked like a gnarled-up shawl in the process of being knit. There we had to be especially careful not to plow into muddy ground.

We moved cautiously along the banks, using the snaking river as our guide. Slowly, gradually, we began to ascend, or so Corrin said. To me the land seemed as flat as the heads on those Flatheaded Indians that he still chided me about from time to time.

By the third day out, I was sunburned beet red and so exhausted that I began to stumble. Finally, I was riding Little Bit, looking off into the eternal distance, everything the endless same, when I felt light-headed and suddenly pitched sideways off my horse.

Hank was close by and saw. He halted the caravan and rushed forward to pick me up.

I came to as he was carrying me to the wagon, and I demanded to be put down.

His soft, weary, midnight face took on a hopeless look, and he said, "Yes, ma'am, Miz Emily. Whatever you say."

I was angry that I was so weak, and angry that I still felt light-headed. It was all I could do to climb aboard the wagon. I was angry that I was useless as far as getting any work done was concerned. I wasn't measuring up, and there was nothing on God's earth I could do about it.

The blisters on my feet required salve. Corrin came to the wagon, of course. He cleaned and dressed them, then angrily took my high-topped, lace-up walking shoes and stuffed them in the bottom of the wagon. He brought out the moccasins he'd purchased back at the fort and helped me put them on, then he laced them. They did feel good, all clean and soft and no pressure at all on my broken blisters. I could even wriggle my toes.

Shirley, who seemed thin and sickly, proved to be a tower of strength. She came to our wagon and kept up camp that third evening.

I lay in the wagon atop a pallet and cried and slept while Corrin ate. Then he forced some broth down my throat and looked helplessly at me.

I sorely wanted to turn back. I regretted everything I had done up to this point that might have brought me to this predicament. I regretted my love for Corrin. I knew that Sally was right—love really was a form of madness, and I had gone plumb, pure mad to come along for this infernal ride.

I slept, then awakened later that evening to hear Corrin and Shirley talking in hushed tones about the state of my health. Shirley assured Corrin that I was just weak and unused to such exertion, that in a few days I would recover and gradually build up enough strength to make the trip. When Corrin asked her—in even more hushed tones and stammering—whether or not I might be with child or otherwise falling victim to one of the female ailments, Shirley chuckled and assured him that female cycles and such did not cause a woman to fall into bed with exhaustion—though she said it in a roundabout way.

"She'll recover. You'll see. She's just worn to the bone from trying to do too much," she explained.

To my annoyance, she was right. I really couldn't keep up with them, but the only thing I suffered from was exhaustion. After a good rest, I awakened the following morning hungry. I ate like a mule skinner, but my feet were still almost too sore to walk. I rode in the wagon all that day and slept well again that night. By the morning after I was feisty and ready to stand by Corrin and try to help him whip the world again, though I was walking on the sides of my feet some—and I held back when it came to walking long distances and lifting heavy packets and all the things I'd tried to do at first.

And miracle of miracles, a change began to take place in me. As my health and stamina improved, my sunburn turned a golden brown, some of the baby fat began to melt off my bones, and I felt better than ever before in my life.

And along with improved health came an improved frame of mind. The prairie, which had seemed bleak and forbidding, now began to reveal all sorts of glorious secrets, from red gold pheasants taking sudden flight out of a patch of ripe green grasses to rich, bold prairie winds that blew up suddenly to ripple the grass like a Spanish fan, showing first the lingering hay color of winter, then the greens of spring mixed with the golden unripe grass in between, then banks of bright spring wild flowers in all colors of the rainbow.

Soon I was strong enough to walk steady again and still keep up with the caravan for short distances. And not long after that, I was getting bored with the sameness of our days.

One afternoon Shirley and I left the party and angled off to look at a bank of familiar greenery. We reached the place—the caravan was still within sight and traveling at an angle that would make it easy to catch up with.

We dismounted to discover mulberries, buffalo berries, greening rye grass, wild oats, and flax, all growing in abundance. The whole prairie was rich with growing things now. We picked the bounty and took back two apronfuls to provide a special treat for supper.

In autumn the grass would be high as a horse's belly, Corrin said as we ate that night, and I told him about what we'd found.

"This prairie is a Garden of Eden once your eye is trained to see the wealth. Adam himself would have been lucky to find himself in such a paradise."

"I don't know as I'd go that far," I said dubiously.

All the same, that flat, wide plain was chock-full of miracles. There were grapes and richly adorned plum bushes that formed hedges too thick to chop through. Vast swathes of goldenrod turned the fields to gold as far as the eye could see, and the horizon was always purple and misty with haze.

"I've seen some beautiful sights here, Emily. Just you wait," Corrin said. He told me about cranes taking flight in vast flocks, their wings beating in a deafening symphony when disturbed in their watery homes; about thundering herds of buffalo as far as the eye could see, majestic and grizzled and mastering the plains till the earth shook beneath their furious passage.

After supper, I sat thinking about what he had said, and I really took time to look at the land around me. As if to honor my interest, the sky began to turn a deep, luminous purple, like the rarest of translucent gems, and I felt it was showing itself off just for me.

Suddenly a fork of lightning shot through the blackening sky, then another vivid fork pierced the darkness, and the heavens lit up in a glorious splendor that illuminated the prairie for what seemed a thousand miles.

"Oh, Corrin, look! Isn't it wonderful?"

But this time he failed to share my enthusiasm. He was frowning hard.

"What is it?" I asked, suddenly frightened by the expression on his face.

"Lightning storm coming," he said, fear growing in his eyes. "These storms can feel like the whole universe is on the rampage. There ain't going to be anything beautiful about this one, mark my words."

Stiff-spined, he hurried away to tie down the animals and make sure the caravan was prepared for the lashing it was about to take.

The storm toyed with us for hours. Lightning cracked through the air. Thunder rumbled so deep and loud that it seemed to rock the earth itself, then echoed off over the land. I had almost given up on the idea of rain when the air grew suddenly heavy and oppressive, the sky burst open, and a blinding waterfall crashed down. I shivered at the raw power unleashed around me.

Nor did that power abate. It rained just as hard all night. Buckets and vats poured down on our canvas tent, puddles grew in the surrounds and overran the moat that Corrin had hastily dug to drain off the water.

We huddled together as the downpour put out the fires, then we all crept to our individual beds. Corrin and I had moved our pallets and belongings into the wagon and had pitched the tent over the double-canvas top to try to save what wasn't already drenched.

The animals whinnied and skittered and tried to break loose from their bonds at every crack of thunder. Some of us spent hours at a time trying to comfort them, the rain cascading off our bonnets and hats and backs and noses. The mules bellowed in fear as the lightning struck over and over again, sometimes lighting up the entire skyline, and the thunderous voice of the prairie sky cracked right along behind it and resounded off the edge of the world.

And then came a new sort of crack that sounded as if the end of the world had finally come. Corrin was gone from the wagon at that moment—it was his turn to tend to the animals—and I peered out, shivering wet, to see a tree alongside the raging river split down the middle. And then the tree was alight itself against the inky night and the backdrop of rain.

And all the folks in the caravan just stood and watched, frozen in fear and awe by the beauty and terror and power of a Creator who had conceived and made such a place.

Corrin ran back, hollering through the downpour. "You all right?"

I nodded and yelled, "My lands, Corrin. Did you see that?"

He poked his head inside the canvas, where there still were occasional refuges of dryness. His face was furrowed with concern. He said, "This grass is drenched, but that may not be enough. Make ready to pull out at an instant's notice."

"Why on earth—"

"Grass fire," Corrin said tightly. "If that lightning hits a spot that's still dry underneath, and the winds come up, it's going to turn into wildfire and lick up the undergrowth all around us, rain or not."

"But surely a fire can't start in this deluge," I said, incredulous.

"Gullywasher like this, the rain comes down too fast and hard to seep into the ground right away. I've seen a storm last for days and flood everything in sight, and I've seen them stop right fast and leave the land nigh unto as parched as when they began, everything running off down the gullies."

But we were fortunate in that respect. The storm kept up for hours, gradually eased, and stayed with us through part of the next day. Then, like all trouble, it finally blew on past, carried by the prairie winds, leaving behind an even broader, angrier, muddier river. The banks were flooded even closer to our route than before. The earth was thick with matted grass and mud that grabbed the wagon wheels and held them. But even that would soon dry out. The prairie had shown us nigh unto her worst, and we had made it through.

For two full days we worked ourselves to the bone to overcome the damage. Most of our goods was soaked through and possibly molding. The sky stayed leaden, and a trace of rain hit us from time to time. When we finally broke camp, we dragged ourselves like a parade of half-drowned, depressed rats.

Nature had toyed with us like a cat with a bug. Even when the sun started to come out, the gold-rimmed clouds still boiled and churned in the vast vault of sky, as if to remind us of what had been and would most likely be again.

13

At best, we made fifteen to twenty-five miles a day. That was more or less standard for a train our size. Sometimes, when folks were especially exhausted, we'd pitch camp early if we came upon a place with ample firewood, grass for the stock, and shelter for us.

Those pioneers who were trying to make it all the way to the Pacific regions went by boat for the most part. The New Englanders were building fine ships that could take them all the way around the Horn, then across the Pacific to some remote place called the Sandwich Islands, I'd been told, so why languish aboard a mule caravan if you could travel by ship instead?

But those few folks who did travel overland to the Pacific had to hurry along lest they be trapped in the Sierra Madre Mountains when the big snows came. Tales of people starving to death or freezing in that region got back to St. Louis every other year or so since the Spanish and old Astor opened up commerce in that part of the world. The overland trip to the ocean was far more rigorous than what we'd undertaken. I was glad we weren't going that far.

We were headed far enough, but we'd have to dawdle endlessly not to reach the Rockies before autumn, and chances were good that we'd arrive while it was still spring. Therefore we didn't push ourselves. The only thing that determined our pace was the abundance of our supplies, the lay of the land and weather, and Corrin's moods.

When we set up camp each evening, several people stayed on guard against Indians. We were well into Pawnee territory. Even if the Pawnee happened to be in a friendly mood, there were renegade bands everywhere, the same as there were outlaws among white folks.

About ten o'clock one morning, Corrin rode up to where I was sitting astride my bay mare. He'd put on his fur cap and all the other gewgaws he'd worn upriver with Ashley, trying to look the part of a mountain man, but if you asked me he still looked ridiculous.

He wasn't asking me, so I hid my smile and pretended that his appearance didn't tickle my funny bone as I gave him a straight-faced look.

He leaned in close. When he spoke, his voice was low and gravelly with concern. "I want you and the other womenfolk to get in the wagons and stay out of sight."

I felt my high spirits sag. "What's wrong?"

"Pawnee," he said with a bitter twist to his lips. "We've had several of them pacing us, keeping just out of sight, for most of the day."

That angered me. "Why did you wait till now to let me know?"

"Because they were far enough away to give ample warning if they were to attack. I didn't want to risk anybody letting on that we'd seen them. Now they could be upon us before you know it."

I looked around at the terrain. Sure enough, we were moving past a region of deeper grassland and gullies, cut out of the landscape by the floods that spilled over the banks of the Platte every spring. There were ample places for Indians to hide and suddenly leap out at us, and I knew from the strained look on Corrin's face that he truly expected them to do just that.

I watched as he rode on down the caravan and instructed each person in turn. I tried to act nonchalant as I tied Little Bit to the back of the wagon and climbed inside. But the minute I was hidden, I peeked back out through a split in the canvas and began to survey the horizon in all directions. Sure enough, there in the tall sagebrush to our north and west I saw something move. I felt a thrill run down my spine. It was bound to be a Pawnee.

Corrin had been helping me learn to shoot, when we could steal the time. I had finally learned to at least load, aim, and fire his extra rifle. I reached for the powder horn, carefully measured out the right amount of powder, seated the ball with the wiping stick, then poured powder into the pan.

I was trembling inside as I finished loading, but my hands were steady as I aimed the rifle. If the Pawnee were going to attack us, I would be as brave as the women in the storybooks. I would defend Corrin and the others with my life.

Aiming at the point where I'd seen movement, I waited and watched carefully, almost afraid to blink lest I miss something. Suddenly there it was again, a bush trembled, I tensed up and almost fired, but my good sense whipped up and held me back.

I'd have to wait till the Pawnee fired first, just in case they weren't on the warpath after all but were pacing us for another reason. Corrin had taught me that too, and I heard his voice that very moment: *Always know what you're firing at and why, before you pull the trigger. More than one head-strong young man had lost his life to a gun accident, and more than one young woman as well.*

Nevertheless, there were Pawnee out there. Real, live Indians, maybe on the warpath.

My heart beat fast—I expected the whole Indian nation to burst out of the bushes and attack us. I shuddered at the thought of the slaughter and the scalping that was about to take place. Yet at the same time I felt eager and determined to hold my own in the fray, even unto death. And even while I felt all that, another part of me was weeping like a little girl, wanting my parents to come and take me out of this, and I was praying to the Lord for all I was worth.

Suddenly the bush moved again, then again, and I got ready to fire. I almost touched the trigger, but in that instant a glorious antelope fawn, golden like velvet, leaped from the brush, rapidly sniffed the wind, then took flight.

I jerked the rifle upward, then lowered it, and sighed as I watched the beautiful creature take to the thicket at a zigzag run. That's when I saw the Pawnee.

There were maybe ten of them, and they seemed to materialize out of the brush at the same time that a full herd of antelope, maybe thirty strong, came pounding through a draw and up the grassy slope. They dodged this way and that as the Indians shouted and yelped and fired and made no bones about showing themselves to us.

One antelope went down. Immediately two Indians were upon it, and then one Pawnee broke out of the pack and rode after the fawn. He was a straight-backed man with a strong face and red and black feathers in his hair, his chest bare except for a buckskin vest, and fringed buckskin pants on his legs. The rest of them were dressed more or less the same. What a sight they were.

He rode hard; the fawn was distant. Then it zigzagged, changed direction, and came directly our way. The Pawnee hunter chased him, his own firearm up and ready to take down the beautiful young creature, when the fawn skittered to a stop, smelling something in the wind, I'd venture. The brave leveled his weapon, had the fawn in his sights, and just then someone else fired. The Pawnee hunter reined in his horse and looked straight in my direction.

I saw Corrin then, sitting astride Packy to one side of our wagon, his rifle still aimed. He had fired the shot that saved the fawn.

The Pawnee sat staring our way for a long time, his gun up as if he wanted to fire back. Likely he was angry that Corrin had interfered with his hunting and was figuring out what to do about it.

The other Indians were over the ridge, pursuing the antelope herd, seemingly oblivious to us, though I wasn't so dumb as to figure they'd let us off that easily.

But that one hunter just sat there, as if trying to make up his mind about something. The fawn danced in place for a while, this way and that. And then it took off at a run, headed south.

The Pawnee raised his rifle again, and again Corrin fired into the air. The brave seemed startled, and his weapon came down.

Corrin rode out toward the Pawnee, sitting straight in the saddle, his rifle pointed toward the sky but ready enough should he need it.

He scared me to death, approaching the Indian that way.

He reached the man and said something, making circles and such with his free hand, and I guessed he was using sign language. All the plains Indians used the same sign, though they spoke different languages. Trappers and other travelers always tried to learn sign, and Corrin said he'd learned enough to get by.

The Indian reacted slightly to what Corrin had said, as if puzzled.

And at that very moment, that ornery Franklin girl Sharon came running up to the far side of our wagon. She ducked under the tongue and hollered at Corrin in a voice like a boat horn: "Pa says to leave them Injuns alone afore they give up on them antelope and come after us instead!"

I leaped from the wagon and grabbed her by the arm—she was a good two inches taller than I was, but I caught her by surprise and dragged her back behind the horses.

I said, "What in thunder has gotten into you?"

She tossed that mane of wheat-gold hair—brushed out and hanging to her waist at the moment—and said, "Mr. McCannon is a fool, Pa says. He'll get us skelped for sure."

She broke loose and took off at a dead run, back to her family's wagons at the end of the caravan.

We hadn't formed the circle that provided protection for the big wagon trains. In the first place, there weren't enough wagons to make a difference. Only four in all, our two and the Franklins'. In the second place, we hadn't had time to even consider such a plan.

Corrin reined in his horse, it reared, and he did look splendid in that moment, and then he rode back to our second wagon, the one holding some of our trading supplies. He spoke with Hank, they unloaded some things, and I realized that he was going to bribe the Indian hunter into leaving us alone.

The Pawnee had been hunting antelope, all right, tracking the herd when they came upon us. But once they spotted us, they'd be no longer content with wild game.

I saw him hand the man a side of beef we'd brought along from the fort. It was bound to go bad soon anyway, even though it had been cured. The Pawnee looked happy, but he was also looking at Corrin as if my husband had lost his senses.

And I reckon he had. That was my first inkling of just what a tender heart that man had—to risk his own skin over an antelope fawn. I'm not sure he always displayed good horse sense, in spite of his good heart.

I knew Corrin was mostly worried about the mules, the packs, and the horses—especially the horses. A fine horse was a treasure to any Indian. They raced them, rode them, nigh unto married them. Once they spotted a horse as fine as the ones we rode, they were bound to feel an itch they'd have to scratch. All the mule skinners knew it. Corrin knew it.

Twilight fell, silent. We put out sentries, then made a fire and cooked supper. We kept to quiet tasks all evening, so as to hear if anything untoward might happen. Nothing did.

Finally we left two of the young men on guard and went to bed. I tried to stay awake to see if there was any activity. I didn't want to miss our first Indian raid, though at the same time I was scared to death it might actually take place. But I was exhausted, as usual, from the tedious journey, and I fell asleep.

The moon was well over on the horizon, and it was moving toward daylight when I awakened to a murderous scream.

I grabbed my flannel robe and stepped into my moccasins—not bothering to so much as tie them, much less lace them right. I scrambled outside to see the two mule-skinning lads who'd been on guard sprinting toward the end of the caravan, while hoofbeats pounded into the distance.

I ran too. I skidded to a stop beside the Franklins' sleep wagon, where Mr. Franklin was standing in his red long handles, Shirley was in her nightgown, white-faced and in shock, and the younger girl was sobbing into her mother's skirts.

"Consarned Injuns came right into the wagon and stole my eldest daughter," Jeb Franklin growled. There was murder in his eyes. "Get your rifles. We're going after them. And when we ketch them, I'm going to hide every blamed coot in the Pawnee village, if it's my very last act on earth."

Doesn't matter, was my first thought. *As soon as those poor redskins get an inkling of what they have their hands on, they're bound to cut her loose come daylight and thank their lucky stars she's gone.*

I was still so disgusted with Sharon Franklin that I almost said it aloud the minute I thought the words. But I managed to hold my tongue at least that once.

Five of the mule skinners went with Jeb and Corrin to track down the girl and the bucks who took her. The rest stayed at camp and huddled around the fire, drinking coffee and muttering about how bad it could get. After sunup, they tended to mending and soaping saddles and other necessary tasks, though all looked miffed that they'd been left behind. They watched the bushes out of one eye, then another, and they kept their rifles and pistols handy.

I was terrified for Corrin. He might be riding into an ambush. The village where they took the girl—assuming that's what they did—might be a thousand strong.

Shirley was crying and apologizing and telling me she knew that headstrong girl had brought it on herself by running around with her fancy hair all brushed loose as if she was trying to snare a husband, Indian or no.

"My land, I yanked her back with a handful of that hair and told her not to show herself, but she's never listened to a thing I say."

"I'm sure it will work out all right," I said and embraced her. But I wasn't really feeling all that positive about things. At that moment, I'd have bet that Sharon could be anything from scalped to enslaved, and not much we could do about it but die trying to free her.

Come noon, it grew hot, and the winds came up, blowing dust every which way. I ate a bit of the antelope stew the boys prepared, then went into the back of the wagon, beneath the canvas, and tried to rest. I prayed, finally slept, and was awakened by someone shaking me hard.

"Wake up, Emily. Oh, I'm so frightened. Wake up—they're here!"

"Who?" I rubbed my eyes, thinking she meant Corrin had returned.

"The Pawnee. Hurry up."

I tumbled out of the wagon as if someone had touched a match to my foot and spilled into the most awful sight I'd ever seen.

All five of our mule skinners were sheltered behind the mules and wagons, weapons drawn, ready for a full-on Indian war. The Indians were lined up much the same, twelve of them in a row, rifles aimed and ready for bear. They were right out in the open, defiantly, as if daring us to take a shot and start the fracas.

Sharon was in the middle of the line of Indians. She stood beside the buck who'd gone after the fawn yesterday, and she looked put upon and angry at the world. The Pawnee hunter stood flat-footed beside her and glared at us, his horse behind him.

185

I wondered if he was somehow getting even, taking our "fawn" because we'd cost him his, though there was bound to be more to it than that. Perhaps he was less interested in war than in wiving.

He shifted his rifle to his left hand, pointed it at the earth, then made some gestures with his right hand that I presumed was sign language, which I didn't have a prayer of understanding. We all just stood there stupidly, not understanding what he expected from us and fearing we'd make a false move.

Suddenly he shoved Sharon forward, so that she fell to her hands and knees. She looked back at him, surprised.

One mule skinner leveled his rifle straight at the brave, but another more sensible lad made him point it back down.

Then I started forward, but the brave reached down and took hold of Sharon's arm, yanked her upright, and pulled her in beside him again, warning me to stay back.

I did, trying to figure it out. What were these fools up to?

The brave and I went the rounds for nearly half an hour. He'd do one thing; I'd respond accordingly. He'd get irritated and do something altogether different, such as shoving Sharon forward or pointing her in the direction of the wagons and pushing her down, then pulling her up again.

Well, I hate to admit how slow I was, but after a while I got the message. He didn't want Sharon at all. He wanted to trade her, just as I'd thought he might—though I reckon her ill temper had little to do with it. I suspect he took her in order to get ransom right from the beginning, since he didn't want to take us all on, and he didn't rightly know which pack mules and wagons to pillage anyway.

I finally negotiated with him, showing him various trade goods. He'd grunt his approval or grunt his disapproval, spitting on the ground.

Each time he spit, Sharon drew up, gave him a disgusted look, and said, "Ugh."

The girl didn't have a brain in her head, not even to be grateful she was getting out of a predicament where she could have easily lost her life. Nor did she stop to consider what it was costing us to reclaim her. She just stood there pouting, and you could see it in her eyes every second. She was thinking about herself only, half irate at being used as trade goods, half excited to be the center of attention. All that girl had on her mind was *me, me, me.*

By the time the horse-trading was done, it cost our party blankets, sugar, coffee, two silver belt buckles, a full keg of white and blue beads, five pairs of buckskin leggings, a small boxful of mirrors, and some chewing tobacco. Only the latter came from her parents' stores.

The brave finally shoved her forward and let her come to us, and the first thing she said to me was, "Why didn't you come after me? You are all so selfish. Didn't anybody even care?"

That did it. I reached out and grabbed a hank of that spoiled child's long blonde tresses, led her around to the back of my wagon, pulled out one of Corrin's belts, and I tanned her hide.

She never so much as fought back, not even a bit—though I reckon if she'd really tried she could have broken loose. But she just stood there blubbering and saying she was sorry and trying to cover her backside with her hands. And all the rest of that trip, every time she looked at me, there was new respect in her eyes.

Two mule skinners had ridden after Corrin, Jeb, and the others as soon as the Pawnee took to trading with me. They found the men just as they were about to enter the Pawnee village, which was indeed some five hundred men strong. They all came hurrying back.

That ornery girl might well have cost folks their lives, if things had worked out otherwise. A hide-tanning was a small price for her to pay for her reckless shenanigans.

14

We reached the twin forks of the Platte on our eighth day after leaving the Missouri. The good Lord had given us swift and safe passage after we met the Pawnee, and we had nary a bit more Indian trouble to slow us down. We were some 433 miles from St. Louis now, an amazing distance. I couldn't believe we had actually come this far.

I continued to walk a good deal, wanting to strengthen my legs and spare my horse. The freshening wind stroked my face, the sun flowed like warm honey to further brown my skin, the moccasins kept my stride strong and supple. The sky was vast and blue and cloudless. The sounds of the mules snorting and the horses huffing, the creaking of the wagons, and the hoorawing of the mule skinners were music to my ears.

The buffalo grass greened up quickly, and our stock fed well. There was ample clear water running in the small streams, though the Platte stayed true to its reputation by remaining so muddy and silty as to be unpalatable.

Then we met up with two more bands of Indians, both small hunting parties. Both were Arapaho and in the mood to be friendly once we handed over a bolt or two of bright red cloth. Both times they rode in and harassed us some, we paid them their ransom, and they rode around the caravan, looking us over till I felt as if they were laughing at us. Then they spurred their horses and rode off at a dead run, whooping and hollering, playful-like.

At the South Fork of the Platte, we stopped. Corrin and I stood together beside the river, looking into the distance, holding hands. I think we were both thinking about what we would find down that wide, yellow-brown branch we were about to follow south.

A long, slender tongue of land lay between the north and south forks. It would be easy to ford the river—or so Corrin and Hank said. They had both traveled through here before at a similar time of year, and they had spoken with dozens of others who had made the trek.

The folks from Fort John who were to meet the Franklin family were nowhere to be found.

Jeb Franklin was aggravated. "They'll most likely be upstream at the Upper Ford," he said to Corrin. "It would only be right for you to accompany us on up there."

"That's sixty miles further on!" Corrin exclaimed.

"It would be the Christian thing for you to do," Jeb Franklin persisted. "So's my wife and girls will be safe."

"What about *my* wife? What about my mule skinners? My first obligation is to my own caravan."

"You cain't leave us out here alone."

"You shouldn't have come alone, then."

Jeb Franklin jutted out his whiskery jaw defiantly. "A traveler ought to be able to depend on his fellow man," he said. "Especially if that man professes to be a Christian."

Corrin fell silent then, and a firmness came to his square-jawed face. He went off down by the river and gazed south, chewing on a twig, hunkered down, drew his finger through the water now and again.

He came back and quietly told us to pitch camp, though it was only just past noon. To Franklin he said, "Like as not your people are on the way here. We'll just set and wait for them a spell and rest up, rather than put ourselves through all that hard, extra travel."

Franklin looked as if he wanted to argue, but Corrin's jaw tightened, and the man quickly looked down, nodded, cleared his throat, and said, "Much obliged."

I didn't mind the wait. As usual I was bone-weary and grateful for a chance to rest. I was also happy for a chance to visit some more with Shirley Franklin before I said good-bye to her. It seemed all I was doing these days was saying good-bye to one person or another. I already had a premonition she would be the last white woman I'd see for a good long while. It wasn't easy to let her go away—all the more so because of that.

We tended to the endless chores of making camp, then set about catching up on other tasks. Shirley and I worked together, visiting and speculating about the future and lamenting the fact that we had to say good-bye.

She had gotten some backbone during those few days on the trail, and she wasn't quite so shy now about standing up to her two snippy daughters. Twice I'd heard her tell them a thing or two, when they went to sassing her. Once I'd even seen her swat one. But I do have to admit she was still as meek as a sheep when it came to standing up to her grouchy, mean-mouthed husband.

But then I reckon the Lord doesn't always solve life's problems all at once. I'd at least helped her get a start on building her backbone.

We washed and mended clothes while the menfolk foraged for fuel and game and the two girls reluctantly peeled potatoes for supper. There was a sad feeling about the camp, almost as if someone had died.

That night I climbed into the wagon and lit the lantern. Corrin and the other men were busy with the stock. I'd brought along writing paper and quill pens and ink. I was going to start a journal.

I dug around in my goods, pulled out the writing tablet, the ink, and a quill. Then I carefully wrote:

June 15, 1822. The South Fork of the Platte River. This was the most beautiful day I have ever seen or am likely to see again. The weather was exceptional, the friendship was splendid. I shall sorely miss Shirley once she travels on, though I shall be glad to see the end of those two ill-tempered girls.

Corrin came in late, tired as all get out from riding down the trail and back, checking out our destination. But he was freshly bathed and shaved. And never had he been so tender, so generous with his love for me. He held me gently and told me over and over again that he was proud of me, and loved me, and was pleased he'd had the wisdom to make me his wife.

Corrin had made the right decision when it came to waiting for the party from Fort John. Sure enough, along about noon the next day, just as everyone was getting cantankerous and snapping at one another, Hank pointed at the horizon.

I could see riders—I couldn't tell how many—headed straight toward us and kicking up dust.

"Indians?" I asked. The thought made me tremble.

"Don't think so, but you can't ever be sure."

The men all readied their weapons and waited cautiously. There was still a chance the Pawnee might ride south and west on either a hunting party or to invade an enemy tribe, but we had more or less left their territory. We were moving into more dangerous lands where the Arapaho, Ute, Cheyenne, and Kiowa raided each other and quarreled over almost everything. All of those plains and eastern mountain Indians were unpredictable, and all of them were capable of burning and scalping and slitting a white person's throat or of befriending one and saving his life. With Indians you just never knew.

Soon the party kicking up all the dust raised high an American flag, as if realizing our concern. When we were certain it was the party from Fort John, Corrin and Jeb rode out to greet them.

They entered the camp and rested for a spell. We helped as much as we could as the Franklins joined this new group. Then they all headed back north, wanting to make it at least halfway back to Fort John by sundown.

We were alone again, just Corrin and I and the other members of the McCannon-Davidson Expedition. And then we too were getting the wagons and the mules in motion, easily fording the shallow river, spattering ourselves with mud. The horses were skittish, the mules worse, the men shouting and spurring their mounts and making more to-do about it than was necessary.

But as soon as we were across the river, I felt my sense of lonesomeness at Shirley's leaving turn into sudden expectation of what was soon to come. It was getting late by then, and we set up camp not far from where the Franklins had left us. I felt somehow elated all that night.

As we traveled the next day, the smell of the air soon changed. It seemed more rarified, cleaner, the dust began to settle down. By the end of the day I could see mountains. Just barely, and just on the far horizon, a thin purple line. When I first spotted them, I rushed forward and told Corrin.

But these weren't our mountains, Corrin explained.

"You're looking at the northern Rockies," he said. "Some good-sized peaks there, beautiful vistas—but too wild to cross at any time of year, much less early spring. No, we have to follow the river south for a ways more till we reach a lower gap.

"We're looking for a Ute hunting trail. They call it the *Hah-oon-kara*. It means 'where the river of blue rises.' White folks like to call it Blue River Pass. It leads through a lush, green mountain valley that will take us most-ways through the Rockies. We'll peel off when we reach the northern part of Bayou Salade and head due west."

"How long will it take to cross?"

"Few days to a week—depends on our fortitude and the weather. But believe me, it's going to be work enough for one summer to get across even the best part of these mountains. We'd be foolish to try to cross them till we reach Bayou Salade."

Bayou Salade. I had heard that name repeatedly since leaving St. Louis—and before, for that matter, from the lips of various thorny trappers and traders. The word *bayou* was, of course, French, and French trappers had no doubt named the region. A bayou was a slack-water slough connected to a larger stream. In this case it would be the wetlands that made the region so rich and that connected with the South Platte River. I reckoned that by *Salade* they meant it was filled up with greenery like the "salad" they'd named it for. The Frenchman who hung the name on it must have been hungry at the time.

Corrin described the region as glorious, a seventy-five-mile-long alpine vale, a bowl surrounded by high peaks and sculpted with rolling hills, rife with beaver and other game. There were rich, deep grasses and sparkling streams that drew the buffalo in vast, thundering herds. Following on the buffalo trail came the Indians—Ute, Kiowa and Arapaho—and all their bloody rivalries.

"The tribes used to slaughter one another all over that country, fighting for control of the region," Corrin said. "The Ute won, though we're bound to see other Indians as well."

"Are they the same Ute as the ones at Brown's Hole?"

"Same type. Different band. Figure it this way: you take a family of crooks back in Missouri—they're bad medicine no matter what their color, compared to the decent folk. Same with the crooked people amongst the Indians. This band is a good sight meaner than most of 'em. I haven't heard of any raids on trappers yet. But it will pay us to stay vigilant."

"When we reach the northern part of the bayou, how far will we be from McCannon's Country?"

As usual, when I called our destination by that name, Corrin chuckled. Then he screwed up his face into mock seriousness. "A sky-high mountain range, sixty thousand rattlesnakes, four hundred hungry grizzlies, and a whole nation of angry Indians away."

That night the sky was clear, and we sat up late and talked. He was explaining to me the methods by which we would cross the mountains when he suddenly changed the subject. "Unless we just decide to stay in Bayou Salade."

I frowned, surprised. "Why would we want to do that?"

"One short word, darlin'. Gold."

"*Gold?* Are you saying there's gold in the area?"

"Some folks say so."

"Who?"

"In the mid-seventeen-hundreds the Spanish did some exploration there. I've read the documents."

"Did they find gold?"

"No."

I laughed. "Then what difference does it make?"

"The Indians paid them for some supplies with gold nuggets," he said. "That kept them here looking for a while till those same Indians decided they didn't like the Spanish nosing around and drove them away. And then a man name of James Purcell found some gold flake in a stream in 1806. That was written up in Pike's journals. I hear tell a few other trappers and traders have struck color in the region from time to time."

"Oh, Corrin. It would be wonderful to find gold. But I can't help feeling that God's plan for us is all the way West in McCannon's Country."

"You may be right," he said and smiled. "Or you may have listened to me just a mite too hard. Anywise, we'll wait till we get to Bayou Salade, then we'll see."

As we followed the river due south, those distant blue bumps beyond the foothills kept me struck with wonder. I watched them grow closer by the day. Finally the hazy blue defined itself into jagged edges etched against the blue sky, snowcaps clinging like clouds to the highest peaks. They grew higher day by day. I couldn't help staring at them for long spells as we labored along in those dry, windy foothills. I kept wondering what lay beyond those mountains.

The thought of all the possibilities made my heart sing and turned me breathless. These were the Far

Mountains, the place I'd dreamed of ever since Corrin first caught me up in his own vision for our future. At last I had come West! The very thought made me feel proud and exhilarated, yet overwhelmed.

Every day I imagined what lay ahead. Waiting beyond those stately peaks was a neat, small fort built sturdily within stone ramparts. The fields around it were planted, the vegetable gardens just beginning to sprout, people waiting for us to arrive with the supplies they needed to make their new homes comfortable. There would be livestock in pens, folks coming and going, bringing in beaver plews and other pelts, buying all sorts of supplies—soon from the McCannon larders, of course.

Corrin could dream his new dream of gold. I was still longing for McCannon's Country.

We reached the pine-clad region north of Bayou Salade two days later. The ascent up the foothills had been so gradual as to seem nonexistent. But I found myself increasingly short of breath.

Corrin explained that we were higher than it seemed and the air therefore held less oxygen. It would take a while for my lungs to acclimate.

"In the meantime, you don't want to overexert yourself, Emily. I've seen people collapse and have a hard time getting over it when they do too much at first."

"But it's not that bad."

"Not if you use common sense. We came upslope fast these past few days. Now take it easy for a while, and give your body a chance to adjust."

Indeed there was an even newer smell in the air. It was crisper, cleaner. The earth was moister. The blowing dust had almost disappeared, to be replaced by the fine, fragile aroma of pine and greenery.

We had reached the high foothills of the Rockies at last. Suddenly the challenge of the mountains, which had seemed distant and fearsome, was up close, immediate, and almost terrifying.

The Rockies were all I'd expected and more. They were so immense as to defy description, and the various colors and hues and shadows brought to them by the changing day was a constantly moving vista of beauty. They were carpeted with tall, ancient forests of pine, birch, aspen, and trees I'd never seen before, which scattered on down into the foothills. I knew I was looking at regions untouched by human footprint since the day God had carefully, thoughtfully created all this wonder.

Here in the lower lands were fields of wildflowers as far as the eye could see, some as delicate as white and purple snowflakes drifted to earth, some as fancy as anything found in a St. Louis garden. There were lavender, yellow, and purple carpets of wild iris. Daisies. Pinks and bluebells. There were new plants to explore and new varmints to learn about, including the curious little prairie dogs that darted their heads out of holes to watch us pass by, grumbled at us, then just as quickly darted back in.

That first night in the high foothills, we camped at the northernmost edge of a long valley. Around and south of us rose an irregular circle of lofty snow-capped peaks. A cascading mountain creek plunged downslope into the Platte, next to where we camped. The Platte itself took on a new, blue-green color. It seemed clearer, cleaner, as if sprucing itself up to honor the beauty that now surrounded it.

The river originated in the Bayou Salade. Its fountainheads came together as mountain rivulets, then streams, tiny creeks, and other snowmelt that found its way through a thousand courses and into the waters that gathered thunder and scope and became the big, muddy South Platte. It was beside one of these feeder creeks that we set up camp, and we'd no more than tended to the livestock when I looked downslope to see Corrin and Hank hunkered beside the rushing stream, shallow pans in hand.

I marched down to watch them. "I didn't know you brought gold pans."

Corrin glanced up at me, sort of cautious, but then an ornery grin came to his face. "I've been thinking about gold for some time, Em. Got some picks and other equipment in the wagon too. Didn't want to find myself unprepared."

Hank watched us, his eyes darting back and forth as if he wondered if we were about to spat. I wondered why he was so cautious concerning me. I had come to know him better, but he was always quiet and overly respectful, as though to keep a wide distance between us. He never addressed me unless spoken to. It was apparent to me that he was indeed a slave who had known his place. To my shame, I had yet to learn to look on him as a person, and I reckon he knew that.

I tossed my head and said, "You'd best find enough gold tonight to last for a good long time, because you have an agreement with me, Mr. Corrin Brevard McCannon. You and I are going on West tomorrow."

I caught the quick, cagey glance the two men exchanged. They were like two boys getting away with mischief.

That evening, after a supper of beans, cornbread, and slab bacon, Corrin and I walked a short distance from our wagons, found a wide rock, and sat down facing the mountains before us. They were glorious.

"I'd like to stay here for a few days and check out the streams," he said, after fiddling with his hat long enough to tell me he was nervous about how I'd react. "I figure I may not get through here again for a while—if ever—and I owe it to myself to see what's what."

I laughed. "I don't really mind, Corrin. You don't have to act so furtive about it. A week or so won't matter, will it?"

"Likely not. But if I strike gold, we'd be stuck here for the summer. I couldn't rightly go on West if there was color here. I'd have to pan it out, then take it back East to sell."

I didn't mention how remote I thought that possibility was. Instead, I remained diplomatic. "We'll deal with that when we come to it," I said. "If you find enough gold, perhaps we'll just buy up the West and let others pioneer it."

"Then we'd be missing out on the best part."

The night was coming on fast, and I shivered. Corrin reached over and pulled my shawl tighter around my shoulders. At that moment I looked upward to one of the rocky spurs that jutted out high above us. I spotted something so wonderful I felt my heart skip.

I whispered and pointed. "Look. What is it?"

Corrin followed my gesture.

"Mountain sheep," he said. His eyes were wide too. "One of the most handsome creatures God ever created."

"Oh, lands, Corrin, isn't that splendid?"

"It is, Emily. God outdid Himself with this creation. And there are herds and herds of them all throughout the mountains."

The bighorn stood on the pinnacle, his neck stretched out, his thick rack of horns wide and regal. Then suddenly the wind shifted, the creature started, jumped, and ran fleetly up into the rock piles.

The next day, and the next, Corrin and Hank panned for gold. I combed the high meadows for edible roots and for flowers to decorate our wagon. I rested, and waited, and wondered what would become of those fools rinsing rocks down at the gurgling creek.

All the mule skinners were busy panning gold too, each young man in a sweat-stained hat, shoulders baking beneath his flannel shirt, all of them suddenly obsessed by the thought of striking it rich. They went through the cook's supplies, borrowed shallow pans and wooden plates, and brought into service everything else they could get their hands on that might pan out some color.

Increasingly I had my hands full just getting them to feed the stock and hunt game. Most of them resented any time they had to spend tending to camp. If they had their way, they'd be at the creek from first light till it was too dark to see, taking time out only for eating.

I sat on the bank from time to time and watched them, while the stream rushed past in blue crystal hues, topped here and there with white water and with a hint of golden rock beneath, though there were smooth red, gray, and brown stones in the channel as well. Corrin explained that the proliferation of gold-colored rock wasn't gold. The gold hid itself good, he said, inside plain gray rocks and made a man work for it unless the stream did the work instead.

"The water will break down the rock after a time and leave nuggets at the bottom," he said. "That's what we're looking for. Nuggets. We find them, we know there's a lode somewhere nearby that they're being washed out from, and after we wash up all the nuggets, we'll go for broke and go find the mother lode."

"Most likely," I muttered.

"What's that?"

"Most likely you're losing your mind, Corrin McCannon."

I was becoming more and more suspicious of all these highfalutin dreams. I was thankful that Hank was kind enough to help me prepare the meals amid all the insanity.

I sorely missed my female friends, and my sister, and my mother. I was set apart from everyone else just on the basis of my womanhood—and even more so because I was Corrin's wife, and Corrin was the boss. So I stayed to myself and worked, and explored, and sat at times and watched the grass spiders spin their webs and the birds in the meadows—and it wasn't half bad at that.

At night, tales of gold strikes abounded around the campfire. There were yarns galore of gold and the Spaniards, of wealthy Indians who hoarded gold and knew all the sources. Corrin spun as much wind as any of them. He was the one who talked most about the Seven Cities and the first Spaniards who had come north looking for them.

Seems this was way back in the fifteen hundreds when the Spanish first conquered parts of Mexico. Some Indian came from the north telling them of finding cities where the streets were paved with gold and houses were made of silver. It hadn't been all that long since the Spanish had ridden into Peru and found the Incas and all their gold, so I reckon the story wasn't so hard to digest back then. And I reckon that's why so many Spanish explorers rode north and straight into trouble with Indian tribes.

"Coronado's expedition was the biggest," Corrin said. "He had two hundred armored men with him, pack animals, artillery, sheep herds, cattle, and they were like a hurricane comin' through," he said.

I was amazed that he was so well educated in history. But then Corrin always surprised me. "The men got angry when they didn't find gold and took it out on the Indians," he said. "Left a lot of bad blood that remains to this day."

"Coronado and his men came through not far from here," Hank commented, also surprising me. "Had some dealings with the Wichitas, I heard."

"Yes, and they were at the Arkansas too," Corrin said. "Panned it and checked out the surrounding hillsides for signs of veins. They didn't find a blamed thing."

He leaned close to me and explained. "The Arkansas River is a mite south of the bayou. On the way to Santa Fe."

"I know," I said with annoyance. I, too, had studied the maps. The Arkansas River Valley was already charted, since it had first been explored centuries before by the Spanish, unlike the regions where we would be going—if we ever left this bedeviled, greed-struck place. In fact, the United States military had ascended the whole course of the Missouri, crossed overland to the Pacific Ocean, and explored the Arkansas and the regions around Santa Fe.

That was way back in 1807, when the folks in the federal government were still trying to figure out what all they had their hands on.

Later, while we were getting ready for bed, I asked, "How much longer will we stay here?"

"Day or two, unless I get lucky."

"But time is moving on, Corrin, and I thought you said we had a lot to do before next winter."

"No rush," he said. "I've got to study things here, make sure I'm not missing an opportunity."

I went to bed irritated with him. I thought I'd married a full-grown man I could depend upon instead of some wild-eyed boy who'd spend his nights telling fairy tales around a campfire and his days swooning over a riverbank filled with nonexistent gold.

And then, the fourth day, I was doing laundry, scrubbing hard and still angry, when Corrin ran helter-skelter into camp, shouting and hoorawing. Men in the distance were coming right after him, throwing their hats in the air, acting like fools down to the very last man.

He skidded to a stop in front of where I was scrubbing twill pants on the washboard and grinned till his mouth looked like it had been embedded with pianoforte keys.

"Here it is," he said.

He opened his fist to display a bright heap of grains the size of seeds, along with other nuggets several times that size scattered among them.

"Color," he said with satisfaction. "Gold. We found it, Emily. We're going to be rich, or I'll know the reason why."

The excitement caught me up too. "What is it worth?"

"In cash money? Maybe twenty, thirty dollars. Around fifty cents to a dollar per grain, but that ain't the point. I'm betting there's plenty more where it came from."

"Will we earn more here panning gold this summer than we would trading?"

201

"Bound to, at this rate. Though I may be sending you back East. This is harder country than Brown's Hole. Arapaho still raid the Ute here from time to time and vice versa. I don't want to put you in harm's way."

I was fit to be tied. "Corrin, you said we were going West together to trade. I will not let you send me back."

"Reckon you will if I can come back to Saint Louis and buy you a fine house like I know you want—land sakes, I'll buy you one of those fancy floating palaces, if you want one. You'll have diamonds, jewels galore."

"I already have jewels," I said flatly. "I left them at Mother's house because you were contemptuous of them, remember? What happened to your speeches about the stars that hang in the sky like the most radiant jewels, and how they're more beautiful than anything man could fashion? What happened to your dreams about going back to McCannon's Country?"

"We'll go on West when we have the money. When I can build a fort of my own, second to none. A man can do a lot more with gold in his pocket than with just a simple dream in his head."

"What about Father's investment money? What about all the goods we brought?"

"We'll trade with the Indians on this side of the mountains, as much as we can."

"I thought you said they were hostile."

"More so than the high mountain Ute, but I figure an Indian is an Indian, all the same."

"I thought you said this band was bad medicine."

"Could be. But if you make sense to them, they're bound to respond in kind, and trade goods will always find a home."

"Then why did you just say they were hostile?"

"I only said there was still trouble here from time to time, and it might be best if I sent you back to Saint Louis."

"Corrin, you are an insufferable fool. If you send me back to Saint Louis, just plan to see the last of me. I have no intention of staying back there while you spend your life out here panning for gold."

He was suddenly shamefaced. "Emily, I love you. I only want what's best. I want to be able to give you the fine things you're used to, the clothes and a good house, the security. I want that more than anything in the world, and I'm not going to give up a chance to provide it. Not if I can get it here panning gold, even if I have to risk my life to do it. But I most certainly am not going to risk your life as well."

"Then you won't be staying here," I said, "because risking your life is going to be the same as risking mine. I'm not going back. Not till you do." I tilted my head back and gave him a hard, angry look. "Maybe not even then."

The next day I went down to the creek bed to watch them. The men worked fervently throughout the morning, as if they were being flogged hard by some invisible whip. Even the two who usually stood on guard had given up their posts and taken to the creek, eager to strike their own color.

Come mid-afternoon, when that hadn't happened, they started getting sullen. Corrin was the only one who had drawn color out of the creek so far, and he had found another panful that morning. Now they were all wanting to pan on his part of the creek, and they moved in closer and closer, grumbling like a bunch of tired mules. And then Corrin found gold again, though not quite so much as before.

The men threw down their gear and stomped into camp that evening. It looked to me as if we were heading for some kind of collision.

Randy Rafferty, a hotheaded young mule skinner, started the whole thing off by hurling his hat to the ground and wheeling around to confront Corrin. "By gum, we were told we were coming out here to work for wages and we'd be given a fair share of what was earned. Now I say that includes a fair share of McCannon's gold." His feet were spread wide as though he were ready to leap on Corrin. His tanned face looked ferocious as a bear's.

Several other boys took up the griping, and things started getting ugly. I stepped away from where I'd been stirring a pot of beans atop the fire, to get out of the way of their steam.

Corrin tried to calm them. "Ain't no point in worrying about something we don't have yet," he said. "I only got—"

"You got gold, right there in that buckskin poke. That's a sight more than any of the rest of us got," Randy said. His hand was on his gun now, and he was toying with it, his face more puckered up than before.

Hank had been standing in the shadows. He cleared his throat, and for some reason that made everybody stop and turn toward him. He was silent for a moment, as if thinking things over. The cry of a coyote came from the prairie east of us and echoed for miles.

On the end of that mournful sound, Hank stepped into the firelight, his old floppy hat half hiding his midnight face. His weariness showed in the sag of his shoulders.

He said, "Beg your pardon, but I feel like I ought to speak up. Looks to me like you boys are about to make a serious mistake."

Randy shot him a sneer. "Why's that?"

"Because you find a little bit of color like Corrin has, it don't mean a thing. If all we can stir up is a few little grains like Corrin's brought in so far, I figure we're just wasting our time with some fluke runoff. In which case we need to be lookin' upstream or travelin' on over the mountains and forgetting about gold."

"Sounds like you're trying to get us off track," Randy said.

"Trying to put some sense into your heads is more like it," I piped up, seeing the looks the boys were sending poor Hank. "Why don't you all settle down and put some food in your bellies, and maybe it will give your brains something to think with. Leastwise it will calm your tempers some. My land. This is the most ridiculous cat fight I ever did see."

I stepped into the middle of them and began dishing up beans and handing around wooden plates.

That gave them something to do besides fight. It set them to grumbling in a different way, but less like they were about to draw down on one another—or on Corrin. The food and a bit more muttering settled them down some more, but they remained sullen till bedtime, all of them shooting Hank and Corrin and me dirty looks. Reckon that's one reason none of us saw the real trouble coming. We were all too wrapped up in our own nasty moods.

15

Our camp was at the base of a high hill that skirted the western edge of the valley floor. Above us were great stands of pine and groves of slender, spring-bright aspen and birch. Downslope was the creek, rushing off through the green meadow and into the main watercourse, the Platte. Beyond that, the horizon stretched off into flatness; then the hills rolled up again at the far side of the bowl.

At first light, I awakened. It was a habit I acquired soon after we began our journey. I enjoyed those early morning moments that allowed me solitude, time for prayer, space to collect my thoughts and consider all that was happening to me.

This morning the air was chill and brisk but refreshing. I was keenly alive as I climbed from beneath Corrin's warm arm, kissed him lightly on the cheek, then quietly dressed. I made my way into the bushes near the stream, where I had set up a small place that allowed me to do a private toilette. It was just light enough for me to be able to see, but for the most part the shadows of night still clung to the land.

I had just dipped cold water from the creek and splashed it on my face when I heard a branch break. I froze, not daring to even breathe. It could be a snake, a bear, a man . . . I tried to peer around without moving.

For a long time I stayed like that, rigid with fear, afraid to move. Finally I heard the horses blowing in their makeshift cottonwood corral and voices drifting on the wind, coming from the camp. I suddenly felt foolish. I had probably disturbed one of the two guards, who had come out to relieve himself. If I had made my presence known, he would most likely have begged my pardon.

Hank and the cook usually made breakfast, so I took my time washing, then made my way back to where the men were in various stages of preparation for the day to come. The sun had cracked the horizon now, and the light was filtering golden through the wide stand of aspen and birch that sheltered our tents. The dew was beginning to bake off the tall grass and weeds that surrounded the camp.

Altogether, our party still consisted of some fifteen men, including the cook, Hank, and Corrin. As usual, they all minded their manners this morning, careful to dress out of my line of sight. Most of them still looked sullen though, and none seemed more amiable than the day before.

I was thinking about that, feeling a mite sorry for myself because I was the only woman amid so much male foolishness, when I looked across the clearing to see young Randy Rafferty step out of the trees, freeze in place, a look of shock on his face, and then collapse to the ground like a deflated balloon.

"What on earth—"

But I had no more time to consider anything. *Thwang!* An arrow rifled through the air, barely missed a second skinner, hurtled past him and thudded into a tree. Suddenly arrows were flying all over the clearing.

And then the Indians set full upon us, some twenty-five of them in the most horrible war paint, screeching and howling, freezing my blood with the rage in their voices and the sudden deluge of blood as they attacked. Arrows struck several more men as the carnage grew.

The attack had come so suddenly and unexpectedly that my senses failed to register the full scope of the horror. For a moment I stood rigid, my fist pressed to my mouth to hold back the scream that kept trying to come out. I saw one young man fly toward a bank of trees, his boots half pulled on. An arrow took him in the back and spun him around. Blood spurted from his wound, and he cried out, then went limp. Another mule skinner was pinned through the shoulder to a tree as he lifted his musket to fire.

The Indians were here, there, everywhere, a nightmare come to life—copper-faced, wearing beaded buckskin vests, buckskin britches, paint on their bared chests, wild feathers and beads in their bear-greased hair.

And then Corrin was beside me. He swept me up like a thin bunch of sticks and ran toward the creek. And when we reached the watercourse, he threw me into the tall bushes and hissed for me to stay still.

"They'll kill us men," he said, "but only the devil himself knows what they'd do to you. Don't move. Don't so much as breathe. I'll be back for you when this is done."

I wanted to tell him to be careful, that I would pray for him, but I couldn't even speak.

The war whoops continued. I heard musket fire, a crack followed by a scream. Another crack. Then another volley. Another. And I knew that at least some of the men had gotten to their guns.

I looked around. I wasn't well hidden. I could see the tops of our tents. Carefully, slowly, I writhed through the brush southward to where I remembered a deep gully filled with high grass. When I reached it, I rolled in, then sat up, and that's when the tears finally burst out of me. I had to gulp and sob them back.

I didn't know what to do. What could I do? How could I help the men? I couldn't even get to a gun. I had never felt more cowardly or more helpless in my life.

I couldn't bear to think what those howls and screams and pain-filled cries above me meant, how they went on incessantly. These were the sounds of death. I had never heard them before, not even in a slaughterhouse or barnyard. The gunfire continued. I sobbed and prayed. And finally the noise died down.

I heard horses running, brush breaking, more howling, and then the air was eerily silent except for one long, keening wail that carried on the wind like the ghost of evil, then faded into the distance.

After a long time, I cautiously climbed up the slope and peered through the grass. Smoke was coming from the campsite—more smoke than could be caused by the campfire.

They were all dead. I knew it. I alone had been spared, and in that moment I wanted to die too. The thought of life without Corrin, the thought of all those young lives lost to such a useless cause as hunting for gold—it was more than I could bear. And I collapsed to the ground, anger and rage and fury at such a world spilling out of me. I cried and cried, sobbing so hard my sides soon hurt, and so intent was I upon ventilating my terror and grief that I barely registered the word when someone spoke my name.

"Emily?"

But the second time I heard it, I fell quiet, almost disbelieving my senses but hearing the wind that rustled through the tall grass, hoping to hear the word again, and hoping it might be on the tongue of an angel.

And then the voice was right beside me, speaking softly. "Emily?"

I looked up into the softly creased, leathery, blood-streaked face of Hank, the runaway slave.

"You aren't going to like what you see, but it has to be done," Hank said as we made our way back to the camp. "We've got eight dead. Three are hanging on, but they're scalped, bleeding hard, and most likely to die. One man has vanished, most likely run off into the woods. And then there's Corrin—"

I felt my heart break. "Is he—"

"Not yet, but I can't say much for his chances."

"Take me to him," I said and broke into a run for the camp.

One wagon was still burning, mules lay dead, the horses that hadn't been stolen had been struck by arrows and limped about, whinnying in pain. Men lay around the site, their clothes ripped from their backs. One young man who had been especially kind to me had an arrow in his chest, another had been thrown into the dying fire and was partly blackened from the flames. I had never seen nor even imagined such brutality, and still I didn't really see it. I made myself look past it, as if I were looking through wavy water. All I could focus on was finding Corrin, as if he were a goal that could get me past all the evil spilled out around me.

Surely there was still breath in his body. I let myself think of nothing but that. He was hurt but not dead. If there was breath, there was hope. I prayed fervently, promising God anything, pleading with Him to please give me back my husband.

I was standing still, looking about, when Hank caught up with me. He led me to Corrin, and I sank to the ground beside him.

Hank had apparently tried to make him comfortable before coming to look for me. I was guessing that Corrin had even managed to tell him where to look. He had been dragged half beneath our wagon. There were blankets under him.

But his face was ashen. His scalp was cut, as if some Indian had changed his mind or had been interrupted in mid-motion. His mouth hung open, and a thin trickle of blood leaked down the side of his chin. I touched his face, and it was cool. The Indians had done their bloody work on him, then thundered away.

"What kind were they?" I asked, sudden rage welling up inside.

"Ute," said Hank. "No surprise. They're about the bloodiest, most unpredictable bunch of redskins around these parts, and from what I hear they think this is their land."

"Ute?" *These* were the Indians who inhabited the region we were headed for?

Hank seemed to read my mind. "Mountain Ute where we're going belong to a different tribe than this," he

210

said. "Reckon Corrin knew there were Ute around here but misjudged their savagery."

I looked at my husband again and felt so helpless. I said, "But why? Because of the gold?"

"Likely as not they didn't even know about the gold. Down here in the foothills there's tribal warfare all the time. Hatred for anybody different."

"And that's why they attacked us? Because we're different?" I was incredulous.

Hank gave me an odd look. "I'd say that's about the size of it, Mrs. Emily. It's a sin, but there you have it. Our strong Christian men just got slaughtered for no other reason than the color of their skin."

We tended to Corrin as best we could. He'd been shot in the side by an arrow, the wound wide and ugly and near his heart. I soothed his head with a damp cloth and prayed with him, talked to him and sang softly, anything to try to get his mind off his condition.

Finally Hank took out his knife, and I held tight onto Corrin's hands while Hank sawed into the wound. Carefully he removed the arrowhead and the two inches of cotton-wood shaft attached to it.

Corrin sweat, his face twisted in pain. He gripped my hands till I thought he'd break them—but just before I was sure that would happen, he mercifully passed out.

Hank told me to stay with Corrin, and he wandered off into the brush, coming back shortly with some heavy river mud. He packed it into the wound, laid matted grass over it, told me to find the bandages.

I complied, then watched as he bandaged the wound tightly. I felt helpless again. As if I didn't know a thing and would never learn.

We went to tend the other wounded men as best we could. But one was already dead when we got to him, one died while we were trying to lift him off the tree stump where he had fallen, and the third one was barely hanging on. We moved him in beneath the wagon beside Corrin. It was a strain that put a stitch in my side, even though Hank rolled him onto a blanket and all I had to do was help drag it.

For the umpteenth time in my life, I wished I were bigger—tall as a sapling, strong as a horse, able to do the sort of heavy work required of a pioneer wife. *Or a young widow,* I thought sadly. How on earth would I even get back to St. Louis if I lost Corrin? And how would I live after that? I was only Emily Anne, puny and small and ignorant of the most basic tenets of survival.

But giving up wasn't an option. I reckon there are times in life when you either keep going or find yourself six feet under. Sometimes those are the only two choices.

The Ute had taken all but four of our unharmed mules and most of our provisions except for the traps and trapping supplies we'd brought along. They'd gone through most everything and left the unwanted goods lying in a heap, along with sacks of flour, slabs of bacon, and other foods unpalatable to them. Reckon they wanted mirrors and cloth and fancy gewgaws but nothing that smacked of good hard work. And they could certainly hunt all the game they wanted, so they had no need for half-rancid bacon.

They had also burned all but one of our wagons, then slit, stole, or burned the tents. They'd generally just destroyed most everything they got their hands on—though thank the good Lord they hadn't taken time to make a thorough job of it. Much was salvageable.

After we had done what we could for Corrin and the young mule skinner who survived, Hank and I set about tending to the remaining stock. We needed to figure out what was left and what we could do about it. After a while, he sent me back to Corrin, and then I heard gunshots. He was killing those animals that weren't going to get well, and he'd been kind enough to spare me more bloodshed.

I was exhausted. But Hank came back and asked for my help, and I went with him to the hillside to dig graves. It was coming on evening by then. I was so tired I couldn't even think. Perhaps that's why I didn't even realize that Hank had also been hurt till he lifted his shovel to dig the third of the shallow graves and a sudden wash of blood bathed the side of his shirt. He dropped the shovel, grabbed his side, and groaned.

I rushed to him. "Hank? What is it?"

"Cut," he said through gritted teeth. "Thought I had the bleeding stopped, but I've broke something open. Help me get to the wagon, please, ma'am."

I braced him and half carried him next to where Corrin and the other invalid lay unconscious on pallets.

He folded to the ground beside them, looking up at me with a pitiful expression. "I'm sorry, Miz Emily. Looks like I'm letting you down too. I—hey, whoa—what you doing? No, don't—"

I laid him flat, all but stepping on his middle in the process. I had to get a good look at that wound. I had to have him in a position where I could work on him, and I didn't have the strength or patience to shilly-shally.

I have to admit I was rough with him. I was somewhat angry that he'd let me down when he was all I had left to count on. But it wasn't that alone. I slapped his face as hard as I could—twice—to keep him conscious, for I didn't have the faintest idea what to do with the wound unless he told me. I was terrified that I'd do something wrong and send him to his grave, and I counted on his wisdom.

Even then, I was somewhat selfish in my motives. If Hank died, that left me alone with two invalids, a whole passel of Indians on the warpath—for although they'd ridden away, there was no guarantee they wouldn't be back—and not enough strength to even saddle a horse, mount up, and ride away. I *had* to keep Hank alive. That was the only way *I* was going to stay alive.

The wound seemed to be a clean one, a knife slit through the side. He told me how to cut hair from the horse's tail to sew it up, how to heat the knife and lay the sides against the wound to sear it shut. He groaned and grimaced and nearly bit his lip in two. Sweat broke out on his face.

Later he grew feverish, talking about the Indian who'd cut him. It seems he'd killed the man, but the Indians had picked up their dead and carried them away for a ritual burial. I admit I had wondered till then why we hadn't managed to bring down a single one of the enemy.

Come nightfall, I built a fire close to the three wounded men. No point in trying to hide—the worst varmints in the region knew exactly where we were. I dug into what was left of the morning pot of grits—it had been knocked downslope and had dirt in it, but there was still food in one side. I ate what I could and then checked on Corrin again. He was still unconscious, but seemed to feel a mite warmer now. I took that for a good sign.

Hank had told me the bodies needed burying lest the bears and wolves come for them and cause us harm in the process. And on top of that, of course, it was the Christian thing to do. But I had used up the last of my energy. Wolves or no, and respect for the dead aside, I had done all I could do that night. I dragged myself back beside the fire, took one last, hopeless look at the three invalids, then lay down on the blankets beside Corrin, drew the tattered covers up over me, pressed in close to him to lend him some of my warmth, and lay there thinking that both of us had just spent our last days on earth.

No matter. This had been the worst day I had ever known. I was eager to be shed of this thing called life, if this is what it was all about. I prayed that the Lord would take us all in our sleep and ease our suffering. I prayed that I would never have to face another sunrise.

16

I awakened next morning to the aroma of boiling coffee. My eyes flew open, and I saw Hank hunkered by the campfire, favoring his wounded side but up and about all the same.

I rolled over and felt Corrin move.

He groaned, and then I felt his arm wrap feebly around me. He whispered, "Mornin', honey."

Tears of gratitude came to my eyes.

His voice was trembly, but he was awake and speaking. On top of that, Hank was up. The sun had risen in spite of my selfish, cowardly prayers.

Even the young mule skinner, a lad named David, was doing somewhat better. We managed to awaken him. He sat up by himself for a spell and told us that an Indian had suddenly appeared, he'd tried to stop him, and several more had jumped him from behind.

He tried to put a courageous face on things—he seemed so young. But when he learned what had happened to the others, he wept and wept, got himself sick again, and curled up and all but passed back out. His eyes were haunted. He stared into the distance as if he were seeing ghosts.

There was still death in the air. We didn't know if the Ute would come back or not, and there was many a good man whose bones needed to be laid to rest. That afternoon Hank combed the surrounding woods and found the body of the boy we thought had run away. The Ute had killed him, it looked like, then dragged him back among the trees and scalped him.

Hank and I worked ourselves nearly into our own graves that day and the next. I did the digging since Hank was unable to handle the shovel lest his horsehair stitches break loose again and reopen his wound. There was no way

215

Corrin could help. It was a good thing I'd gained so much strength on the trail.

One way and another, we got the boys put to rest, prayed over them, wept over them, and stayed so confounded busy that we didn't have time to truly grieve or worry about ourselves. We needed to get out of the bayou as soon as possible, and the only way to do that was to dig those graves, bury our dead, somehow put a pack train back together, and head north, back toward the region that would take us on West.

Thank God, Corrin was sturdy, and he healed fast. Every day he seemed to be stronger, though it took him several days to get back on his feet, and it would take a good deal longer before he was his old self again.

The hardest part for him was the grieving and the guilt that seemed to grip him and refuse to let him go. Night after night he'd confess how bad he felt and how he had failed us all.

Finally he said, "I should have listened to everyone and come alone. At least I wouldn't have brought you into this muddle."

"And you'd likely be dead by now," I said. "If I hadn't been here to help you get well."

"I'd deserve it. If I hadn't been so confounded greedy, if I'd have been thinking about something besides gold, those boys would still be living. If I hadn't jumped into the front of the battle I might not have been wounded first, so that I couldn't defend them—"

"But Corrin, they're dead and buried, and we're going to have to say good-bye to them and to what happened here, or we're going to end up in the same place they are. And much as I'd like to just sit here and give up, I don't see how that's going to help them one little bit now."

The next afternoon I caught him staring sadly into the distance. I brushed the hair back from his still feverish forehead and said, "I'll give you a shiny new copper for your thoughts."

"They aren't worth a copper, nor am I. It's my fault, Emily. I've failed miserably. I don't know if I can ever face those boys' families, knowing that I let them die like that."

"Corrin, you're going to have to get hold of yourself and face the facts."

He frowned, seeming puzzled by my sudden flash of temper. "What facts?"

I was bone-tired and fed up. "The fact that you're not God," I snapped.

He stared at me. "What?"

"I said, you seem to think you have the powers of the good Lord Himself."

"What in thunder are you talking about?"

"You keep saying it's all your fault. That implies you have the power over life and death."

"That's foolish. I only mean it was my fault because I was careless of the men in my responsibility. I was chasing after gold when I should have been watching my boys' backs."

"Could be, but you didn't kill those men, Corrin. The Utes did. That part's *their* fault. Reckon if you'd expected such a thing to happen, we never would have come. And since you didn't plan it, and likely couldn't have stopped it, I don't see how you can say everything's your fault."

"But I *could* have prevented it—by watching closer, by taking a different route, by not wasting the time looking for color . . ."

"Oh, pshaw. You could have never been born too. Come on, Corrin. Sometimes you just have to accept the fact that the Lord sees things through a whole different lens from the one we look through. He allows what He allows.

"Those boys have gone home to be with Him—they were all good Christian men. They went in an awful way, but that wasn't your fault. You didn't shoot a one of them, and you did your best to stop it once you saw it coming. You almost gave your own life trying to save them. So just stop feeling sorry for yourself, accept the fact that some things

217

are beyond your control, that well-meaning people do make mistakes, and let the poor dead rest in peace so the rest of us can get on with what we have to do."

Truth to be told, I didn't feel indifferent about things. My hardness and resolve were born of necessity, for I saw Corrin wasting away because of his guilt feelings. In my heart of hearts I sometimes blamed him too—for stopping so long to look for gold. But I didn't love him the less for it, and I didn't want to see him humiliated. I just realized that he was human, that he could make mistakes. I was beginning to learn that, if I was going to find safe passage through this world, I'd best rely on the Lord Jesus and no one else, since the Lord was the only one who'd never make a mistake in judgment.

When we finally had some parts of the camp salvaged, repaired our one remaining wagon, loaded up the four mules and six horses that had survived the onslaught, we were almost ready to pull out.

In bed that night, Corrin said, "I've decided we should go back to Saint Louis."

"Absolutely not."

"But why go on West? It will be harder now. Nothing to do but trap, now that most of our goods is gone."

I thought for a long time before I answered, then I said, "I'll tell you the truth. I don't want to go on. I'm afraid with every breath I take. Every time a tree trembles, I jump, thinking we're under attack. I dream of the bloodshed every single night, but—"

"That settles it. We're going back to Saint Louis."

"No, Corrin. You brought us this far, and we're seeing it through."

"Why are you so confounded stubborn?"

"I don't know why. But this is our destiny. I pray and pray, wanting to stop this journey now. But the feeling just keeps getting stronger that we're on the path the Lord chose for us and we'd best not head off in any other way."

"It's all in your mind."

"I wish that were true."

"We're going back tomorrow," he said mulishly. Then he turned his back to me and quickly fell asleep.

We pulled out the next day, cautious, watching every ripple of aspen leaf, every movement in the tall grass. We didn't know if the Ute might still be watching us or if other Indians might appear. It was a full day's ride to the northern part of the bayou where we would turn upland into the mountains, headed for the place the Utes called *Hah-oon-kara.*

"Where the river of blue rises." What a beautiful name. But as Corrin said, this was an ancient Ute hunting trail. The lush, green upland valley we'd travel through most of the way was also a Ute resting place, and we were likely to run into more Indians.

"No other way to get through unless we backtrack—go on up the Platte to the northern Sheets-Kadee, then come back south," he said. "By the time we do that, summer will be over. Besides, we don't have enough supplies left to go that route. Everything says we go back East."

"No," I said. I was determined. Though I couldn't have told anybody why, it surely had to do with the Lord's ability to see into our futures, even when we didn't have a clue.

But at that moment, all of this distilled down and manifested itself as the stubbornness of Emily Anne McCannon née Davidson. For although I was beat up and battered some by life at that point, I was still and for certain *me.*

The more Corrin wanted to return East, the more I insisted we go West. Soon Hank and David were agreeing with me. Corrin was too weak to stop us, and we just up and took him.

We started up the mountain early the next morning, when the dew was still on the grass and the birds had just started singing. It was hard going, but we had a double hitch that allowed us to put two horses on the one small wagon.

Corrin rode inside—against his will. We nearly had to tie him up, what with his not wanting to make the trip and not wanting to have to ride in the wagon. But he was too feeble to climb that grade, even if he refused to admit it. And he was too feeble to take off on his own. So he sat in the wagon and grumbled and called us fools and hollered at us. I had never seen him in such a cantankerous mood.

Finally he climbed down and demanded that we turn around.

I'd had enough of him. I stopped in my tracks and gave him a tongue-lashing he'd never forget. He stood open-mouthed, likely never expecting me to tear into him like that. Meekly he climbed back into the wagon and fell silent. But I caught him darting a puzzled look at me now and again.

Come mid-morning, we stopped to let the horses rest and to make some coffee and eat hardtack. Climbing the grade was the hardest work we'd come to yet, and every last one of us was already tuckered out before we even started.

We were also depressed, considering what we'd just come through. No matter how much I tried to accept what had happened and get on with things, I kept thinking about those boys, each one precious in God's sight, all of them with families and futures. At times it would overwhelm me, and then I'd have to just stop, catch my breath, push back the tears, and force myself to go on.

The wagon was our biggest problem. The two horses were mismatched. They had a hard time pulling in tandem, and the grade was just too steep. Finally the wagon slid off into a ditch cut by the rainfall, and I gave the wagon wheel a tongue-lashing too. Not that it did much good.

Hank, David, and I worked until we were sweaty and filthy. At last we just gave up. We unhitched the horses, padded a saddle so that Corrin could ride comfortably, loaded down the other wagon horse with what it could carry, put as much as we could on the other pack animals, and left the rest beside the trail for the Indians or whoever else would find and make use of it.

When we reached the top of one final, steep grade, we were in high country. Once in a while we could see mountaintops around us, most of them deep in snow. Up here there was still an occasional snowbank beneath the trees, and the ground was damp from the winter runoff. There were great forests of birch and larch and aspen, with pines and spruce laced in between and an occasional glade rich with tall grass, cold ponds of snowmelt, meadows splashed with purple mountain lupine, lavender chiming bells, sky-blue forget-me-nots, and pink and maroon primrose. The birds sang endlessly, clearly glad it was spring. I recognized the familiar calls of a finch and a jay, a lark and a pippin and a sparrow. I paused to collect a basket of rich, ripe chokecherries to prepare for our supper.

Soon the mountain foliage grew thicker. Varmints started and ran as we trespassed on their terrain. I spotted numerous tiny, rabbitlike critters with small round ears that Corrin said were conies. He told me they made little houses that looked like haystacks, though I didn't see any and thought he was joshing me. He told me they called with a shrill, high whistle to alert each other. I did hear that sound, so I reckon that much of what he said was the truth.

It got so I was spying something new and delightful nearly every few feet. I saw gophers and mice, rabbits and squirrels. It broke my heart when Hank traipsed off by himself, then came back with several tiny rabbits, shot dead and dressed out. But hunger has a way of searing a person's conscience. I helped eat them all the same.

We forced our way through about a mile's worth of heavy undergrowth, which was harder going than the grade. We were all cut up, scratched, bruised, and with blistered hands from moving deadfall and logs and such.

But at last we came to a place where the various treetops were laced so thickly that the sun couldn't reach the undergrowth, and it had all but died out. This was a heavenly place, with an occasional sun shaft bursting through to light a ferny glade, but otherwise the forest was all tall pine, spruce, and occasional clumps of bright green aspen and birch. The firm, clean, pine-needle-covered ground was so easy to walk on that we soon felt chipper again, thinking the hard part of our journey was finally done with and we'd reached the doorway to paradise.

We were just considering stopping for the day, making camp and resting beneath those trees, when we saw the forest brightening before us. So we pressed on to find ourselves stepping out of the dense wood.

And then we were looking down into a wide green bowl, a lush valley with a bright blue river running through it—the sky was blue, the birds were still singing, the sun suddenly broke through the clouds. I was never so glad to see a place in my life as that valley.

Even Corrin welcomed the sight.

We made camp right there on the edge of the bowl, where we could see all around the valley, from the jagged rise of mountains on the west all along the north-flowing *Hah-oon-kara*. The Blue River. Nothing had ever been more accurately named.

Hank and I cooked a meal, and Corrin became more personable when the vittles calmed his temper. After a while he was back to his old self and talking as if nothing amiss had happened all day.

"No recent sign of Ute," he said, and I knew he had been carefully watching for them. "But this is one of their favorite camping places. We'd best not stay here long."

"How do we get past those jagged mountains?" I asked.

"Follow the river north. When we almost reach the end of it, we'll cut west, and there's a pass through. It requires more climbing, but it will bring us out into a valley that takes us downslope for a ways. We'll make it—you'll see."

I knew right then that Corrin had changed his mind about going West. The excitement had captured us all once again. There was no stopping us now. We were going to make it all the way across the Great Divide, all the way through the pitfalls. We were going all the way to McCannon's Country.

17

By the first of June, all the men had ceased shaving. Their hair was long, their beards getting thick. Corrin's was rust-red, just like his hair, and he cut a pretty figure. They'd all taken to wearing the buckskin-fringed garments they'd purchased back on the Missouri, partly because the Indians had taken most of their store-bought goods. They looked, acted, and smelled like mountain men.

As for me? I didn't know what I was or where I belonged anymore. I just got up and did what I had to every passing day, enjoyed what I could of it, tried not to work myself clear to death, and ate and slept when I could. I had taken to wearing men's clothing—pants and flannel shirts—with the moccasins Corrin had bought for me. The Utes had taken most of my fine dresses, but I didn't mind anymore. I was looking for comfort, not prettiness. I wanted clothing that was functional, easy to care for, and I didn't have to give a hoot about what anybody thought of me.

I had given up on anything complex and was learning to live simply but well. I watched carefully as the men shot wild game, cleaned, and preserved it. Soon I was helping them. I watched Hank and Corrin scan the sky for rain or other weather as they searched the woods for animals or Indians. By watching them, I was learning what to look for and where to look. I was beginning to understand the savagery and beauty of this place and how to survive within it.

We followed the Blue northward till we came to the end of the valley and the mouth of the sandy creek that ran into it. The Blue made a turn and flowed south here, becoming darker. A ways down, Corrin said, the waters turned reddish, and the Spaniards had named the river Colorado—for the color red.

"Some folks say it goes all the way to the sea," he said, "though you couldn't prove it by me."

There we turned west, past the towering jagged peaks that had blocked us from the land beyond. Here the mountains tapered off to low hills, and we easily made our way through.

Our journey was a good one. We found ample water, grass, game—even several herds of buffalo, regal and stately, not a bit afraid of us. We rode close enough for them to smell us and look up from their grazing, but they had no reason to fear. The woods were thick with animal life, with birds, with nature's buzzing activity. Though the snow was still melting off higher up, the lower reaches we stayed to had mostly thawed, and spring was in full bloom.

Corrin grew stronger day by day. Hank mended too, though he stayed silent, taciturn, and sometimes moody.

The boy David had been taken on as a full partner by the other two men. He was quiet also, and I knew he thought a lot about what had happened to his friends. But he was a hard worker, polite, friendly, and downright funny now and again with his lank brown hair, his oversized nose, and his ability to mimic nearly anyone in the most amusing way.

By the end of the week I was wondering if we were ever going to get through the mountains. Not that I really wanted to. It was beautiful up there. One day I discovered a red fox hiding in brambles beside a quiet stream that held sunlight like gold and was as brilliant as any diamond I'd ever seen. The grass was long and lush, the birds filled the trees. Deer were everywhere, and so were beaver dams, which set the men to talking of stopping for a spell to trap—until they thought some more and realized we might still be in the region of those same Ute who'd attacked us. That kept us moving on.

Soon we were climbing again, the vista changed, and a whole new range of mountains spread out to the north in front of us.

225

"Oh, Corrin. Do we have to climb them too?"

"We're skirting the south of them. This is the last of it, Em. We're moving downslope from here on, though we'll still find some hard going from time to time."

At that moment, a herd of elk erupted from the trees below, racing against some invisible foe. They were regal, bearded animals, more powerful than deer but just as stately, smaller than buffalo but just as strange to me. Both Corrin and I were struck dumb with the wild, awesome beauty of the moment as they charged across the meadow, running from who knew what or to who knew where, their heads held high.

I watched till they were gone, and I had a sad feeling as they disappeared. "If I died at this moment, I would feel complete," I said, leaning into Corrin's shoulder.

"There are elk aplenty where we're going, Em. You'll most likely be looking at them all your life—probably raising your children on their meat."

"I don't ever want to shoot one," I said. "They're too wild, too regal." I looked out over the mountain range that shadowed the woodland from which they had appeared. "I am going to name those mountains after them and never forget this moment."

"So be it." Corrin laughed. "Those are now the Elk Mountains. I'll be sure to put it on our map."

"Not Elk. That's not quite right. No, we shall call them the Elkhead Mountains. So we will remember how beautiful their antlers are in spring and how proudly they hold their heads."

"Then that's what the mountains are called," Corrin said. "At least by us. Come on. Hank's got the coffeepot on, and it's getting cold out here."

The sun shone brightly on the camp next morning, and the Elkhead Mountains loomed beyond in bright relief, reminding me with pleasure of the day before. Our spirits were high; we had almost reached our destination. We filled ourselves with flapjacks, the last of our slab bacon, and some

beans left over from the night's meal. Then we were under-
way.

Two days later we reached the mouth of the Yampa,
well down the western slope of the Rockies. Bear River,
some trappers called that watercourse, though Corrin said
the name was confusing, since there was a Bear River up
north, named by the Indians. Since the Yampawah tribe of
the Utes was prevalent in this land, the name *Yampa* helped
to define the territory as well as describe a kind of root
found growing in the valley.

I didn't care what the river was named. I was just
glad to be there, almost "home." We followed the river westward for one day, two days, and finally were in the middle
part of the valley, or so Corrin said.

This was a land where the grasses and natural hay
were belly high, where the river ran through cottonwoods
and chokecherry bushes, where the lower mountains rose up
on all sides—ah, what a beautiful, gentle place.

We made camp at the confluence of the Yampa River
and a wide, rushing creek. I'd seen beaver ponds throughout the bayou and the wetlands beside the Blue River. But
they'd always been distant. Now I finally saw my very first
beaver up close.

I had walked off a distance when I heard some small
critter splashing in a stream. I listened to the gurgling of
creek water over a riffle in the rocks, then followed the
sound down to where a bunch of the busy creatures were
industriously building a dam.

I approached carefully, intent upon seeing how they
did it. But careful though I was, I must have made some
sound—or perhaps they caught my scent. A large beaver,
who had been laying willow twigs atop the lodgelike structure, suddenly stopped, tilted his head, then slapped his big,
flat tail on the water. That sent the others diving beneath the
surface and into the underwater doorways of the wooden
shelters built into their dam. They seemed so clever. I really

didn't want to trap them; I wanted to let them all live, let them all enjoy God's country as much as I was beginning to.

God's Country. McCannon's Country. It was all the same, and so far as I was concerned, we had at last arrived.

"It's been flooding," Corrin said as he tramped around looking for a dry enough campsite. "Creek and river have had this place covered over recently. But there's enough dry land to shelter us for one night."

"Why can't we stay longer?"

"No time," he said. "We're behind as it is."

"I saw beaver, Corrin. You could trap them."

"It's not that easy. First you have to lay a trap and bait it, then you have to wait while they find the traps and take the bait. That doesn't generally happen overnight. No, we'd best head on down to Brown's Hole and get ourselves settled."

That evening as I was cooking supper, I chanced to look up at just the right time to see a bold, stately buck elk stride proudly out of the woods, then stop to haughtily appraise me.

I touched Corrin and nodded toward the beautiful creature.

"It's a sign," I said. "This is it. McCannon's Country."

Even my whisper carried enough to startle the majestic elk. He spun and darted back into the forest. We heard the brush break as he ran away.

Corrin looked around him. "This country is beautiful, all right. But it wouldn't do to settle here."

"Why on earth not?"

"The Ute, for one thing. This is some of their prime hunting ground, and I'm not familiar with the bands who mostly hunt here. For another thing, the winters set in about October, and you don't see anything but snow again until early April most years. The winters are harsh here, Emily. You wouldn't survive the first one."

"I want to stay here." Intuitively, with absolute certainty, I knew this was the place where I belonged. "We could build farther uphill, above the flood plain. We'll call this tributary Elkhead Creek."

"Can't do it," Corrin said. "Come on. We've still got a good long ways to go if we're going to reach Fort Davy Crockett this week."

Some twenty miles west, we reached the end of the Yampa River Valley. The river itself meandered on west through a green swatch of bottomland, but the surrounding terrain turned brown and unwelcoming. In front of us the hills spread out in a pastiche of flat adobe, sagebrush, and sandstone. I was looking at some harsh, hard land.

"Why on earth are we leaving all the greenery and beauty and going off into this wilderness? I thought we were headed for the mountains."

"There is another range beyond this. That's where we'll find the fort."

"Corrin, I don't want to go there. I mean it. I want to stay here. We could build a cabin, trap right here—you could go down to the fort to get your supplies and such . . ."

He shot me a puzzled look. "I've never seen you so persistent. What on earth has gotten into you, woman?"

"I just know this is where we belong. Let's stop."

He looked around him and stretched. He was almost completely healed from the arrow wound, stronger and more supple than ever. He scratched at his shaggy head. "I'd be tempted to listen if I didn't know better. I agree this is some of the most beautiful country I've ever seen, and it does have a good feeling to it. But you don't know the Ute, Emily. I've heard that this Yampawah band is a good deal more peaceable than the band we encountered in the bayou, but you never really know what they'll do."

"What about the Ute in Brown's Hole? Isn't it the same with them?"

229

"But I know them. They aren't going to attack us—at least, not if the same ones are there. And I don't ever want to take a risk with you again."

He convinced me to travel on. And so we spent three days crossing flatlands, trekking through juniper-clad hills, fighting dust and rattlesnakes and sagebrush. And finally we reached the region that held Brown's Hole.

It was a wild and beautiful place. But even if things had been as I expected, and I'd arrived at a clean little fort with gardens and all that, it still would have been a great disappointment to me after passing through those glorious, pristine mountains and thinking they would be my new home.

18

It was June 10 when we finally reached the eastern-most boundary of the Ute Mountains. Deep, wild gorges cut through the rough terrain, which was a mottled mixture of grays, browns, and greens, softened here and there by wonderful cuts of soft green meadow and stands of cottonwood, willow, pinion, juniper, even aspen and pine. This range of the Rockies seemed to be harsher than the one we had recently come through. The approaching lands looked far from hospitable.

That final morning, we passed over broad, sandy wastes. Sparse grass sprouted here and there. Our stock had a hard time finding forage. This unfriendly place was too dry to attract any game, our meat supply was dangerously low, our beans were running out. I was seriously worried about our destination.

The broad, purple backs of the Ute Mountains grew higher by the day, but they never became more welcoming. This place was nothing like what I'd imagined it to be.

Mid-morning, we crossed a swift, reddish stream that Corrin called Vermillion Creek. It had recently overflowed its banks. We followed it downstream toward the Sheets-Kadee, the Green River. We flushed a cloud of birds from the bulrushes and watched them wheel away into the sky, as if the last trace of life were fleeing the land.

Numerous brush-lined creeks rushed into the river, churning and roiling with mud. When we reached the river itself, Corrin paused on a little knoll and looked around him with a shocked expression.

I didn't know what to think.

He peeled his hat off his head and stood with shoulders slumped. "I'm sorry," he said. "We shouldn't have come."

I was sorry too. I had expected to arrive at one of the soft, green bowls in the mountains, such as the one that held the Blue River. I had imagined a log-and-stone fort with turrets and a wide gate, people to welcome us, a hot bath, a hot meal. I had expected a languid, green-hued stream, lined with trees and grassy banks.

Instead, we were looking at a mud-filled monster of a watercourse churning sluggishly through a desolate valley. The river was so silty it looked like dirty laundry water. It had broken free of its banks to flood out in wide, stagnant, unpleasant pools all across the central valley floor. There were deep holes, yellow-gray with mud; shallow stretches that showed a sickly green, as if the algae had grown giant-sized; whirlpools in places where sandbars guided the water into a languid spiral motion. Sagebrush and greasewood bushes stuck above the water, and the smell of stagnation was everywhere.

"Where is the fort?"

Corrin gestured with his head. He looked as if some giant weight had broken him in half. "Down there."

I looked downstream to an especially broad bend in the river. For the first time I noticed several groves of cottonwoods, drowned halfway up their trunks. Everything else was below the waterline. I could just see the outline of what appeared to be a low building of wood and clay with a wide wing, flooded almost to the rafters with ugly, yellow, muddy water. There wasn't a sign of life anywhere.

I turned to Corrin. I knew my eyes were wide with shock. I felt as if my heart had suddenly frozen in my chest. "Oh, Corrin. Oh, what have we done?"

"It's my fault," he said with pain in his voice. "I didn't think ahead. I should have realized they were building on the floodplain."

"But—where are they? Thompson and Saint Claire?"

"Looks like they've flown the coop."

I felt my lip quiver with the threat of tears, but I managed to hold them back. "What will we do?"

He spread his hands wide, helplessly. "Move on, I reckon. What else can we do?"

I turned away. I couldn't look at him. We didn't have enough supplies to last a month. And move on to where?

He cleared his throat. "When I left here, this whole valley was green, and the river was about a tenth this size. You should have seen it then, Emily. It was green and clear, there was pastureland as far as the eye could see, beaver streams galore farther upriver—"

"Where's your cabin?"

"Don't matter. No point in lighting here."

"Is it flooded out too?"

"Not likely. It's farther up into the trees." He indicated a slight rise where cottonwoods grew thick, knitted in with aspen, larch, and willow. There were cottonwoods of every size in that region, from gnarled old-growth timber that looked like giant briars, to a full forest of stately trees with trunks five feet in diameter and more than seventy feet high.

I was suddenly excruciatingly tired, and a heavy pain had entered my back. "Let's find the cabin and rest, while we decide what to do."

"Wait here," he said, "while I see if it's still standing. The way things are going, you never know."

He and Hank walked off into the cottonwoods. David seemed heartbroken as he tended to the stock, and I just stood there, letting the tears stream down my face now that Corrin couldn't see me cry, and looked out over that ugly flooded-out valley.

Minutes later, Corrin came back. "It's gone to seed," he said, "but at least there's a bit of a roof left. Might as well come on and take a look—you've already seen the worst you're going to see today."

The cabin was desolate and lonely. It had half a stripped-bark roof and empty holes where oiled paper had once formed windows. But Corrin had done a good job of building the walls—they were straight and undamaged.

233

The place had been sitting empty and abandoned for two full years. It was obvious the critters had used it for a shelter from the rain and snowstorms during that time. Mice and pack rats had filed squatter's rights on the deserted premises, presumably along with other neighboring varmints such as skunks, badgers, and prairie dogs who had wandered in and out at their own discretion. These uninvited creatures had called this place home ever since Corrin left it. As was to be expected, they'd forgotten to clean house when they moved out.

I carefully looked the cabin over. It would be a huge job, repairing it enough to make it livable. Waist-high Johnsongrass and Russian thistle with a scattering of new-growth sagebrush had almost taken over the outside and would have to be cut out with a grubbing hoe or ax and burned. The roof had partially collapsed from snow weight and would have to be patched somehow. The plank floor had many holes, and there was about three inches of dried manure scattered around in the two small rooms.

But with a lot of hard work it could be made habitable. At least I'd have some walls around me and a roof of sorts over my head for a week or two, while we tried to regain our strength and figure out how to get back East.

For that's what I wanted to do now. Go home, oh, home. How I longed for the comfort and security of my parents' home in St. Louis. And I knew I needed to get a handle on my mule-headed stubbornness. Corrin was my husband. I should have listened when he tried to leave me there. I should have listened when he wanted to return after the Ute attack. I had to admit it. Once again I'd gone off hot-headed, made demands, talked the men into a foolish act, and I'd gotten us all into a pickle this time. A serious one. It could even cost us our lives.

We moved the pack train near to the cabin and set up camp. I was feeling worse than I was letting on, and the pain in my back was shooting spurs out in various directions now, all the way around to my abdomen. I told Corrin I wasn't feeling well, then lay down on a pallet in a glade a short distance from the cabin. I tried to rest as the men took in shovels and started pitching the manure into a heap at the side of the door.

The smell of the dried stuff was unpleasant, but I turned on my other side and soon got used to it. I was half asleep, trying to ease the pain in my side by pulling my knees up to my chest, when another smell began to merge with it.

Smoke! I sat up straight.

I looked west, toward a higher forest of cottonwoods and sage, and was surprised to see a smoky column drifting lazily above the treetops, as if wafting up from a campfire. Then a dog barked in the distance, the sound carried on the wind. We didn't have a dog.

I stood up, spun on my heels, and took off at a dead run, straight into the cabin.

Corrin stopped with his shovel in midair. "What in blue blazes—"

"It's the Ute. We've stumbled upon an encampment!"

The men grabbed up their weapons and followed me outside. Corrin took one look at the smoke curling up and shot Hank a peculiar look that could have meant anything.

I was shivering inside, afraid to go with them, afraid to stay alone. At any moment, I expected braves to leap from the trees and begin their carnage, just as they had done in the bayou.

Instead, a man in buckskins stepped out of the trees and almost made my heart stop beating.

Corrin raised his rifle and sighted.

"Hold up thar, you flea-gnawed varmint!" the man called.

If this was an Indian, at least he spoke English! And with the Tennessee accent I'd heard not long ago from Davy Crockett himself.

What a sight. He wore a tobacco pouch and a large knife, and his gnarly face was clean-shaven except for a long

235

mustache, though his dark, tangled hair was shoulder length.

The man laughed, the roar coming from his belly and roiling up till it erupted in a long, rollicking howl that almost doubled him over. Apparently he found the situation funny, though I failed to see how, considering that his own rifle was nowhere to be seen and Corrin's was still aimed dead at him.

Corrin's eyes squinted up, and he peered at the man. "Phil? Phil Thompson, that you?"

"The same as, you hide-tanned bait for bear. What in blue thunder brings you all the way back out here to the Hole?"

Corrin set his rifle butt on the ground. A grin broke through his scowl. "I came to trap and trade," he said. "I took you at your word."

It was the other man's turn to squint. He walked up and was beside us now, and I saw he was much younger than I'd initially thought. Probably about Corrin's age.

He said, "Which word was that?"

"You and Saint Claire said you were building a fort."

Thompson looked puzzled. "Well, we built one too. Didn't you see it?"

"I saw what's left of it."

"So?"

"So I came back in good faith, planning to help you with your work."

Thompson shrugged, as if it didn't matter a hill of beans to him. "So here you are. Help away. Why don't you start by bailing out that water near the fort's front gate. Dip it over there into that gully, and we'll be back in the trapping and trading business in no time. Say—who's that young'un you got with you?"

Corrin looked around. "Young'un?"

"That little varmint you got there beside you. You bring your kid sister along?" He chuckled at his wit.

236

Corrin drew himself up, as though he was about to get riled. "That's my wife, Emily Anne."

"Wife?" Thompson turned and looked full at me, and I felt the blast of his breath. This coot was knee-walking drunk!

"I am small but full grown, thank you," I snapped.

"Right feisty too," Thompson said. He offered me a lewd wink.

Corrin stepped between us. "Where you camped, Phil?"

"Upstream. With my own wife, though I picked me one of the wilder kind."

"You married a squaw?"

"Shore did. Best little filly you ever did see. I moved in with her band when the river flooded and left me high and dry. We just pulled back into the Hole and set up camp."

"Where you been?"

"Trapping upriver."

"Where you getting your liquor?" Corrin asked.

The question worried me. I was afraid that Corrin was going to join in some revelry and give up on everything else. Though to tell the truth, I was at the point of giving up, myself.

"You want a swig? Come on back to camp, and we'll have a hoedown," Thompson offered.

I shuddered at the thought of our men getting drunk with a band of Ute Indians.

But Corrin had better sense than I gave him credit for. He said, "No, sir, I have enough problems. But I want to know where you got it."

"Some fellers set up a trading post at the head of the Green. Going to make it a yearly trappers' rendezvous."

"Which fellers?"

"Don't reckon you know them."

"Folks from American Fur? I ran into some of their bourgeois, who said they were planning to move in on the Tetons."

"American Fur moved in all right, but they're a bit farther north. Heard they was up there, though. And then pretty soon, lo and behold, here comes Rocky Mountain Fur with supplies for the new trading post and sech, trying to beat out American and them others who'd like to be in the middle of the trapping up at the headwaters of the Sheets-Kadee. You ask me, the competition's getting fierce around here."

"How did you find out?"

"Band of Ute rode in and told us about it—that was about the time the floods hit. Me and mine rode on up and took a look. Traded our winter's plews there and got set up right fine for summer trappin'."

"You have supplies?"

"Some." He looked suspicious, peering at us out of his bleared blue eyes, as if he suddenly thought we might try to steal from him.

"Who came in with Rocky Mountain Fur?"

"A whole blamed expedition of them. Said they came up the Missouri headed for the Three Forks, but Ashley decided—"

"Ashley?" Corrin was dumbstruck.

"Shore nuff. Reckon you know of the man? Been trapping in these mountains off and on for a coon's age. He put himself a big party together back in Saint Loo last April or so and come back West. Some of them went on north, but the party broke up somewhere upstream, and some of them went into the Green River region to set up shop."

"Which men are among them?"

"Young whippersnapper name of Jim Bridger, for one. Ain't no more than eighteen and tryin' to call the shots already. Not a bad hunter though. And a few others."

"You say they have supplies for sale?"

"That's what they're here for—to trap and trade with the Indians. They're all but setting up a full-time trading post up there at the mouth of the river."

"How many days' ride?"

238

"I'd say five up, five back, if the weather holds. You can follow the river valley plumb near all the way."

Corrin turned to me. "We've found the supplies we need to start over," he said.

"But what about money?" I asked, when Thompson was gone.

"I have that buckskin poke full of gold nuggets," he said smugly.

I'd forgotten all about that.

He showed me the sack that night, spreading out the nuggets on our pallet. It looked like a good deal of money now. A treasure, but still nowhere worth what we'd paid to get it.

Corrin looked right proud as he showed it to me, as if he'd finally managed to do something right. "Don't let on to Thompson that I have it, though," he warned me.

"Why not?"

"Can't tell you, really. There's just something about that man I don't fully trust."

I felt the same way. But to give Thompson credit, he was always fair to us, though he drank a good deal more than I liked to see. Corrin said he hadn't been like that before the fort flooded out and he lost everything he'd worked for.

But of course I didn't know all that when I first laid eyes on old Phil Thompson. Seems he had indeed been born in Tennessee, same as Davy Crockett. He'd earned his reputation back in 1811 by crossing the Rocky Mountains all the way to Oregon, which made him a bit older than Corrin after all. He was among the first to strike up trade with the Indians in the area.

Well, I suppose hard times will bring out either the worst or the best in a man, and those were hard times aplenty. But I'd been on the receiving end of enough gossip not to want to carry on the tradition of gnawing and chewing and pawing over every little thing a person does that doesn't suit the crowd. I was going to be charitable to Phil Thompson.

But if I'd had my jewelry along, I'd have buried it and left it hidden all the time I was there, just to be on the safe side.

19

We were all curious about the Indian camp, so we walked up to take a look. Corrin kept assuring me there was no danger, since he knew these folks.

"I know them as well as I know your family, Emily. Maybe a good sight better. They lived right outside the camp for the two full years I trapped here."

Somehow that didn't take away my fear. I had seen the Ute only once. That image would terrify me for the rest of my life. I wasn't eager to see another one.

But Corrin was right when he said there were all kinds of Indians, just as there were all kinds of people of every skin color. Those Ute back in the bayou had been the equivalent of a band of pirates on the high seas. These folks here, he said, were the equivalent of a group of easygoing Mississippi River folk. They were a long ways from lazy—they'd have starved to death if they had been. But it seemed that after they took care of their basic needs, the farthest they cared to look was to their next meal.

The Indian camp consisted of six wickiups—shelters built of poles and reeds plastered together with mud and grass. They looked something like huge woven baskets without handles set upside down.

"The Ute use hide tents when they travel," Corrin explained, "but when they settle for a spell they build these more permanent shelters."

In wintertime, he said, they made these warmer by adding on bearhides or buffalohides they'd traded from the plains Indians—or sometimes they went across the mountains to hunt buffalo themselves. They had horses, of course. The Spaniards had brought horses not far south of here a century and more ago. The Ute bred fine horseflesh and traded horses to the lowland tribes for other necessities.

They were industrious in their own way, even though it looked to me as if they didn't do much actual work.

The women were all dressed in tanned antelopeskins and deerskins—some of it looking as soft as silk and adorned with dyed porcupine quills. There were perhaps a dozen women in all in the camp, ranging in age from young to old, all of them stopping to look at us—and especially at me—as if we'd sprouted horns.

A passel of children ran among them. There were dogs, and Corrin told me that sometimes the women used them in the stewpot. That broke my heart.

I saw a woman cooking over an open fire with a wicker basket hanging from a stick directly above the flame. That astonished me. Corrin explained that the baskets were specially treated and were woven so well they were watertight. My admiration for the abilities of the Mountain Ute grew by the moment.

The Indians were fit to be tied when they laid eyes on Hank, the runaway slave.

Thompson got a good laugh when his brother-in-law, a tall stripling called Goes-for-Broke (renamed that by Thompson, I might add), walked cautiously up to Hank and tried to wipe the color off his face. He'd wipe, then look at his hand; wipe, then look at his hand; then step back, puzzled.

Hank just gazed at us all out of his sad, old eyes and acted as though he couldn't have expected much better from us. He must have put up with a lot by then.

I was learning about that too—about human nature and respect for my fellow beings and all that. From the Indians I learned it was always a mistake to jump to conclusions. From Hank I learned that the color of a person's skin had nothing at all to do with the quality of the soul inside.

And I also learned that black folk were put on earth for something besides tending to white people's needs. It made me ashamed to realize I'd treated our house servants like little more than furniture that moved when I needed something. I *had* been spoiled and simpleminded before I left St. Louis.

Hank and I became good friends, and I loved that old man dearly. I was soon grateful to Corrin for his judgment in bringing him along.

We stayed busy those first few days, cleaning the cabin and then building a matching place for Hank and David. Thompson and his brethren didn't come back to help, after they all had an initial look at us. I hadn't expected any better, since Thompson was staying drunk and his adopted family seemed to be in a nonproductive mode as well.

The weather was exceptionally fine as we laid out a rectangle of rocks for Hank and David's cabin.

And speaking of David—he took to the work right well. He had grown a long blond mustache by now, and I saw some of the younger squaws looking at him and giggling. He was going to like it just fine here, from what I could tell so far. I was grateful for that too. Another pair of hands was sorely needed and sorely appreciated.

I did my best to show them all how much I appreciated them by cooking up great pots of antelope stew and by combing the surrounding area for berries and seeds and other edibles that Hank and I could incorporate into a decent meal.

By our third day of building, the cottonwood logs for the men's cabin were laid up to just above David's head—he was the tallest of the three. When they put up the logs, they quickly chinked them with dry grass mixed with mud that would dry nice and sturdy. They built a sod roof and a rough log door that swung on hide hinges.

I wished we had some oiled cloth—we'd brought some but the Ute in the bayou had taken it. The cabins were both dark inside and primitive—nothing at all like my mother's fine house back on the Mississippi River. I thought at times that she'd faint dead away if she could see where I was forced to live.

243

Our own cabin consisted of the two-room structure Corrin had built two years before, then shoveled free of dried manure. The wood floor was scrubbed clean. I felt blessed at that. Hank and David's cabin had only a dirt floor, smoothed out with water and then swept to hold back the dust, while I had a whole layer of wood between me and the insects and the outside dampness.

Corrin built a large log bed with a straw mattress inside our second room. That and a few of his trapping supplies were about all the room would hold. In the main room, the men built a table with a split-log top and benches along both sides. Our two other chairs were tree trunks, with part of the wood left higher to provide backs. I had a three-legged stool to sit on while I cooked at the sod fireplace, and a cast iron pot that we'd managed to get all the way from St. Louis. Once we got settled in, it seemed as if I spent most of my time at that cook fire. Folks were always hungry, and there were never enough hours in the day.

One night, when the cabins had been finished for several days and supplies were running even lower, Corrin lit a tallow candle and set it in an alcove, then sat down beside me and said, "I've got to go north and meet up with Bridger to get us restocked. I don't like the way you've been looking lately, Emily. I don't care to take you along."

"I know, Corrin. I'm still having trouble with my back. Reckon it was just the stress of the trip. I'll be fine here. I'll take it easy while you're gone and let my back mend up."

"Are you sure you'll be all right?"

"I'm certain. Just take David and let Hank stay with me."

The candle made his shadow loom large behind him; it seemed almost ghostly.

"Wish I knew why you've turned so pale."

"There's not as much sun here as on the plains," I said, though I knew that wasn't the reason.

"You're still tanned. Just sickly looking behind it—"

244

"Pshaw, Corrin. Next thing you'll be telling me I look puny and sickly and all those things Mike Fink said to me."

That got a laugh out of him, and he soon changed the subject.

But I knew something was wrong. I had missed my monthlies, and the pain in my back and abdomen came and went something fierce. I didn't know what could be done, though, and so I spent a good deal of time in prayer. In the meantime, Corrin had more than enough to worry about. I didn't want him to worry any more, especially since he couldn't make anything different anyway.

He and David mounted up and rode out the morning of June 26.

That afternoon I was working at the north end of the cabin, chopping some small cottonwood saplings that were threatening to wrap around the only window on that side of the building.

Hank was down at the creek, getting a bucketful of still muddy water. We had to let it settle for several days, strain it through cloth, then boil it before it was drinkable.

I chopped with the hoe, taking out some greasewood, then stopped to slap at a mosquito that was trying to sting my neck.

My body suddenly bent me double with the most ferocious pain I'd ever known. As I reached out to catch myself, something seemed to burst inside me, and I felt wet. I looked down and was shocked to see the skirt of my one remaining calico dress suddenly soaked through with blood.

My knees turned to molasses. I couldn't stand up. Thick sweat broke out, poured into my eyes. I touched my dress and saw my hand come away red.

I was terrified. My first thought was that the Ute had shot me with an arrow.

But when the fire started inside me, as if something was grinding inside my middle, I knew this wasn't anything the Indians had done.

245

I had suspected for some time that I might be pregnant, though only a few weeks along. Now, in that silent, terrifying moment, I knew beyond a doubt that I had just lost my and Corrin's first-conceived child.

Finally the worst of the pain passed, and I managed to open my mouth and scream.

Hank came running.

I heard him speaking, though I couldn't tell what he said. I felt him lift me, felt myself gently placed on our straw mattress. "I lost a child," I managed to mutter.

His kind, worried eyes went wide, and he inhaled slowly. In, out . . . in, out . . . thinking all the while. It seemed to take an eternity for him to breathe in, then breathe out again. And when he had at last exhaled completely, he said, "I got to go get one of the squaws," and was gone at a dead run.

To my surprise, two women arrived—one an elderly, dour-faced woman with steel-gray braids, the other the young, very pretty woman Phil Thompson had married and who was called Sky Feather.

They murmured over me in Ute-Aztec. It was only gibberish to me, and I hated to have them touching me, removing my bloody clothing, looking at me, and saying things I couldn't understand.

But there was nothing in the world I could do to stop them. I barely had enough strength left to breathe. And I was grateful too, for they seemed to know what they were doing.

Soon I felt them bathing me in soothing warm water. They dried me, and padded me tight, bound my midriff, then dressed me in one of Corrin's flannel shirts. One of them put a blanket over me.

The other raised my head, and a warm pungent liquid began to flow down my throat. I managed a few swallows, then a few more, and almost instantly I felt the pain begin to subside.

Then I slept.

I awakened in the middle of the night to find Hank there, a fire built and him lying on a pallet on the floor, sleeping fitfully.

I tried to get up to go relieve myself, and the moment I stepped onto the floor the pain returned, so much so that I screamed.

Hank jumped up and grabbed me and settled me back down. Phil Thompson's wife came in, her hair all tangled. She must have been sleeping in the other room in her deerskin dress. She and Hank carefully helped me out to our small privy and stayed right outside while I went through agony again.

Back inside the cabin, she fed me more bark tea—willow bark combined with roots and herbs to take away the pain and make me sleepy.

This time I managed to thank the young woman, who nodded as if she understood, then stood looking patiently at me, her dark, alien eyes appraising me dispassionately as she fed me yet more tea.

I slept for a long time then. The next morning most of the pain in my body was gone. But as the physical pain disappeared, the ache in my heart began.

I could sit up and eat some warmed-over stew. Hank stayed with me every moment he could, while still tending to the necessities of survival. I grew stronger throughout the day.

We tried to entertain ourselves that evening with the sights and sounds of the creatures. They came in the evenings to drink at the small creek that meandered across the corner of the cabin site. We watched them till a deer and her fawn came down to the river to drink, and then an audible sob grabbed my throat.

Hank looked helpless, as if he didn't know what to do.

I said, "Oh, Hank, I couldn't have been over a month or so along. But it was a child. It could have been our first child. Oh, Father in heaven, what did I do wrong?"

Hank scowled. "Reckon it was beyond your control," he said.

I looked at him intently, wondering about his history. "Did you ever have a child?"

"Several."

"What happened to them?"

A pained look came into his eyes, and I swear I saw them blur with tears. "Shipped off downriver by the master," he said softly. "Sold, sold, sold."

My heart suddenly broke for him instead of for me. "I am so sorry. So very sorry. Oh, Hank, I have learned so much from my friendship with you. How could we white folk ever be so thick-witted and selfish and wrong?"

The next night we walked out and quietly sat and watched the evening fall on the sloughs and grassy meadow. As the sounds of day quieted into a soothing, cool solitude, we were entertained by a chorus of frogs singing from where the floodwaters had receded to leave behind cool, verdant ponds. Night brought out the crickets, with their friendly chirruping. Then came the evening swallows and night birds, the restless hooting of an owl, and an occasional mournful howl of a coyote wandering in the shadowy hills nearby.

During the stillness of such evenings, tranquility and peace folded down like a curtain. The night noises seemed amplified and carried through the serene quietness with great clarity. God's nature appeared to be at peace with man.

But though I sat quietly and seemed to be enjoying the solitude, I was at war within myself.

I blamed myself for losing our child, for being too blind to realize what was happening with my body. A litany of guilt played itself out over and over in my head. I should have known. I should have told Corrin. I shouldn't have worked so hard. I should have taken more time to learn what I was doing. I should have stayed in St. Louis where I belonged.

The constant barrage made me grim and angry. I didn't want to see anybody, didn't want to talk. When Thompson's wife came by and offered to show me how to make deerhide moccasins, I all but snarled when I told her I was too busy.

Corrin came back two days later, leading two new pack mules heaped high with all sorts of necessities and even a few treasures. He was delighted to see me, but I couldn't even look him in the eye.

"What's the matter?" he said, suddenly anxious.

"Nothing."

"Emily. Look at me."

He cupped my chin in his hand and lifted my head up so I had to meet his eyes. But still I looked away.

"Why are you angry?"

"I'm not," I snapped.

"Then what have I done? Why aren't you glad to see me?"

"She's been sick," Hank intervened.

Corrin's concern was immediate. "What's wrong?"

"Pretty much done with now," Hank said, embarrassed.

I said nothing. I wanted to break down and tell Corrin everything, have him fold me in his strong, brave arms and make everything all right. But every time I tried to speak about it, the words caught in my throat.

I am ashamed to admit I had to let Hank tell him what had happened.

"Oh, dear Lord," Corrin said in a half-lament, half-prayer. "Are you all right?"

"I'm OK," I said, though I knew I wasn't.

Corrin had his arms around me by then, and he held me and promised it would be all right, that we'd have more children. "At least you're still alive," he kept saying over and over again. "No telling what might have happened. At least you're still alive, and the child wasn't very far along. We can both thank God for that."

249

I tried to respond to his sympathy. But in truth I hated him right then for not sharing in my grief.

It was your child too, I thought later, as he went about the business of unpacking items, then repacking them in a smaller trap bag. He had already told me that as soon as he was back he'd have to head straight upstream to trap some beaver before the summer season was over.

The least you could do is grieve for our lost child, my heart said.

But he was busy. He and Phil Thompson and Hank were exploring the fort—what part wasn't still under water—and making plans to rebuild it, though on higher ground if Corrin had his way.

I stayed angry at him, hiding it behind a show of quietness and as much solitude as I could muster.

If Corrin wasn't grieved, then I would grieve enough for the both of us. And in that terrible, angry moment I made a vow.

I vowed I would never for the rest of my life let myself stop grieving for the lost child who had died inside my womb.

20

Our cabin was located on a slight rise above the small basin where the river meandered through the greening meadows and on down the valley. Most of the higher ground was dry now and thick with fresh growth.

We could just see the drowned fort from our front door. Day by day more of the bedraggled cottonwood structure emerged as the water receded. And then one morning I awakened to see that the entire building was showing; the river was all the way back inside its banks. It was as if one of those giant lizards Corrin spoke of had lumbered past while we slept and sucked the floodplain dry.

With the first of July, the soft, hot winds came. The valley began to dry. But even the end of flood season didn't cheer me up. Depression settled down around me like a leaden cloak thrown over my shoulders, and it was far too heavy for me to remove even if I'd made the effort. For some reason I didn't even want to try.

Corrin tried to cheer me up, but he was gone a good deal of the time. He, Hank, and Thompson were trapping upstream in a variety of tributaries that flowed down into the Green.

Corrin told me how they did it. They'd hike until they found the beavers' ponds and dams, then wade into the stream and set their steel traps. They'd fasten a trap-chain to a stick and affix that to the bottom of the stream, then set a little twig baited with beaver musk atop the trap. When the beaver came for the bait, it would trip the switch, panic, and dive, get snared by the trap and thereby drown itself. All in all, I didn't find it a pleasant business, considering my affection for animals, but when it came to survival, most things weren't very pleasant in those days.

The men would tramp in and out of any region rich in beaver, set traps all up and down the streams, come home and rest and tend to things here; then after a few days they'd hike back in and check the traps. They skinned the beaver where they caught them and brought only the skin, the tail, and the musk glands back to us. The pelts were cured, then stored for sale at a later time.

The tail was a delicacy and was eaten right away, though I didn't care for it myself. The first time Hank cooked some, it nearly made me sick. It was fatty and had a sweetish taste. But the Utes considered beaver tail a treat, and the tails were never wasted.

As for the musk, it was used for bait, and it sold on the market at around three dollars a pound. What the men didn't use in their own trapping would be sold at that tidy price when they disposed of their pelts at the fall rendezvous.

Thompson's wife, Sky Feather, and the brother-in-law, Goes-for-Broke, had the job of handling and storing the pelts once they came in. They had a work area set up near the Indian camp. David, the young mule skinner, helped them. He also helped me and otherwise tended to the stock and other things at home while the other men were gone.

I watched Sky Feather and Goes-for-Broke prepare the pelts one day. It was dirty work and a job I was glad to miss out on. They scraped any remaining flesh from the inside of the hide, then stretched it tight on a big semiround device made from sturdy twigs. Then came the job of curing, drying, and marking the furs with their own private sign.

Some trappers who didn't have a home base buried their pelts, then retrieved them on their way back to rendezvous. The trouble with that was that every now and again someone stumbled onto the cache and robbed the trapper of his year's work. I'd heard that the men who worked for American Fur were especially fond of doing that and had been known to spy on other trappers in order to commit that very crime.

I soon grew restless in spite of my deep depression. Though there were bear, wolves, coyotes, and even cougars in the region, I took to wandering around to gather firewood, to look for berries, and to otherwise make myself useful. But no matter what beauty I discovered, no matter how busy and tired I kept myself, the depression remained, like some foul invisible creature that had leeched onto my back in order to weigh me down.

It was worst at night when Corrin was gone. I would sit with David on the front stoop they'd built for me, and we would look at the lonesome world around us. The stars would materialize in all their glory on cloudless nights; sometimes it seemed as if I could reach up and grab a handful and fling them to earth like diamonds.

David said they had been set in order by the Creator just to remind mankind of how puny, small, and insignificant we were. He was given to deep thinking and profound conversation. And he was also proving himself to be a hard worker who made pleasant enough company.

He knew I was hurting, and he tried to cheer me up. But he was a serious sort of person, and joviality came hard to him. Anyway, nothing could make me cheerful. The exhaustion of the trip West—the desolation of what we found once we got there—all combined with the loss of my child to turn me into a miserable, melancholy, bitter woman.

And then one fine morning I heard a horse nicker outside as I was dumping my dishwater out the window into the gully. Then I heard a strange voice call, "Halloo!"

I stood stock-still and silent, listening.

"Halloo," the voice called again. "Is anybody there? Mrs. McCannon, is that you in there?"

I reckon they'd known someone was home from the smoke still drifting up from the sod fireplace after I'd fried some duck eggs for breakfast. But who in thunder had come to visit us way out here?

I quickly dried my hands on the back side of my britches, then hurried to the front door.

I opened it and stopped, thinking I had finally lost my mind. I actually rubbed my knuckles into my eyes, then looked again. And lo, the apparition was still there.

I was gazing at a whole caravan of the strangest creatures I'd ever seen. I had never so much as imagined such a sight. It was like something straight out of a storybook with fairy tales and goblins, except that a real person headed up the mirage.

Jim Bridger himself stood there, decked out like an Indian, with a tall, gangly man beside him.

That alone was enough to strike me dumb.

Bridger wore a dressed deerskin shirt, open at the throat, and buckskin leggings with fringe down the side, all of it heavily adorned with red, white, and blue beads and fancy starbursts of white-dyed porcupine quills. His feet were shod with heavy buffalohide moccasins, and an ammunition belt hung at his waist alongside a buckskin sheath that held the bone handle of what looked to be a humongous knife. A hatchet was stuck into the belt on the far side, and he also had two deerskin bags looped over his shoulder— one for powder, one for tobacco, was my guess. He was leaning on his rifle, which was pointed at the sky. And if the sight of him hadn't struck me speechless, the rest of the procession most certainly would have.

Behind him were two pure white horses, mud-spattered yet regal. They were adorned with fine silver-trimmed bridles and saddles, the kind the Spanish make in Santa Fe. Bridger held the bridles, and beyond the horses I saw a two-wheeled wagon of the sort you expected to see on St. Louis streets. This one was painted white and was trimmed in the colors of the American flag. Beyond the wagon, several buckskin-clad white men sat uneasily astride their assorted horses. And behind them stood a half dozen well-loaded pack mules and two spindly-legged dogs that looked as if they'd been freshly rescued from one or another Indian camp.

After a quick glance to take it all in, I returned my gaze to Bridger and to the straw-haired apparition with watery blue eyes who stood nervously beside him.

This second man was dressed even more outlandishly than Bridger himself, and he wore a haughty expression on his face besides. The man stood a good six inches taller than Jim, was thin as a rail, and sported a white-blond handlebar mustache that drooped to his narrow, receding jawline. He was tanned nut brown and wore a buckskin outfit similar to Bridger's, though it was far more ornate. His stovepipe beaverskin hat was what topped the cake, though. It marked him for a dandy, in spite of his attempt to go native. And it looked as out of place as a flea in a frypan.

As I appraised him, he suddenly stepped forward and gallantly took my hand, making a grand flourish of the gesture. I was too stunned to even protest.

He then bowed and brushed his lips almost to my hand, barely missing it. He let go of the hand, bowed again from the waist, and doffed his hat. Then he stood straight and, with a pronounced German accent, said, "And so I meet the illustrious Miss Emily Anne Davidson. I have heard of your adventures." There was haughty amusement in his eyes.

I thought for a second that he was being disdainful of my appearance—I was wearing trousers again and a raggedy blouse I'd cut down from a dress ripped up by the Utes in Bayou Salade.

But then I realized that he'd heard something overly familiar about me. Could he have heard about the episode back in St. Louis, when I was dragged down the river in that bright red petticoat? If so, how?

I looked at him, then at Bridger. "Jim Bridger?" I said stupidly.

"Yes'm," Jim said with a lopsided grin. He was enjoying my reaction to him and his strange little parade.

"I am pleased to see you again," I said to him. "And thank you for your help with regard to my river adventures."

"Don't look at me," Bridger said, taking it wrong. "I didn't know nothing about them pirates and what they did to you until the prince here come along upriver and brought the Saint Looey gossip with him."

The dandy bowed again and butted in. "I, madame, am Prince Paul of Wurtemburg, nephew of the King of England and fearless explorer of America's Far West." He huffed up, as if waiting for me to make a fuss over him.

"A prince?"

Jim Bridger rolled his eyes upward and stared at the sky, a deprecating grin on his face.

"Ah, yes, I am a prince," the man said. "And I bring greetings from your illustrious father."

"From my father?" Why was I so addled that all I could do was repeat everything he said?

"But of course," he replied with a little flourish. "On my way up the Mississippi from New Orleans I stopped to visit Saint Louis for a number of days. You have become the object of much admiration back there."

"Me? Admiration?"

"Ah, yes. I was told you are a brave young lady. I believe you foiled a bunch of river pirates, if I am not mistaken." But he wasn't talking about that at all. I could tell by his eyes. La, but people did love to dig up my misadventure, then hash it over as if there was something to be learned by it.

"How did a prince such as yourself come to be out West?" I said, in order to change the subject and hide my embarrassment.

"I traveled by boat all the way up to the Three Forks of the Missouri. From there, my guides brought me down the Green and to Rocky Mountain Fur's new camp, where

I enlisted the aid of young Mr. Bridger to get me the rest of the way here."

I was almost struck dumb again. "You were coming *here?*"

"Why, of course." He tilted his head and gave me an indulgent look. The kind you reserve for small children and mental misfits.

"You mentioned my father," I reminded him.

"Oh, yes. I had occasion to meet him in Saint Louis while I was outfitting for this expedition. I requested audience with a man who would know the terrain and was introduced to him."

"Father has never been out here."

"Oh, I understand that. But he certainly has commerce with men who travel far and wide. It is for that reason I solicited him, and he shared invaluable wisdom with me. He also asked me to bid you hello, should I pass your way."

"Did you see my mother? Or my sister?"

"He advised me that all is well with your family. Though they miss you sorely."

Somehow that news from home was just the thing I needed to perk me up a bit more. Though I had been gone for only about two months, it seemed a lifetime had passed.

He glanced around the muddy valley, then his face pinched up, and he said, "We have matters to discuss with your husband. Is he here?"

I grew guarded at the question, then looked again at Jim Bridger. David was just up in the timber, cutting logs. But aside from that, I trusted Bridger, although I was certainly skeptical about the so-called prince.

I said, "Corrin has gone trapping. Is there something I can do?"

"This man is looking for the giant lizards," Bridger piped up.

That struck me totally speechless.

The prince apparently realized my consternation. He hastily explained. "I had occasion to encounter a gentleman in Saint Louis. A professor under contract to the United States Government, a man with snowy hair and piercing blue eyes. He said he knew you?" He made it a question, then peered at me so I'd have to answer.

With sinking heart I remembered the rough map of Brown's Hole that Corrin had drawn for the humbug professor that night on the riverboat. That old scalawag had a hand in this, that much was for sure.

"We met him briefly," I said. "I suppose he sold you a map?"

Those princely eyebrows darted up like a hawk's wings, and he seemed surprised and pleased by my insight.

"Why, that he did," he said, "though it took a good bit of persuasion and more than a glass or two of whiskey for me to convince him to sell his treasure."

"Treasure?" I repeated.

What had the old fraud done now?

I said, "Don't tell me you're here looking for gold."

"Ah, but I have all the gold I'll ever need. I am, after all, a prince." He smiled indulgently. "Besides, treasure is all in a person's eyes, Mrs. McCannon. To me, treasure is knowledge, it is wisdom, it is understanding the geography and origins of this great world. Which is why I have come to explore the Far West and this land of giant lizards. I would be most generous to anyone who could take me all the way to where they are."

I shook my head in disbelief. Here was a full-grown man—a man who claimed to have no end of money—who had nevertheless fallen for the most ridiculous story I had ever heard.

I searched his cold eyes and saw nothing, then searched Jim Bridger's for a clue. But Bridger merely gazed upward at the heavens, as if to say he was humoring the prince but didn't require me to do the same.

"When will Corrin be back?" Bridger said, suddenly earthbound again.

"Tomorrow at the latest. Maybe even this afternoon."

"Then we shall take the opportunity to rest up," the prince said to Bridger. "So when he returns, he can guide us the rest of the way."

"Don't know if he can do that or not," I said.

"Why, pray tell?" Those fair eyebrows darted up and arched imperiously as he looked down his thin nose at me.

"He has to trap."

"I'll pay him better than he'd earn at trapping. I am eager to make this discovery, and I won't stint when it comes to paying those who help me."

Well, we could use money all right, I thought, though I didn't know if Corrin would want to earn it by coddling a fool. I told them it was all right for them to pitch a tent and sleep nearby and wait for Corrin to return. Then I went back into the cabin, sat down to a cup of tea, watched them set up camp, and thought long and hard about the professor and the trip out here, the prince and Jim Bridger, and my husband.

I thought about Corrin most of all and wondered why he seemed to have a way of getting us into the strangest fixes by doing the simplest things.

I didn't think about my recent grief or my vow to wallow in it. Not until late that afternoon. By then it had mostly drifted away, like a thundercloud that dematerialized as it blew on past with the wind.

21

Corrin, Hank, and Phil Thompson arrived that evening as the sun was sinking behind the mountains.

By then Bridger, Prince Paul, and their several hired men had set up camp a short distance downhill on a flat place beside the stream. Fancy white tents were pitched, tables with folding legs were set out—such luxurious things those men brought with them! Tallow candles were lit, and a feast was soon in process.

I was down there, of course, marveling at their stores and sharing in their bounty.

The prince's underlings set out a fancy fare of fish packed in cans—I had never before seen such a thing, though I had heard that folks were beginning to use that newfangled method of storing foods. They had beans in a can too, with pork, and ripe cheeses of various types, well preserved. They served up hot skillet biscuits and fresh honey they'd taken from a hive up north a ways. Crackers and salted meats obtained at Bridger's trading post made up the rest of the meal, and they even had some dark green bottles of English ale and ginger beer.

For a woman used to fresh game, corncakes, birds' eggs, wild root vegetables, and not much else, this was a feast fit for a prince, all right. Some might even say it was fit for a king.

To dress it up some more, Prince Paul set out a silver dish of fancy peanut brittle, taffy, pralines, and other delicacies, and I was fully engaged in enjoying the sweets and listening to his far-fetched tales of adventuring all over the world when Corrin stomped into the midst of the outing.

He took one look at me sitting wide-eyed and listening to the prince's tall tales, then marched straight up to Jim Bridger.

"I demand to know the meaning of all this."

Bridger grinned wickedly. It seems he enjoyed getting a person's goat. "Corrin, I'd like to introduce Prince Paul of Wurtemburg, nephew of the King of England and fearless explorer of America's Far West." They recited it the same way every time, as though the whole blamed thing was a part of the man's title.

"A prince?" Corrin said with surprise.

I smiled and bit into a candy.

"And a famous explorer," the prince said immodestly. He stood and extended his hand for a shake, then gave Corrin a little bow to top it off. "I am extremely pleased to make your acquaintance, Mr. Corrin McCannon. I have traveled a good many miles to meet with you and solicit your help."

The flattery and the warm tone of voice worked right away on poor Corrin. He was exhausted, trail-sore, curious, and blinded by the sight of such a circus setup in his own backyard.

Before long, a campfire had been built, buffalo hides had been spread out around it, and the host ordered up some brewed coffee after Corrin wisely refused his offer of ale. Soon we were all sipping on the warm, fragrant liquid, and the men were talking about the most foolish things.

Thanks be to Hank, who'd had the good sense to tend to the pelts, then join us only after the work was done. Even the usually sober-headed David seemed caught up in some kind of spell by the time they finally got around to the subject of giant lizards again.

"I've never actually seen them," Corrin was saying. "But my sources are good."

"You heard it from the Indians?" the prince asked.

Corrin nodded. "From two Utes who trapped here a few years back, though I haven't seen them since. And I heard about it at the deathbed of a trapper who died from the colic too—though he was raving a mite, and I can't vouch for the truth of anything he said. He kept saying the place was bedeviled."

"How far is the journey?"

"From what I hear, not far. But it's plenty rough."

"You ever been there?"

"I been planning to go have a look but haven't yet found the time."

"What kind of terrain? Canyons? Impassable rivers?"

"Can't say. I've never been up that way, though I'm told it's canyonland for a while, then it flattens out some, and the region itself is mostly red rock slabs and sand rock."

"As I told your wife, I would be most generous to anyone who could take me all the way to the area." The prince's eyes fairly glittered.

"I could likely get you there, though I don't know how much we'd find," Corrin said.

"It's a chance I'm willing to take," said the prince. "If it turns out to be true, I shall have justified every year of my explorations in one fell swoop. Ah, if only I could find the remains of but one giant dinosaur, my scientific reputation would be made."

Finally I'd had all I could stand. I stood, puffed up my cheeks in disapproval, and said, "You can't be serious."

Both men looked at me as if they'd completely forgotten I ever existed.

"We are not so poor yet that we have to reduce ourselves to the level of flimflam artists," I said to Corrin in my most poisonous tone of voice.

He blinked but then gave me a mild, unperturbed look. "I told you about the so-called giant lizards, Emily."

"You told me a bunch of hogwash."

"Could be," Corrin said, still unperturbed. "But maybe not too."

"It's all nonsense. Am I to understand that you all plan to go off hunting dinosaurs? That these are the giant lizards I've been hearing so blamed much about?"

"There's only one way to find out for sure if they exist," Corrin said in a brand-new tone of voice.

"Do you expect to capture them dead or alive?" I asked with bile in my voice.

At that moment I wanted to throttle my husband for even considering such an expedition. The summer was now halfway over. Thompson and his Indian family were still planning to build another fort before snowfall, and they'd need every pair of hands they could find. I had been told by everyone that the winters here were deathly cold, and we needed to either do something to fortify ourselves against the coming chill or pack up what was left of our decrepit selves and go home before we froze to death. Add to that the fact that if Corrin didn't bring in enough beaver plews before snowfall, we wouldn't be able to sell them come spring, and it would be a bitterly poor, bitterly cold winter anyway.

But I might as well have saved my breath for all the good it did to quarrel with Corrin at that moment. He had that faraway look in his eyes again, and I had most certainly seen the results of *that* before.

For another hour or so, the talk continued. They discussed giant reptiles, giant flying birds, certain bones and such that had been found in various remote parts of Africa and Europe.

"I have been told the bones range from as small as a chicken to larger than a good-sized house," Bridger said, getting in on the conversation.

"I don't know about that chicken part, but I've seen so-called dinosaur teeth in Europe that are as long as your forearm," the prince said. "I have heard of flying species and land-bound. Those particular teeth were said to have come from a brute called the Tyrannosaurus rex. An eater of flesh."

"Ever heard of any live ones?" Bridger said.

I knew he was having some fun with them, but he managed to sound as serious as all get out.

263

The prince finished up yet another cup of ale, and he paused and considered that question for a very long time. A coyote's howl back in the wilderness broke the silence, then wailed off into the distance. Finally he said, "Rumors have drifted back from the upper Amazon. Tales of certain swamp creatures with all the characteristics of dinosaurs. I tried to put together an expedition for there last year, but, alas, I couldn't find anyone who would join me in the challenge."

I listened with growing animosity toward all the tall tales. And then, about midnight, I excused myself and went back to our cold, empty cabin and climbed into what might as well have been a widow's bed.

I felt sorry for myself and reached out to grab hold of that familiar old feeling of depression. My mind rummaged about looking for it, and it just wasn't there. The feeling was flat-out gone. I didn't know if it had been replaced by excitement or by anger, but it was gone all the same. The good Lord sometimes answers prayer even when you don't have the sense to utter one!

By the time Corrin came dragging his tail home about an hour later, I had done my thinking. As he lit the tallow candle and sat down on the bed to try to make up with me, I came right out and spoke to him in no uncertain terms.

"If you are going gallivanting into the mountains looking for giant lizards and such, I am going with you, no matter what you say."

He looked surprised, then pleased. "Do you think you're up for it?"

"Certainly. My body has completely mended."

"It will be a hard trek."

"No harder than sitting here day after day and wondering where you are and what wonderful adventures you're having," I said.

He laughed, then took me in his arms and kissed me on top of my well-brushed head.

"I swear, you're beginning to sound like your old feisty self again," he said. "And I'll tell you what. If it takes a giant lizard or two to perk you up, I promise to find you a whole zoo full."

"I doubt if you'll find a one, but I want to be there to see you fail."

"I wouldn't have you miss it for the world," he said.

We left the wagons and most of the prince's supplies at the cabin, with men to guard it all, and departed early the next morning just as the sun was winking above the rimrock and hills.

Riding horseback and leading two pack mules, six of us followed the Green River due south. After a while we left the relative greenery of Brown's Hole behind and meandered along beside the yellow-green river, amid burned yellow hills and gray rock outcroppings thick with cedar, piñon, juniper, and sage.

The ride was easy. Little Bit was well rested and ready for some exercise, since my illness had kept me from riding her for a while. We stopped mid-morning to eat, then traveled on in high spirits.

But by high noon the July sun was beating relentlessly on our heads, and we soon left the easy terrain behind. We set off cross-country, looking for an easier way to our destination. As if a spell had been placed upon us, we suddenly came upon a pair of huge, abrupt cracks in the earth and found ourselves descending into red-rock canyon country. Dismal, deep, impenetrable canyons blocked our passage and turned our journey into a trek through a very dangerous maze.

The river rushed through the first canyon, but even the water had changed. Now it was deep green and angry and rushed with great velocity through the narrow, dark-floored channel. We dismounted and led our horses along precarious rock walls and alongside steep juts of rock. Now and again someone would get too close to the edge, and rocks and debris would slide over the edge to fall with a resounding noise into the ravine far below.

By nightfall we were all exhausted and irritable, and we headed for our tents after eating hardtack and hot beans. The prince, Jim Bridger, and their two men kept shooting Corrin looks that told me they were clearly nettled. Corrin had told them it would likely take no more than a day to reach the region he'd heard about, and already they were complaining.

We slept in sleeping rolls, fitfully, atop gathered leaves and twigs. I awakened time and again to the mournful howl of a coyote, who seemed to be protesting our invasion of his land.

At the crack of dawn, we were up again. I was sore and miserable, and a fine drizzle ushered in what promised to be a gloomy day. We ate, climbed back in the saddle, tried to be civil to one another, and set off on our questionable adventure once again.

Finally the sun burned off the drizzle, and the slope leveled off some. The canyons were replaced by broad, rocky hills, some with giant slabs of rock tilted on their sides as if a giant's hand had pressed them together and left them broken and upturned to jut into the hot blue sky. Finding a zigzag trail to the bottom, we passed through a smaller canyon, forded a thin little creek, then came back up the other side on a long series of switchbacks. Little Bit was edgy from the heat but seemed otherwise to be weathering the trek just fine.

We found ourselves on an old Ute hunting trail and followed it along the edge of the rimrock, up through the boulders between two sage-clad hills, then down the other side.

"There's been a slide up there," Corrin said, reining in and using his hand to shield his eyes while he peered at a region of tangled rock and trees.

"Rain washed out the underpinnings," Bridger agreed. "Looks like we might be able to get past her, though."

We rode forward, dismounted, and led the horses over scree and sharp pebbles, going so slow it nigh unto drove us all mad. For the most part, we weren't even speaking to one another by then—not even Corrin and I. It was as if some dark wind had swept in to rile our moods, along with the hot sun that baked our faces. I think we all knew that anyone who dared set off the tinder in our moods at that moment was likely to find himself in the middle of a raging blaze of anger.

We finally made it past that obstacle and were on raw red rock, so smooth that the horses had an even harder time keeping their footing.

So intent was I upon leading Little Bit and making certain she didn't stumble or get a pebble embedded in her quick, that I missed the first sight of it.

I only looked up because Corrin yelled, "There! Look there!" His shout was so loud that it echoed like thunder and reverberated back to us.

I stopped short with the rest of the party and followed his gaze.

Then my heart lurched in my chest, and my breath came short. I dropped Little Bit's reins and hurried to stand beside my husband, suddenly needing to feel his warmth and strength.

My words came out as a breathless whisper. "Stop, please. Don't go any closer!" I grabbed his hand and tugged him back to me.

He put his arm around me, mindful of my terror. Then he gazed around at the rest of the party and appraised them with a wide smile.

They all stood with mouths agape, staring at what was in front of us—most of all the prince, whose mouth hung ajar like an opened door to a root cellar. He kept trying to shut it so that he could say something but apparently wasn't having any luck.

In that moment the earth was revealing a terrible and powerful secret.

Two upthrust buff-colored shale and rosy sandstone walls loomed high above us—still at a considerable distance but not so far that we couldn't see that the walls were embedded with enormous bones. They were so huge they literally stood out in relief from the rock wall, a fissure in the earth having opened in that particular place to spill out the secret that God had kept there since the beginning of time.

We were gazing upon the sketchy outlines of giant flying reptiles, looking at massive forebones from some great lizardlike leg. From the size of the bones, the creature must have been all of seventy feet long! We were all spellbound by the discovery and spoke in hushed tones when we could speak at all, as if we were in the presence of something spiritual.

We saw the remains of a forty-foot-long creature— even part of a jaw was visible, with sharp, curved, daggerlike teeth. All sorts of prehistoric animal life were mixed up in a jumble. I didn't know the names of them. All I saw in that moment was a terror that had once been a fanciful dream— a joke. Now, it shook the very fabric of my universe.

There truly *were* giant lizards! It hadn't been a prank after all. And if that part of my belief was so easily discounted, what on earth else did the Lord have in store for me that I couldn't so much as even dream about? I was deeply shaken.

Slowly, gradually, fearfully, we traveled close enough to finally be able to reach out and actually touch the wonderful fossilized bones fixed in the ancient stone. And when I felt the smooth, cool texture of something that horrible and that long dead, the sensation made me shiver.

I knew in that moment that I never would understand more than just the very surface of this wild and crazy world into which the good Lord had deposited me. I was awed, overcome, at the majesty of a Creator who could design such a terror, then turn around and form something so tender as a little bird—for at the moment I was considering all this, a tiny white-breasted wren flew into a juniper and chirruped, as if to bring me back to life.

That night, as we camped within sight of the immense concentrated deposits, the moon came out and shone high over the rimrock and cliffs surrounding the site. Our mood was elated, everyone was animated, talking incessantly, almost as if we had approached the edge of hysteria.

Later, I slept fitfully and kept awakening to turn over and stare at the looming rockface that held the marvelous bones.

That next day we began our excavation. It was hard, tedious work. The men used pickaxes and shovels to break away the rock from around the bones—even shattering one of the bones itself, which sent the prince into a veritable fit.

By the end of the day we had a half dozen or more good-sized bones for the prince to carry back with him. He planned to take the find to people back East and convince them to mount a full-on scientific expedition to unearth the rest of whatever miracles the region might hold. He was joyous, bragging, kicking up his heels, and bossing everyone around something ferocious, as if his most-dreamed-of ship had just come in.

Corrin was pleased. A scientific expedition would mean more folks out here to take advantage of the supplies at nearby Fort Misery—as I couldn't help but call it now. Anything that might bring a taste of civilization to our doorstep was just fine with him.

And as for that recently drowned so-called fort, I wished I'd seen the last of it. Corrin had been right long ago, when he told me that misery rode in and out of the region on a regular basis, whereas Davy Crockett had never so much as laid foot in the place.

22

We left part of our supplies cached beside the buff and rosy sandstone and piled one mule high with bones. Then we set off to retrace our steps to Brown's Hole.

As we rode along, I could see the vast range of blue mountains to our west, the dry, flat sagebrush desert to our east. I looked longingly at the horizon past it. That desert separated us from the soft green mountain valley where I longed to be.

In spite of all that had happened since I'd arrived in Brown's Hole—or perhaps because of it—I still yearned to settle back in that grassy, welcoming place beside the watercourse that ran into the Yampa River. The place I had named Elkhead Creek. At unexpected times the desire would well up and set my heart to longing for that place. That was on my mind as we rode along. The future. Where we would finally end up, for I was sure that Brown's Hole was just one chapter in what would be long and interesting lives.

Corrin led our small caravan. Bridger had taken off ahead to try to find an easier way back. The prince and his men rode along behind Corrin in single file, the pack mules behind them. Hank and I brought up the rear.

We were moving along a series of switchbacks again, heading down into a canyon, when my horse suddenly stopped, bucked, catching me off guard, and threw me sky high. I landed square in a patch of sagebrush between two large bushes.

I heard Corrin holler, "Whoa! Hold up—we got some trouble back there!"

I only half heard him, though. I was busy staring at the cause of Little Bit's panic. A thick, four-foot mountain rattler was coiled not two feet from me, back in the shade of the sagebrush. It was grayish-green with wide black spots, a nasty little triangular head, and icy dark eyes. We had interrupted its midday nap, though I couldn't for the life of me tell why the rest of the party had moved on past and I was the one whose horse was startled by him.

Of all the things that frightened me, snakes were at the top of the list. I felt my hands go clammy, my breath come short. The critter might as well have already bitten me, considering its effect on me at that moment.

I wormed a hand slowly around, feeling for the firearm I had holstered to my side. I'd practiced with it some, and Corrin had agreed to let me carry it on this unusual journey.

I stared the coiled snake square in the eye, managing not to blink, as my hand moved closer to the pistol, closer—

"Blasted woman anyway," the prince snarled, leaping from his horse and running toward me. "I knew we shouldn't have brought anyone so feeble along."

He startled me. He startled the snake.

And in that instant several things happened. The snake's attention was diverted from me to him. It uncoiled quickly, slithered beneath the brush, emerged on the far side, and recoiled itself, ready to attack this newer, louder enemy.

Just as the prince's leg hove into range of the rattler's fangs, I grabbed my pistol, fired, and caught the snake square in the middle, in mid-motion, exploding it just a split second before it would have plunged those fangs into Prince Paul's leg.

You never saw such a surprised look on a man's face in your life as when he heard that blast and saw the snake blow apart. He leaped backward and nearly fell. To be truthful, I was surprised too—that I'd even hit the nasty reptile.

But that was only the start of it, because the deafening gunshot spooked the horses.

Corrin had reined around and was heading back toward us, a frown on his face. His coming to help left the lead horse in the hands of one of the prince's young hirelings, and apparently the man couldn't handle the horse when the gunshot frightened it. It pitched him into a gully and took off down the steep switchbacks at a dead run. The rest of the party either clotted up alongside the trail to get out of the way or else barreled along behind. Men and supplies flew everywhere, people shouted, horses whinnied, mules brayed.

The mules went too. Right out from under my nose they bolted and took off running, faster than I'd ever seen a mule move, trying to get away from that gun blast and trying to catch up with the horses.

I watched helplessly as the poor critter that carried the bones stumbled on a sharp rock and pitched to one side, barely missing going over the canyon wall. At the same time the whole blamed bundle of bones shifted to the same side. The strap broke, and the pack kept on going, airborne, in a wide arc that sailed it out over the river till it lost momentum and suddenly plunged straight down three hundred or more feet into the swift, raging white water below. It was gone almost before we saw it land.

And then the prince began to avail himself of every curse word mankind had ever invented, a good number of them directed at me. He didn't even look again at the dead rattler that lay at his feet.

It took a while to get the caravan reorganized. I spent part of that time using Corrin's sharp-whetted knife to slice off the snake's rattler—to keep as a reminder of what can sometimes jump out of the bushes at you when you're least suspecting.

The prince was all for turning right around and going back, but there was no way Corrin would let that happen—especially after the vile words the prince had said about me, blaming me for coming along and spoiling things. Corrin was stubborn-jawed and angry and not about to help that fool a second longer than was necessary to get him back home.

We were running low on supplies anyway, and the mule that would have carried back the bones was crippled and had to be shot.

"I'll get you back to Brown's Hole—then you're on your own," Corrin said to Prince Paul.

"Then I'm not about to pay you," the so-called nobleman said.

"I'll take it out of your hide then," Corrin said. "I ought to anyway, after the way you treated my wife. I ought to scalp you like my wife just scalped that snake."

The prince fell silent then, and I knew the argument was over. He would pay up, and he'd soon be out of our hair. I could tell from the fear that came into his eyes when he saw the look in Corrin's and heard the knife-sharp edge in his voice.

And in that moment I was prouder of my husband than I'd ever been of anyone in my life. And I knew that though he made mistakes—my land, didn't we all?—I was bound and beholden to respect him in the same way he respected me.

Strangely enough, I hadn't realized until then just how much he did respect me. But right there and then I saw, as if for the first time, what a truly fine and decent man I had married.

23

When we got back, a new face had appeared in the Hole. Prewitt St. Claire had returned. He was a mid-sized, dark-haired, mild-mannered fellow. He had been up the Yellowstone, trapping with yet another partner of theirs, a fellow named Craig, who had gone downriver to sell their beaver plews.

They had set to cleaning up the muck around the fort. They were planning to rebuild it.

Corrin argued with them, saying it made no sense to rebuild that miserable edifice on a flood plain. "Same thing will happen again next spring," he said. "You've just got it set too close to the riverbank."

"Likely not," Thompson argued. "Goes-for-Broke says this was a hundred-year flood, and it ain't likely to happen again for at least that long."

"How does he know? Was he here a hundred years ago?"

"Don't get feisty on me now, Corrin. It's *our* fort, and we say it goes back up where we started it. Them timbers are still strong, and they dried out right well. The foundation has drained nicely, and the mud's almost gone. Ain't no point in starting over when we can make do partways with what's already here."

Corrin argued some more, but his words fell on deaf ears. And so they kept on building in that same dreadful region, cleaning out the previously drowned building and otherwise staying occupied.

The prince and his entourage pulled out the second day after we came back from the dinosaur find. He hadn't said another word to either of us in the meantime. He paid Corrin, but through Jim Bridger—who apologized to us, though he did admit he planned to help the prince return to collect more bones, once they rode back up to the company trading post and resupplied themselves. He was already tired of working for Ashley and Rocky Mountain Fur, and he wanted to put together his own fur-trapping enterprise.

So their caravan departed, and though Jim Bridger was to be our friend for the better part of both our lives, we were lucky to never lay eyes on that so-called prince again.

I did hear later that he wandered on north and hooked up with the British who ran the Hudson Bay Company, then roamed around a bit more. Reckon he may have spent the rest of his born days trying to convince everyone that he'd discovered giant lizard bones in the far Rocky Mountains in a place that was bedeviled. And I truly hope that everyone spotted him for the ill-mannered fool that he was.

Watching the raising of the fort took up a good deal of my time during that next month. The men worked hard, and before long they had a hollow square of one-story cabins with roofs and floors of mud set up where the first structure had been.

The Ute came in to watch. And when the buildings were done, Thompson moved his wife and her family into two of the cabins, which brought the rest of them down from their slightly higher camp. They set up their conical skin lodges among the trees around the fort, and before you knew it I was a part of a thriving little community made up mostly of Ute and trappers and a packrat or two. This particular band of Ute seemed pleased that the white folks had chosen to settle in the region—which is why I was surprised to learn that other Ute nearby were anything but pleased.

Corrin wasn't worried, though. He trapped and spent any free time improving our cabin against the coming winter months.

And then one day he came in and told me he and Hank were going back up the Yampa to trap along Elkhead Creek, where they expected to get a heavy haul of beaver-hide. Then they could take some time off before snowfall to prepare for the hardest months. We had only a month or so before the big storms could hit.

"Would you like to come?" he asked.

We packed up and left the next day, and after a hard two-day trek we found the very spot beside Elkhead Creek where I knew we would someday build our family home.

When I told Corrin that, he thought I was dreaming. "I already told you, Emily. Winters are too harsh up here."

"All the same," I said. "This is McCannon's Country. Our time at Fort Misery is only a prelude to our settling here."

He merely shook his head and fondly kissed my forehead. "You certainly have big dreams."

"I reckon it's true," I said.

That night I sat beside the campfire for a long time, just thinking. This world is truly a challenge.

Still, I was learning a few things, such as, if things get rough—well, don't give up.

I was learning that you never know what you're going to find on the other side of the next step you take. Who would have ever thought there really *were* giant lizards imbedded in stone out here?

I was learning that there's joy and adventure aplenty even in the midst of hardship, so long as Corrin and I just keep on taking that next step.

But surely the biggest lesson I had learned so far was that I had married a good man. One who was far from perfect, but then I was hardly perfect either. I still needed to get a rein on my temper and learn to be half of a team instead of acting like a bossy mule.

And as I slid into the sleep roll beside Corrin, I knew the good Lord would be with us through all of it. He'd take us to wherever we needed to be next, if we'd let Him. He'd see us all the way—safely home.